OCTAGON HOUSE

PHOEBE ATWOOD TAYLOR

OCTAGON HOUSE

An Asey Mayo Cape Cod Mystery

A Foul Play Press Book

THE COUNTRYMAN PRESS
Woodstock, Vermont

This edition published in 1991 by Foul Play Press, an imprint
of The Countryman Press, Inc., Woodstock, Vermont 05091.

ISBN 0-88150-194-8

Printed in the United States of America

10 9 8 7 6 5 4 3 2

OCTAGON HOUSE

1. WITH undisguised pleasure, Asey Mayo abandoned himself to a prolonged survey of the outside of the new post office.

Opened the day before, that post office had played the beanstalk which overnight sprouted Quanomet into the headlines, lifting it forever from its unquestioned position as Cape Cod's forgotten hamlet. For twenty years, while other sprightlier towns continued to burgeon and flourish, Quanomet had steadily withered and decayed. Finally, when people recalled the place sufficiently to mention it at all, they spoke in tones of deepest condolence. Poor Quanomet, they said, Poor Quanomet, it's Gone to Seed.

But Quanomet, thanks to the post office, had sprouted.

Twenty-three versions of the sprouting reached the ears of Asey Mayo, just returned to his home town of Wellfleet after a two months' absence, even before he had the key in his back door. With the twenty-eighth description of the Quanomet flurry, Asey changed his traveling clothes for corduroys and a blue shirt, and forthwith set out to view for himself the post office and its mural.

Ordinarily Quanomet would have been thrilled to the core by the picture of Asey rolling along Main Street in his newest streamlined Porter sixteen roadster. But that Friday

noon, Asey was not even noticed. He got only the shortest
of nods from the state cop who was helping unsnarl traffic
in Depot Square. Reporters, who usually dogged the heels
of the man they had popularized as "The Hired Hand de
Luxe," "The Hayseed Sherlock," "The Homespun Sleuth"
—today they dismissed Asey with a lanquid wave.

Parking his roadster in the square's last available slit of
space, Asey joined the crowd milling towards the post
office.

The building would have inspired unabashed awe in a
good sized metropolis. In Quanomet it assumed an aura of
complete unreality. For each individual member of the
town's all year round population of eight hundred, Asey
estimated offhand that the post office lavishly provided an
area of six square feet, apiece.

For the most part the structure was red brick, but here
and there whimsical areas of concrete had been introduced.
The front pillars were dazzling chromium, the steps pink
granite, the windows were strangely barred casements. A
self-conscious placard announced that the architecture was
Early Colonial Modified.

"Modification my eye!" Asey murmured. "It's out an' out
repeal. Wow!"

Inside, sitting on the marble floor, he found most of the
summer residents of the Cape, gazing up in spellbound
fascination at the mural.

One brief look convinced Asey that the twenty-eight descriptions he'd heard were just a bunch of shabby belittlings.
No living man could describe that mural, and if he could,

no one would believe him. Even staring at the central panel somehow smacked of fraud.

Peace, her wings protruding from beach pajamas, was starting a side chancery on a clam digger, who resented it vigorously. Ignoring three heavily armed apes in gas masks who belabored her from virtually every angle, Peace beamed down at a stalwart youth whose full nelson on Capital was definitely getting results. Capital, Asey decided, was a mighty sick man.

From the clam digger's left knee tottered a leering British Grenadier, and a pirate hugging a mussed Red Cross nurse. Near her, two tired women stirred something steaming in a kettle. Out of the steam emerged a Model T Ford driven by a child who looked like Shirley Temple. Myles Standish sat in a cramped position on the spare tire, making faces at John Alden and a tubercular Indian.

"Whee!" Asey said. "Wheee!"

He didn't realize that he had spoken out loud till the girl standing beside him chuckled.

"Say it, Asey," she advised pleasantly. "Don't try to hold in. It's dangerous."

"D'you suppose," Asey asked, wondering who she was, "that feller with the scythe who's floatin' on top—is he death, or the tax collector?"

"He's father, and I think he's got grounds for libel. Have you come to the Civil War yet?"

Asey shook his head and tried to figure out where he had met this girl before who so obviously knew him. She had a nice voice and a nice laugh, a well tanned face and wide brown eyes—probably, he decided, she was a friend of young Bill Porter's wife, although her blue denim shirt and dungarees were the general store and not the specialty shop variety.

"Well," she said, "the Civil War's a fat Aunt Jemima in the far left panel, frying pancakes. Grant is badly burned."

In the general shushing that followed Asey's unrestrained roar of laughter, he and the girl tiptoed outside to the pink steps.

"I shouldn't have let myself go," Asey said, leaning weakly against one of the chromium pillars. "What's that artist wastin' his time on federal pictures for? With a sense of humor like that, he'd ought to be sellin' things over the radio. My, my, I'd like to meet that man!"

The girl looked at him quizzically. "I don't think," she remarked, "that you would. Not unless you've changed a lot since I knew you. You see, the artist has no sense of humor. Not a whit. As far as he's concerned, that's the History and Customs of Cape Cod, just as the title says. He means it, earnestly."

"Go on!" Asey didn't believe her. "He don't!"

"He's Jack Lorne, my brother-in-law," she said, "and it pains me to say I speak the truth about him. After the tumult and the shouting die, come over to the house some day, and I'll take you over to their place and introduce you. That is, if you'll promise not to hurl anything very large. Most people want to."

"What house do I get you from," Asey's eyes twinkled, "to go about meetin' him?"

"You mean, who am I anyway? Oh, Asey, I'm so crushed! I was so sure you recognized me. I live in Octagon House—"

"Octagon House!" Asey said. "The old eight sided Sparrow place—why, I ain't thought about that in years!" He caught himself just in time to keep from adding that he thought it had long since fallen down. "That makes you Pamela Frye, an' you mustn't hold my not rememberin' against me. It ain't often that a spindly little shrimp like you was, Pam, grows into such a nice lookin' young lady as you are. Sure I remember you now. I taught you to sail a boat."

"It's still the thing I do best."

"An' you used to drive me crazy," Asey said "always wantin' to go ashore to hunt for ambergris. Mornin', noon an' night, you combed the shore for ambergris."

"And I still do," Pam Frye said. "I still do, in spite of what everyone, including my excellent and talented sister, says. Look, come over in a few days and I'll show you Jack Lorne and the bewitching Marina. Don't look so puzzled, you knew her too. She was plain Mary Hosannah Frye in those days, but she's turned out to be the bewitching Marina Lorne. You'll recognize her. She's that, quote, beautiful tawny creature, unquote, that lives in the tobacco ads."

"A model, huh?" Asey asked, recalling vaguely that the other Frye child had been weedier and more gangly than this one. "Well, well."

"Yes, she's the figure of Peace, inside in the mural. I'm one of those weary wenches next the kettle, but happily no one's recognized me yet. No one ever recognizes my modeling. I'm simply tanned, not tawny. Sister turned out to be a Sparrow, you see. I'm just an old Frye."

"You model, too?" Asey, whose curiosity rarely got the better of him, unashamedly pumped. The girl interested him. Somehow he got the impression that she lived in Quanomet all the year round, but he could not imagine what possible charm or opportunity the place held for her.

"Oh, I do almost anything to earn money," she told him with complete candor. "In a nice way, of course. I've done any number of things for Peg Boone's stuff. I'm ladies with dishpan hands, and dirty sheets, and sometimes I'm personally unclean and have to be told about it—oh, Lord, it's nearly one o'clock! I've got to dash. I must—"

"Wait a second," Asey said with sudden inspiration. "If you still like sailin', why not come back to Wellfleet with me, an' help me try out this new craft of mine that's just been delivered? I need a crew—"

"The new *Mary B?* Oh, Asey, I saw her Monday, in the creek— She's a beauty! I'd love to go. But I've got this new crop of boarders to feed—"

"Of boarders? Whose boarders?"

"Father and I and Octagon House," Pam said, "we have boarders, with stewed prunes for breakfast. Our first two— boarders, Asey, not prunes! They came today, and it behooves me to put my best foot forward, like whipped cream with jello. They're very nice—more decent than most, and father can't be trusted to cope with a whole meal. He's absent minded. Look, will you ask me sailing next week, when Quanomet's back to normal? Is that a date? And in return, I'll display the Mighty Jack and the Bewitching Marina."

As she paused to light a cigarette, it suddenly occurred to Asey that never in all his life had he heard such hatred as Pam's quiet voice held while speaking of her sister and brother-in-law. Its bitter intensity shocked him.

"I'll even show you," she went on, "Father's collection of odd and curious clocks, and—oh, look at those damn tourists eating their filthy lunches in the old cemetery! What horrid people! What lice! I suppose it's what comes of headlines."

"The headlines won't last," Asey assured her.

"You don't know the half of it, Asey. Behind all this happy blithering of the summer folk and the tourist trade and the outlanders, this town is torn wide open. Quanomet's in upheaval."

"What's it upheavin' about?" Asey inquired. "The new P.O.?"

"That, and the mural, and Jack Lorne. They never did want the post office, they loathed the thought of the mural, and they've cordially disliked Jack for the five years he's been here. And in the mural he's been unwise and misguided enough to caricature half the town. Those daubs of his are just mocking burlesques—didn't you get that part?"

"I didn't look long enough," Asey said. "But come to think of it—"

"Yes. You go gape again at the side panels," Pam said, "and you'll see why fifty per cent of Quanomet itches to tar and feather Jack Lorne, and why the other fifty per cent is convinced that tarring and feathering is far too good for

him. What's going to happen when they finally come to their senses and begin to realize that Jack hasn't the brains to be that malicious all by himself, without outside inspiration!"

"Who prompted him?" Asey knew the answer even before he asked the question.

"Three guesses," Pam said tartly. "Thank God, the town likes Father even though they secretly think he's slightly daft, and I play the church organ and help run the Women's Club, so I'm reasonably safe. But what's going to happen to the rest of the family, I can't bear to think. Quanomet's aroused for the first time since I've known the place. It's on the warpath. And some of the mutterings are downright ugly. And if these headlines keep up—"

"They won't," Asey said. "They can't."

But they did.

Once in the headlines, Quanomet stayed there. Those piercing optics, the Eyes of the Nation, focused themselves on the town. It became, as a Boston newspaper grudgingly admitted, a cynosure. In twenty-four hours, the average blindfolded resident of Walla Walla or El Paso could have navigated Quanomet's Main Street with greater ease than he could circle his own back yard. Aunt Nettie Hobbs, the Pickle Lime Lady, was Woman of the Week in three news magazines, banishing the budget and a couple of wars way back among the dandruff cures.

The continued headlines, of course, were not due to the post office, or even the mural. But like the Octagon House and the Pickle Lime Lady, they continued to provide an important and bizarre background. They were what the press meant when it referred to the Incredible Background of These Startling Incidents.

The first incident which startled Asey Mayo happened in the bright moonlight at two o'clock that morning as he rowed back to his landing.

His mind occupied almost entirely with the new sailboat which he had just returned to her mooring, Asey didn't see the figure lurking in the shadows on his wharf until a hand reached out and grabbed the prow of his sharpie.

Shipping his oars, Asey jumped lightly onto the landing.

"What the—who—Pamela Frye, that ain't you?"

"Yes, Asey, I—"

"What're you doin' here this time of night—look, child," Asey discovered that she was trembling from head to foot, "what's wrong?"

"Asey, you know today—you laughed about my always hunting ambergris, and I told you that I still did, and—"

"But God A'mighty, child, you ain't found some!"

"Asey, I have! I did, this afternoon, on Quanomet Point. A huge lump. It's a hundred pounds, anyway."

"What!" Asey did some rapid calculating. "That's more'n fifty thousand dollars' worth—no wonder you're quiverin'! I know what you want. Sure, I'll help you lug it to Boston, an' get it to the right place, an'—"

"But that's not what I've been waiting for, Asey. It's about me and Sister. She—"

"Your sister Marina? Oho," Asey said. "Did she find it with you?"

"No, but she helped me take it home. And tonight I went over to get it, and—Asey, she's been killed!"

"What?"

"Murdered. And they say I did it!"

2.

ASEY stared for a long moment at her face, chalk white in the moonlight, and then drew a long breath.

"Sit down, Pam," he said gently. "Here, on this clam dreener, before you tremble yourself off into the water. Now," he made fast the sharpie, "tell me everything, just as short an' sweet as you can make it. Begin back with the ambergris—ambergris—honest, that amazes me more'n the rest!"

"But it's the rest that matters—that's the worst," Pam said. "Asey, they'll be after me now. Hunting me. It *was* my knife that killed her, you know. Jack Lorne recognized it. He knows it's my knife. There—there isn't any way out of it!"

"Pam Frye," Asey spoke almost in his quarterdeck voice, "snap out of it! You didn't kill her, did you?"

"Of course not! Of course I didn't. But," she added honestly, "I've often wanted to. I wanted to this afternoon."

"There's a vast difference," Asey said, "between feelin' an urge to kill someone an' actually killin' 'em. If you didn't kill her, don't worry."

"But I did want to, and it's my knife, and they think I did. They're hunting me now, probably. I heard them a thousand times while I waited in the last hour. Somebody's sure to come to you and tell you and ask your help, even though they don't know I'm here—" Pam's voice broke. "They'll arrest me and—"

Asey held a match for her cigarette.

"In another half minute," he said, "I'm goin' to begin to wonder if you didn't kill her— Pam, I know you're all worked up, but you've got to quiet down an' tell me things. Until you do, we can't get any place at all. Begin with the ambergris."

"I found it around five this afternoon," she made a valiant effort to pull herself together. "On Quanomet Point. I thought at first it was a lump of tallow—oh, Asey, after all these years, I couldn't believe it! There it was, staring me in the face. A chance to get away from that Godforsaken town, and that tumbledown rat trap of a house, to get Father away, to go places and do things—art school, everything. I just sat down and bawled. As hard as—as I'm bawling right now."

Asey lighted his pipe and waited for her tears to pass.

To a certain extent, he thought, he understood how the girl must have felt. That afternoon he had driven past Octagon House, as massive and ark-like as it had been when he first saw it years and years before. The sides facing the road were bravely painted, the lawns and the flower beds were well kept. Even the stiff-necked iron stag by the elm tree seemed to be doing his gallant best to bear up past tradition.

But the rear of the house was bare of paint, and the back porch sagged. The old octagonal barn was warped to a circle that hovered uncertainly on rotted underpinnings. No electric wires, he noticed, ran to the house. That meant kerosene lamps and a hand pump and all the drudgery that went with old time housework. And a casual inquiry had brought forth the information that Pam Frye, at twenty-three, lived there throughout the year, supporting herself and her father, and somehow keeping the old place going. They were completely ignored by the bewitching Marina, who went her gay way—

"I'm pulled together now," Pam said. "Asey, after I finished bawling, the problems involved suddenly burst on me. There I was, three miles up the beach. The tide was coming in, lickety larrup. The ambergris was almost awash. I couldn't carry it, or even lift it. I didn't dare leave it, to go back for a barrow, or a car, or anything. And I began to wonder what would happen if anyone came."

"Uh-huh," Asey said. "It ain't like fifty thousand dollars' worth of stocks or bonds registered in your name. If you happened to meet someone who felt like claimin' it, an' if they happened to be bigger than you—"

Pam lighted another cigarette.

"You have," she said, "hit the nail squarely on the head. I did a lot of hard thinking. Funny that in all these years of hunting, I never once considered aftermath and transportation problems. Anyway, the lump wasn't staked, or above high water mark. The sand was soft there, and I couldn't see any footprints. But I'll admit the wind was whipping so that it practically had covered my own prints in the sand. On the other hand, anyone who might have found it before me wouldn't have left it, any more than I intended to. Don't you agree?"

"Right," Asey said.

"Well, I got a stick from some dune drift and levered the lump up above the highest water mark of kelp and seaweed, and then I sat down and got my breath and wondered where to go from there."

"Think of cuttin' it up?" Asey asked.

"Oh, yes. I thought of that. I usually wear a sheath knife, like the one you've got on your belt. Awfully handy, from cleaning fish to digging weeds and cutting roses. But I'd forgotten it, then of all times. I even remembered just where I'd left it on the back porch, too. And—"

"That's the knife that killed Marina?" Asey interrupted.

"Yes. Well, there I was, and there was the ambergris I've hunted all my life, and there was the tide, bounding in. I thought of swimming it back, but three miles is too much for me, and if anyone picked me up from a boat or anything, they could claim salvage. And—do you happen to know Rodney Strutt?"

"Young Rodney? No," Asey said, "I don't, but Bill Porter claims Rodney'll be the first of the idle rich they rend limb from limb, come the revolution, and a good thing it'll be."

Pam nodded approvingly. "That's Rodney. He's got a shooting camp beyond the point. I noticed fresh tire marks —he keeps a beach wagon with big tires to taxi his bunch over and back. After considering that angle, I decided I'd practically rather shove the ambergris back into the water than ask Roddy or his pals to help. I've had my little run-in with Roddy, like the rest of the local gals. In Quanomet," she added parenthetically, "mothers don't caution their young daughters about sharks, quicksand, or highway traffic, they just say, 'Look out for Roddy.' And then, by God, Roddy's beach wagon bounded up in front of me, and in it was Sister, apparently on her way to Roddy's."

"She plays around with him, does she, huh?"

Pam shrugged. "Father and I decided years ago that we were happier not knowing Marina's playmates. It's all very well to take up the white man's burden, but you have to draw the line somewhere. Well, there was Sister, Asey, and she caught on about the ambergris. Her eyes gleamed like— like a tawny tiger—I never saw a tawny tiger, but that's the only way I know of describing her. And—somehow—I don't honestly think I ever hated her more than I did that moment."

"Would the ambergris mean so much to her? The money, I mean?" Asey asked.

The moonlight caught Pam's twisted smile. "Her modeling and Jack's painting would keep Father and me in utter luxury. But Sister and Jack have expensive tastes, and they're usually more broke than we are. Sister caught on, all right. Don't think she's anyone's fool. I knew there wasn't any use haggling with her. I said, 'All right. Half if you take it back.'"

Her cigarette butt described an arc into the water.

"And Sister said," Pam continued, "that I could go to hell. She said she was the only one who could get the stuff back, and without her I'd have nothing. In short, she would have it all, herself. And that was that."

Asey grunted. He hadn't liked the sound of the bewitching Marina when he first heard about her. Now he gave up being open minded and let himself hate her, thoroughly and forcefully.

"I hope," he said, "you knocked her teeth out!"

"I picked up the stick I'd used as a lever," Pam said, "and I don't know where I got the strength, but before she had time to understand, I had that lump of ambergris down in the surf."

Asey's eyes narrowed. With fifty thousand dollars and all that it meant staring her in the eye, this amazing child preferred to throw it away rather than let her sister get it—

"Yes, I'd rather have lost it entirely," Pam echoed his thoughts. "So would you. When Sister saw that lump hit the undertow, she was out of that beach wagon in a flash, yelling for me to get it. And that time, *I* did the laughing."

"Didn't she go for it?" Asey demanded.

"Sister," Pam said, "is afraid of water—don't you remember how she kicked and screamed in boats when she was little? She's terrified of water. She can't swim. And let me tell you, Asey, the primitive emotions that got aired on that beach—I felt like something out of one of those earthy novels, all heaving breasts and stark urges. We ran the gamut, Sister and I did. And the ambergris bobbed on the surf."

Asey puffed at his pipe till the bowl burned his fingers. He marveled at Pam Frye, and the impersonal way she could describe such a scene, as though it had happened to two other people entirely. It was, he decided, the Cape Cod half of her speaking. Her mother's family had been an indomitable tribe.

"Go on," he said.

"I knew the lump would float back in with the tide," she said. "But Sister didn't stop to figure that out. After she got exhausted, I said I'd get it, if she'd promise to take it back for me for five thousand dollars. And she put that in writing, Asey, on the back of a grocery bill. I've got it here. After that, I marched into the surf and fished out the ambergris. She helped me get it to the beach wagon, and we covered it with a tarpaulin, and started home. She was a rag, emotionally, and I was a pulp, physically. The surf out there is something awful, and fighting the undertow almost caved me in. Well, so much for that part."

"Did you trust her?" Asey asked.

"Trust Sister?" Pam laughed. "Don't be silly. Of course not. Halfway home, she said we mustn't tell a soul. I agreed we mustn't. Then she said, let's take it straight to Boston, now. And the air was full of the smell of old rats and mice. I said we couldn't, without my telling Father. Otherwise, he'd have the police combing the Cape for me when I didn't return to get dinner. She said that mustn't happen, and I kept on agreeing. It was dawning on me, Asey, that she hadn't an idea in the world of letting me have my ambergris, after all. It was one of those things you could feel. Like when you want to go somewhere, and someone doesn't want to, and they don't do anything, but you just know that you'll go over their dead body. It's hard to explain—"

"I get it," Asey said. "What'd you decide to do?"

"Two things, to get home as quickly as I could and tell Father, and somebody else—I sort of decided on this boarder named Carr who came today with his grandmother. He's a teacher, around thirty, and an awfully decent sort. And I intended to call Hank Stevens, he's a chemist and works for Joralemon's in Boston. He's a friend of Father's and mine, and he knows all about my ambergris hunting. I thought, if someone on this end knew, and someone in Boston, I was pretty well protected. I also wanted to get the stuff to Boston, pronto. I don't know why I didn't think of you then. I wish I had."

"It wouldn't have done you any good," Asey pointed out. "I've been frolickin' around in the boat since afternoon. What did you tell Sister?"

"I said, as if in a burst of light, that I'd get the boarders' dinner, and then tell Father that I was driving up to Boston with Mary Kean. She has a flower shop and often drives up to the florists' market, and I often go with her, and Sister knows it. I said that in that way Father wouldn't suspect a thing. We could start at eleven, park in a garage, then go to Joralemon's early. She agreed very quickly. Thought it was a peachy idea. That convinced me she had some plan afoot. But I figured, if she wanted time to connive, I could take the same time and thwart her connivings. And I did want to get the ambergris to Boston and into someone else's hands before the reporters got wind of it. Wasn't that right?"

Asey hesitated. "Well, I don't know. Myself I'd—but I s'pose the instant the news got around, Lord knows how many claimants'd come poppin' up."

"Exactly, as you said, it's not like dealing in registered bonds. So, we went to Sister's garage, and shifted the ambergris from Roddy's beach wagon into Sister's—hers hasn't soft tires—and covered it with the tarpaulin. Just as we finished, a roadster drew up with horns blaring, and one of Roddy's pals leaned out and yelled at her and said, for God's sake where had she gone with the beach wagon, they wanted it, and he had Farbstein waiting for her, and Farbstein was flying to New York in half an hour with someone, and what the hell, didn't she want to see him. And at that point, Marina could have screamed."

"Why?" Asey demanded.

"Because all her life she's wanted to model for Farbstein, more than anything else. Her life ambition. Apparently some of Roddy's gang had collared him, and there was her chance—she's tried to get to him for years. There was Farbstein, the unapproachable, and there was me, and there was the ambergris. And there was the lad in the roadster, yelling for God's sake to make up her mind. She did. She grabbed the car keys, and said she'd be back by eleven, and off she went in the roadster. And there was I."

"Why didn't you," Asey demanded, "take the ambergris, and beat it?"

"I can't drive," Pam said simply. "We never could afford an automobile. I beat it home to tell Father and talk with him, thinking we might harry this amiable boarder into taking the stuff to Boston in his coupé. And I found a note on the door, saying they'd gone to a clambake, and the movies later. Shall I pass over the dismal hours till eleven o'clock?"

"What did you do? Whyn't you snake the ambergris out of the garage?" Asey demanded. "I would have. I—"

"So would I, but, Asey, do you know Aunt Nettie Hobbs? She keeps the Woman's Exchange. She—"

"I know her," Asey said. "I know her! The old gabbler! Did she—"

"She came, Asey, to call. She came as I finished reading the note and was just starting for the wheelbarrow. She stayed. She talked. She ate supper. She stayed. She talked. I could not get rid of her. I have never been so mortally rude to any living person. And she stayed. I couldn't tell *her,* naturally. It'd be like inviting the world to share my ambergris. I couldn't leave her—although I did, once, around nine o'clock. I whipped over to the garage and the ambergris was still there. It was then that I slid the garage doors off their rollers—I knew Sis couldn't get 'em on without help. That was my one and only hope, that Sister, in her general greed, wouldn't tell anyone. I prayed that she wouldn't. And Nettie stayed. She left at ten-thirty. She told me, in parting, I was the most nervous thing, I needed a good tonic, and I didn't seem myself a bit. Asey, can you figure Nettie's story when this breaks? That alone'll hang me. The second she disappeared down the road, I grabbed the barrow and legged it to the garage. And there, on the floor—there was Sister. Staring up—oh, that—that face, Asey! She was so beautiful, you know, she really was. But her face—then—it was awful. I know now what people mean when they say someone was rooted to the spot in horror."

"And the ambergris?" Asey demanded.

"It was there," Pam said. "There, in the beach wagon. Just as we left it. There it was. And there she was. And I looked at it, and I looked at her. And I thought of the things she'd done. She broke Mother's heart, Asey. Mother never got over that—well, I won't go into it. She took every cent Father had, literally, when she first ran away from town. She stole his first editions, the pride of his life, and pawned them. But mostly the things she'd done were things you couldn't put into figures. She did something to Father that he never got over. Something to his ambition. Something to his pride. The more I thought of what she'd done, the—well, I didn't feel sorry for what had happened. That sounds inhumanly hard. I suppose it is. But little sister's had to live in the dregs of what Marina left behind. That's enough to make you a little inhuman, I think. And the irony of it got me, too. She couldn't even die, I thought, without a last final blow at us— for how *could* I take the ambergris then?"

"I hope," said Asey, "that you did, Pam, just the same."

"I did, because I knew I'd never have a chance to get it later. Not with Jack Lorne, and the police. I took it. Then I phoned the state cops. We had the phone put in again this morning. We can only afford it when we have boarders. I told the cops to come to Octagon House, then I dashed back to the garage. Jack was there, in the most terrific frenzy I ever saw. He pointed his finger at me and said, 'You did that. It's your knife'—I hadn't even noticed that before, Asey. But it *was* my knife. I knew the notched handle. 'You did it!' Jack yelled. 'You were jealous of her, always. It's your knife! I've called the police and told them so! I've told them you're the murderer!' "

Pam lighted another cigarette.

"And when he said that word, murderer, all of a sudden I thought of you. I suppose I connected you with murders. Anyway, I raced out of the garage. He tried to follow me, but I tripped him. I cut through the woods until I was so breathless I had to stop. I was just behind Chases'. I sneaked into their barn and stole Billy Chase's bike, and pedaled over here. That's your story. I hid the—"

"Wait," Asey said softly, in her ear. "What kind of cigarettes are those you're smokin'? Luckies?"

"Yes, have one?" Pam tossed him the package. "I hid—"

Asey's hand went over her mouth. "So you pedaled here, did you? Quite a ride. Must be five-six miles, an' most of it uphill."

Pam listened in bewilderment as Asey, his hand still covering her mouth, casually chatted on about her feat of bicycling over. He was sniffing the air, and automatically Pam sniffed, too.

She understood then the reason for Asey's hand on her mouth.

He had caught, before she had, the whiff of Turkish tobacco smoke that meant that someone, very near, had been listening to every word. That someone, very near, was waiting for her to tell where she had hidden the lump of ambergris.

3. "YESSIR," Asey continued blandly, "after all you been through today, Pam, I should think your trip over would've been about the last straw. Say, you got a match? I thought I had a pocketful, but this old pipe's run through 'em all."

He removed his hand from her mouth.

"I've got a new flap of 'em somewhere on me," Pam said, slightly dazed at the natural and familiar sound of her own voice. "Wait'll I fish around."

"When I ask," Asey whispered in her ear, "where's the ambergris, you be real reluctant. It's in your house? Then you say, it's in the woods behind the garage. Act up! Thanks," he added aloud as she gave him the matches. "Now, Pam, before we do anything else, we'd better settle up the ambergris part. Where'd you hide it?"

"Do—do I have to tell you?" Pam asked.

Asey announced with some firmness that he was sure he was as safe a person as she was like to find. "An' certain," he said, "I'm sure the clam dreener ain't goin' to town an' spread the tidin's."

"Oh, I didn't mean to insinuate anything about you," Pam said hurriedly, noting Asey's grin and his nod of approval at her acting. "I'm sure enough about you. It's just—well, after what I've gone through, I sort of hate to tell anyone."

"Uh-huh," Asey said, "but we got to get to it—real soon. I s'pose you took it over to your house, didn't you?"

"No," she said, "that's the last place to keep anything safely. We have hideous rats, you know. I didn't dare take it there. I wheeled it in the barrow out to the woods, about halfway between the garage and our place. There's an old summer house there, filled with trash that never gets taken to the dump. There was an old linoleum rug. I set it on that," it was easy to romance, she found, once you got started, "and then covered it, and put things around it. No one's gone near that summer house for thirty years, except a vast family of skunks that live there. I knew they'd take care of the rat problem for me. I don't know from experience if rats like ambergris, but our rats eat anything, and there's no reason to suppose they wouldn't eat ambergris if they got the chance."

"I see," Asey said. "Well, we'll go after that directly. But first off, we got a mighty heap of thinkin' an' plannin' to be done. You sit there, please, while I brood some."

He closed his eyes and listened.

A soft wind murmured in the tall pines nearby, and little waves lapped at the wharf piles. Beyond, on the outside beach, the surf boomed dully. A whippoorwill called plaintively from his orchard. Two dogs yelped furiously for a minute and then were abruptly silent.

Something nearby crackled. No, it was only his imagination. No, it wasn't either. Something—someone—was moving in the shadow of those tall pines at the foot of the landing.

Casually, Asey turned his head and stared, but his eyes couldn't penetrate those deep shadows. Probably the fellow was crawling on hands and knees through the thick quiet layers of pine needles, screened by the beachplum bushes that fringed the shore.

It was a physical effort to check his impulse to start out in pursuit. If only, Asey thought, he were alone! Somehow he'd get the fellow. But there was the girl to consider, and other little items, too. This fellow could see them, but they couldn't see him. He was probably armed. Asey had nothing more vicious at hand than a clam hoe and a pair of oars. If the fellow wanted to take a pot shot at Pamela Frye, there was nothing to stop him. If he suspected that they knew of his presence, Asey decided, Pam was the logical person to pot-shot at.

Nearly a quarter of an hour passed before they heard the sound of a car starting.

"No lights?" Pam asked.

"He don't practically need 'em on the road," Asey said. "Not hereabouts. He'll put 'em on when he comes to the curve—see? At that speed, he'll be hob-nobbin' with the summer house skunks in about seven minutes flat, or else the angels'll be measurin' him for a harp. I hope for his sake that he knows the road."

"Aren't you going to follow—whyn't you go after him while he was here? Who is he? Did he hear us? Who is he?" The questions tumbled over each other.

"Offhand," Asey stood up, "he's the feller that killed your sister. That's my guess. I didn't go for him, 'cause I felt you wanted to live to enjoy your ambergris fortune. Pam, this is very enlightenin', this is—come on. Let's wander up to the house—"

"Did Sister tell someone, d'you suppose? Did he hear us? What'll we do now?"

"Sure he heard," Asey said, shouldering his oars. "Sound carries real nice on the water. I guess, Pam, I'll collect an arsenal, an' go prowl round—except there's this problem of you. If you come, that means subjectin' you to the cops. An' if this feller finds the summer house bare an' void of ambergris, he's goin' to track you down an' choke the truth out of you. It's better that you stick here with me. An' better that the cops don't get—wait. Wait up—"

They stopped at the end of the landing.

"What," Pam asked dismally, "now?"

"Listen," Asey said. "Cars. Hear? Several of 'em, an' bein' driven at a pace so's to endanger. See the lights now? Comin' to my house—"

"Cops," Pam said. "Cops. Exit Miss Frye, with gyves or handcuffs. Anyway, you've heard the truth, and you're one up—there go the brakes, they're stopping in front of your house. Thanks, Asey, you—"

"Wait," Asey said, "I keep wonderin' why you've got to be carted off, when you'll be such a nice drawin' card for this lad—oh, drat, I left a note for Syl stuck in my door, sayin' I'd be in the *Mary B* or at the wharf—here they come! Pam, how much spirit you got left?"

"Practically none," she told him truthfully.

"You can't get up the path, now—Pam, will you take a duckin'? Till we see what they're—"

"Asey!" It was Hanson, the police lieutenant, who yelled.

"Up to," Asey finished swiftly. "Get in the water, keep under the wharf, out of sight. Can you?"

"I'll try it. Take this," she passed over a slip of paper that he knew was the agreement Marina had written on the ambergris sharing.

"Quick—"

She slid over the wharf and into the water as Hanson yelled again.

"Asey! Asey Mayo! For God's sake, why can't he—Asey!"

"Hello!" Asey said, blinking as a flashlight hit him full in the face. "Tryin' to blind me, Hanson, or bust my ear drums?"

"Asey," Hanson said, "we've got some new business for you. Dull as ditchwater it's been since you've been gone, and now you're back, things happen. It's a nice murder. Marina Lorne, she's the wife of that artist that did the Quanomet mural, she's been stabbed out in her garage. One of old man Frye's daughters—lives in the Octagon House, you know? Well, it's the other daughter's knife, and they hated each other like poison, and Jack Lorne says this other daughter's been jealous of him and his wife, and Nettie Hobbs was over at Octagon House tonight, and she says this other daughter, Pam, was nervous as a witch, almost out of her mind. And—"

"In other words," Asey interrupted, "Pam Frye killed her sister Marina Lorne."

"Yeah. She beat it when Lorne accused her. It's a cinch. Nettie saw her go to the garage around nine, someone else saw her come out. It's all plain as daylight."

"Then why," Asey said, "tear over here to tell me about it, Hanson? Why—"

"Because," the stocky figure of Dr. Cummings, Asey's own doctor, the district medical examiner, loomed in the path, "because, God damn it, I made him, Asey, that's why! Because I made him. Listen to me, I'll stake my life that Marina Lorne was stabbed by a left handed person. Got that? Well, I know Pam Frye. She's right handed. And she busted her left arm last winter. And furthermore, I don't care if Nettie Hobbs *saw* Pam Frye kill her sister, I wouldn't believe it, do you hear me?"

"Most everyone," Asey said gently, "from here to Provincetown heard you, Doc."

"Damn it," Cummings stamped onto the wharf, "damn it, I don't care if I wake up the whole bloody town, I don't care if I wake up the whole bloody Cape! I'm mad. I'm so mad I can't talk. I'm so mad that words dry up within me. I'm speechless. I'm speechless with violent and uncontrollable rage!"

For ten minutes Dr. Cummings proceeded to enlarge on the extent of his speechlessness and the violence and fury of his anger. Underneath the wharf, in water up to her armpits, Pam Frye writhed in silent laughter. Dr. Cummings' chronic attacks of speechlessness had intrigued her through measles, mumps, whooping cough, appendicitis, a broken arm, and a large variety of assorted stomach aches, contusions and abrasions.

"What you're drivin' at, Doc," Asey stemmed the apparently endless flow of words, "is that you don't think that Pam Frye killed her sister, an' Hanson thinks she did."

"In a nutshell, yes. It's a physical impossibility, Asey. At least it's impossible for Pam. I'll swear she couldn't have struck a left handed blow with that force. She has a strong right arm, and she's very right handed. And besides, it's a psychological impossibility. I know Pam Frye. I know she couldn't kill anyone. And God knows," Cummings added wrathfully, "if anyone ever presented two people with adequate motives for murder, Marina presented 'em to Pam and Aaron Frye! Asey, what I want you to do is come over to Quanomet and convince this crackbrained, dunderheaded outfit which laughingly calls itself the police, that Pam Frye did *not* kill her sister. My God, I'm exhausted."

He sounded it, Asey thought.

"Where's the girl?" he asked.

"She's beat it," Hanson said. "She wouldn't beat it if she wasn't guilty, would she? Innocent people don't run away and hide. They—"

"Pfaugh!" Cummings snorted. "Why you cops stick to these outworn clichés, I will never know! If you were confronted with the murdered body of your sister, and her husband screaming that he'd told the police you'd killed her, I venture to say, my fine fellow, you'd run! I'd run myself. Anyone would. Anyone with a grain of sense—"

"Listen," Hanson said, "she ran away, and that's enough for me. And she won't get far, because she doesn't know how to drive, and she hasn't any car. And she hasn't any money. Lorne said she'd try to get away in her boat, so we've got that guarded, and we've got her house guarded. We're stopping all cars up at the bridges, up Cape, so she can't bum a ride and get away. She's crazy about her father, and sooner or later she'll get in touch with him—he didn't know about it, he was away. We'll get her through him. Now, Asey, I want you to come over and talk with Lorne, and this Hobbs woman, and see the body, and convince this pill peddler he's crazy. A woman in a fury can do anything, even to stabbing with her left hand—why, we had a woman in East Brinslow, she—"

"She doubtless," Cummings said icily, "murdered her husband with a razor blade held between her teeth, being armless and legless. I've no doubt at all. Ripley's cartoons are full of just such quaint coincidences. The fact remains, Pam Frye did not kill her sister, and Asey, I want you to come and prove it!"

Asey yawned elaborately, while Hanson and the doctor stared at him in surprise. It was not Asey Mayo's custom to greet cases with such languor.

"As a matter of fact," Asey said, "I got back here in town today after four rough days up from Jamaica, an' I been out in my boat since early afternoon, an' to be downright honest with you, I'm sleepy. An' furthermore—"

"What!" Cummings raised his voice. "What—? The fact that Pam Frye is shortly going to be arrested by that brainless thing—that doesn't move you any? Asey, you've got to come!"

"An' furthermore," Asey continued tranquilly, "I'm sort of sick an' tired of doin' Hanson's work for him. He says this is clear as crystal, you say it ain't. Can't you compromise on the girl's husband? Honest, I'm sleepy, an' this don't move me much one way or the other. Kind of a commonplace murder, when you come right down to it. Girl stabbed. That's all there is to it. Girl stabbed. Now, if you had quintuplets hung in a row, or someone stood up against the mural an' mowed down with a machine gun, why that'd be diff'rent. But—girl stabbed!"

The doctor gaped at him.

"Well, really," he said. "Really! If that's the way you feel —come on, Hanson. Let's battle it out to a finish—ouch! Ow! My God, Asey, why can't you fix your damned wharf? I nearly broke my neck on that loose board!"

Asey watched them stride up the path—listened to the cars as they roared off in the direction of Quanomet.

"Okay, Pam," he said. "Come on out. Are you frozen?"

She swung herself up on the wharf. "No, the water's not so cold—Asey, why'd you do that? Why didn't you go over?"

"Because," Asey said, "I didn't want to leave you wanderin' around loose to catch pneumonia, or meet up with our fine feathered friend the listener, who ought to be comin' back pretty soon to find out more about the ambergris, I think. Hustle up to the house. We got things to think about."

Pam chuckled. "Now that the sheer terror is beginning to

wear off," she said, "I'm almost enjoying myself. Cummings —isn't he an old lamb? I nearly giggled out loud when he yelled at that loose board—he really didn't trip, you know. I was right underneath. He just yelled because he was sore at you, and he had to take it out some way."

"He yelled," Asey said, "because I pinched him from the rear. He'll be back shortly, an' find out what's goin' on. The doc's got consid'rable more brains than most folks, includin' Hanson, suspect."

Up in his house, Asey unstrapped a suitcase and rummaged through it.

"Here," he said triumphantly, producing a pair of flannels, "I knew these was in the clean lot. They got shrunk so they're about your size, an' here's a shirt. An' a sweater I was bringin' home to Betsey Porter, but your need's greater'n hers. Upstairs, first left, there's a bathroom. Take a hot bath, please, an' a cold shower, an' I'll leave some food in the bedroom next door. You stay up there while I do some organizin'."

There was cold roast beef in his refrigerator, potato salad and a custard pie—all donations from his cousin Syl's wife. With the deftness acquired from his earlier days at sea, when he was a cook, Asey dressed up a tray, brewed coffee, and concocted a hot toddy.

He never thought to pull down the shades in his kitchen, nor did it occur to him to look outside the window, where a figure watched with interest as Asey left with the heaped-up tray for Pam.

Asey returned, sat down at the kitchen table and ate his own meal. At its conclusion, he toyed with the carving knife beside the platter of beef.

Knives. He knew all about knives. He had learned about knives in a series of installments over a long period of years, and from a strange and widely scattered assortment of people. There was that Jamaican cook and his razor sharp cutlass, and the dagger of an Italian mate, and the stiletto of that Spaniard in Hong Kong. The Spaniard and Asey had got to be friends, later; he'd taught Asey a lot about knives, and knives needed knowing. Practically any fool could pull a trigger, but a neat stabbing, such as this seemed to be—that took a bit of skill.

Asey balanced the carving knife. Somewhere around the house he had a jackknife with a six inch blade. For fun, he'd get it out. Probably he'd be no use with it. You had to keep in trim to play with knives.

The watcher outside stared intently, and fondled the gun in a hip pocket. Actually neither Asey nor the girl had to be killed. Asey would be put out of business, and—well, if there were trouble with the girl—

Slowly the gun was raised.

Asey continued to finger the carving knife. It had on the whole a nice balance. He flexed his wrist, and then on sudden impulse hurled the knife at the bread board, hanging on the wall next to the window.

Instinctively, the watcher ducked.

"Huh," Asey said to himself with quiet pride, watching the knife quiver in the exact center of the soft pine board, "it must be like bicyclin'. You don't forget."

He wrenched the knife from the board, and standing in the far corner of the room, hurled it twice more. Both times it hit within a quarter of an inch of the center.

The watcher returned the gun to his pocket.

A few minutes later the knocker on Asey's front door sounded.

4. THE insistence of that continued rat-a-tat did more than jerk Asey back from his reminiscences and his knife throwing; it made him keenly aware of his stupidity in shilly-shallying when he should have been indulging in a good dose of constructive and thoughtful planning.

"Fool!" Asey murmured to himself. "Dum fool, you even left the shades up!"

And anyone over two feet tall, approaching that side door from the back of the house, might well have been watching him for the last twenty minutes.

Asey gritted his teeth and summed up his own mental caliber in a few terse nautical phrases.

En route to the door, he detoured into a bedroom and rummaged in a traveling bag. Finally he brought forth his favorite Colt, the old single action Army forty-five, which he thrust into his belt.

To think of it! To think that he could have sat there like a lump, fiddling with that knife! As if he hadn't a single care in the world.

The trail of reproachful murmurings accompanied him as he slid through the dark hallway; he would have greeted with merriment, at that moment, any suggestion that his knife fiddling had probably saved his skin.

Snapping on the outside light, he peered through the curtained side glass at the stranger who stood on the millstone doorstep.

Definitely the young fellow did not belong to Hanson's outfit, nor could Asey recall ever seeing before that longish face, and the thick horn rimmed glasses. It was possible that he might be a messenger from Dr. Cummings—the doc was always commandeering tourists to do his errands, and this one had the usual raw and untanned look of the newly arrived summer visitor.

Of course, Asey thought, there was the possibility that this fellow might be the prowler who had overheard Pam's story, and crawled off through the pines. The immaculateness of his white linen suit cried out that he couldn't have crawled through anything, let alone a hundred yards of dusty pine grove. But that was no conclusive proof. He might have a car stuffed full of clean white linen suits for just such crawlings.

Asey swung the door open wide.

"Mr. Mayo?" the young man smiled. A pleasant smile, Asey conceded, and a quiet, well bred sort of voice.

"I'm Mayo."

"How do you do? My name is Carr. Timothy Carr. I'm a boarder at Octagon House."

"Yes," Asey said, in a tone that said perhaps he was Mr. Carr of Octagon House, and perhaps he was not.

"The police have been here to see you? And the doctor?"

"They've been here."

Asey's grudging taciturnity did not appear to bother Mr. Carr in the least.

"That's fine," he said, "because it'll save me any amount of explanations. Of course, as a matter of fact, I knew quite well that they have been here. Mr. Mayo, I'd like to come in and talk with you about this affair. I know it's not a socially accepted hour for calling, and I understand that you are weary to the point of exhaustion. But I told Mr. Frye I'd talk to you, and—"

"An' what?" Asey demanded.

"And I intend to," Mr. Carr smiled his engaging smile. "I fully intend to, even if I have to stand out here and yell through your splendid paneled door. It would distress me to have to yell, but on the other hand, I promised Mr. Frye."

He spoke very quietly, but he obviously meant what he said. It was the sort of tone young Bill Porter used during the Porter factory strike, when Betsey called him The Blithe Bulldog.

Asey grinned. "Come on in," he said, "an' talk."

"Thank you. And I have a verbal message from Dr. Cummings, too," Timothy said as he followed Asey into the living room. "He'll be over shortly, just as soon as he can get away."

"If you'd told me that first," Asey said, "you'd have got in quicker."

"I know, but I'd have been entering under false pretenses," Carr said amiably, sitting down on the couch and watching Asey draw the window shades. "I do really want to talk with you about this affair, and the message was incidental. I was coming here anyway. And besides, I wanted to find out if you were as adamant about playing with the case as that

policeman seemed to think. Gran and I—that is, my grandmother and I, we both decided you were faking, and now
I'm sure you are. Gran's an old Asey Mayo fan, she reads
every scrap she can find about you in the papers. I've often
had to restrain her from framing you and hanging you on
the walls. She claims you have things up your sleeve. Do
you?"

"What did Hanson say?" Asey countered with another
question.

Timothy Carr polished his glasses. "Hanson," he said,
"probably has a heart of gold. He must have some redeeming
feature, and God knows his teeth aren't it, or his brains.
Look, to begin with, Aaron Frye is frantic. Naturally. Then
Hanson set a copper over him, and forbade his stirring from
Octagon House, which made him more frantic. Gran and I
worried about him, and the only way we could calm him at
all was to promise that we'd come to you and ask your help.
Hanson said we couldn't go, but the doctor took our part,
and gave me that message when Hanson was otherwise
occupied. That sums up the details."

He paused and pulled out a cigarette case. The initials,
Asey noticed, did not stand for Timothy Carr, unless Mr.
Carr spelled Timothy with a G and Carr with an M.

"What," Asey asked blandly, "d'you propose should be
done about things—are those Turkish cig'rettes that you're
smokin'?"

"Won't you have one of the filthy things?" Timothy got
up and offered him the case. "They're Gran's fault, she has

an elderly beau in the tobacco business who gives her these in carload lots. We'd much prefer plain common cigarettes, but Gran says we can't hurt his feelings. What she really means is that she'd smoke salt hay to get his opera seats on alternate Wednesdays."

Asey declined the cigarettes and lighted his pipe. Mr. Carr, he thought, was as left handed a young man as he had observed in some time.

"What," he asked casually, "did you say your name was?"

"Carr, Tim Carr—oh, you saw those initials? That's Gran again. She gave me this case when I was twenty-one. She brooded a week to find a suitable sentiment to have engraved on it, and with great simplicity she landed on G. M. Grown Man," he explained. "I suppose on the whole it's better than 'To dear Timmy from his doddering Granny,' which she'd seriously considered. She—"

"I see," Asey said. "You're quite a southpaw, ain't you?"

Tim Carr stared at him.

"You certainly take everything in!" he said with admiration. "I'm left handed, but I'm really not grist to your mill, you know. Gran and I are alibied by the movies, thank God. But that left handed item is one of a number of odd and instructive details I wanted to talk with you about, if you'd care to hear 'em. Things like how I fell in love with Marina, and my offering to kill her, and Gran seconding the motion, and all—shall I go on?"

"Just why," Asey inquired, "are you so lush an' lavish with your information?"

"Whenever it seems likely that I shall become involved in a situation," Timothy said, "I find it's simpler to tell than wait to be found out about."

"A noble an' high-minded sentiment," Asey commented, trying not to look at the pine needle that was caught in the sole stitching of Mr. Carr's brown and white saddle shoes. "Almost lofty."

"Yes," Timothy agreed, "it's the type of homely honesty I try to implant in the young, and it gets me promoted to a mastership over much worthier folk. I'm a teacher of mathematics, by the way, in Banks and Webster's swanky little prep school on upper Madison Avenue. Everything pointed toward my becoming an architect, originally. Everything except the depression, and that pointed to a job. Once I got into this quadratic surd business, I never dared leave a regular salary. Just another square peg. I'm quite sure," he added, "that you don't care a rap about my career or my early youth, but if going into them will melt those base suspicions gleaming in your eyes, I certainly shall go into them at great length."

"Just what makes you feel that you'll be involved in this business?" Asey asked casually.

"All the murders I've read about, in fiction and in the papers," Timothy said, "always dig up vast quantities of details concerning bystanders. All bystanders, innocent or otherwise. Gran and I are bystanders, in a sense. Amazing how one slips into the language of murder, isn't it? Gran just called it Foul Deed. Anyway, when people begin delving into Marina, they'll find us. Bellowing with rage and screaming murderous threats. It just seemed simpler to tell you first."

"If you and your grandmother," Asey said reasonably, "disliked Marina so much, what in time did you come an' park yourselves practically next door to her for? What made you come to Quanomet?"

"You don't think we knew she was here!" Timothy said. "Perish the thought! We came because Gran had flu last month, badly and expensively, and we needed cheap country for her to rest in. Gran found the Fryes' ad, and we both liked it. It said, 'Old fashioned boarders wanted, for impossibly inconvenient house with no modern improvements whatsoever. Oil lamps, outhouse, pump. Prunes for breakfast, catch your own fish, dig your own clams.' It had a curiously honest ring. And then when I found out it was an octagon house, that clinched matters. Wild horses wouldn't have kept me away. I've always been fascinated by octagon houses, I don't know why. Maybe I got scared by one in childhood, or something. Anyway, I've collected a lot of junk about them. Pictures, photographs, floor plans, clippings, articles and stuff. The old Orson Fowler book. So Gran and I came—"

"Fowler," Asey said thoughtfully. "That name seems familiar. Who was Fowler?"

He knew perfectly well who Fowler was, for up in his attic were a hundred odd Fowler books, the legacy of a great-uncle. Most of them concerned phrenology, but the rest covered practically everything from bee-keeping to the evils of tight lacing, tobacco and strong drink.

"Fowler," Timothy said, "was some lad." And forthwith he embarked on a discussion of Fowler, his invention of the octagon house, the gravel wall mode of building, and the general sanity of Fowler's architectural ideas. "Of course," he said, "sanitation, drainage, and his strange notions of sanitary disposal, those licked him. But if more people had had such thoughts about architecture eighty years ago, when Fowler thought up his octagon, lots of countryside would be better looking. Now, I—"

"Yes," Asey said, a little disappointed that he had not been able to catch Mr. Carr, "but let's get back to Marina Lorne. You knew Marina in New York. You must have known where she came from."

"She never mentioned Cape Cod. Never. I thought she came from the Middle West. She called herself Marina Fern. Not Frye, or Lorne. Fern, like the plant. She was modeling at an art school I went to at night. Jack Lorne was in one of the classes, by the way, but I didn't know that then. Or that they happened to be married. Those were points she didn't bring up. Well, I fell for Marina, and not even Gran's japing snapped me out of it. In fact, I didn't emerge till the day I found four hundred dollars of mine, and all of Gran's jewelry, missing from our apartment. That emerged me at once."

"Why?" Asey wanted to know. "Most anyone might steal—"

"Yes, most anyone might, except that Marina was the only person who knew about that money of mine. I'd sold some drawings—a major miracle, I never sold any before or afterwards. And I'd told Marina about it, and how I'd hidden it, and how I was going to take Gran on a bust of a trip. Gran didn't know a thing about it."

"What'd you do?"

"For three days I detected," Timothy said. "Marina had disappeared, no one at her boarding house knew where she'd moved. The third day, I found a key shop where the man had made a duplicate of our key for her, and the time he made it checked with Marina's going and coming to our place one day. She'd apparently taken Gran's key from the hall table, gone, had the key made, came back and left Gran's in its place. Carlton—that's Gran's tobacco beau—he found most of the jewelry in a downtown pawn shop, and gallantly redeemed it. We never could have. At art school, shortly after, someone displayed a post card from England. 'X marks our room, wish you were here, Marina and Jack.' And I discovered they'd been married a couple of years. That week Jack was awarded a prize for some splendid work— happened to be copies from some stuff of mine, with a lot of polishing and embellishments. Stuff I was saving up for a scholarship competition. Marina, someone said, had helped him a lot. I thought so, too."

"I get," Asey said, "the idea. An' you didn't do anythin' about her?"

"There wasn't anything to be done, then. We were too damned poor—and, well, there was the other angle. I would have looked like a fool, and Gran would have had to be dragged through the courts. No, there wasn't anything to be done then."

"Did you keep track of the Lornes?" Asey asked.

"Yes, through friends of theirs I knew. When they returned to New York, I took Gran and Carlton and paid Marina a call. She was wearing Gran's diamond rings. It was a splendid interview. I held her, and Gran removed the rings. Then Carlton said gently, we'd like the four hundred dollars, and the money paid for redeeming the jewelry. She was frightened to death, and wept and wailed and said they were penniless, and Carlton said, very well, the police could take a hand. She had two hundred cash, and so we took that and then snatched a few pictures off the walls and called it a day, after much rhetoric from Gran and me as to what physical damage she would suffer if she crossed our paths again. We discovered later that the original stones had been removed from the rings, but by that time the Lornes had flitted again. That, in brief, is why we don't like Marina—"

"An' when did you discover she was here?"

"Tonight, when we came back from the movies, all God's children roamed the grounds and vicinity of Octagon House, and a woman named Hobbs was having hysterics and saying she'd just come back for her pocketbook, but she knew all the time, she knew, she knew! And police raced around, and finally we got someone to tell us the trouble. They said Marina Lorne had been killed, she lived in the Cape Cod cottage at the corner, beyond. Gran asked who did it, and they said her sister, Pam Frye. That was the first we knew of Pam and Marina and Mr. Frye being related—"

A horn outside blew three strident blasts.

"Who's that?" Asey asked. "Someone at your car?"

"Oh, it's Gran," Timothy said.

"Out in the car? Whyn't you bring—"

"She thought she'd better not come in, she has Emma with her. Emma Goldman. Her cat. It's a red Persian," he added in explanation. "Emma hates police. One stepped on her tail when she was a kitten, and she's never forgotten. Gran was afraid she'd scratch the cop staying with Frye, so we brought her. And Aaron Frye's parrot drives her frantic—"

"Do you mean that your grandmother has been sitting out there all this time, holding a cat?" Asey sounded incredulous.

"Oh, Emma's trained to a leash," Timothy said. "Gran always trains her cats to a leash. There goes the horn again— I'll dash out—"

Asey started to follow him, but remembering Pam Frye, he first ran upstairs to the bedroom.

There was a note stuck on the door. "Dear Asey, I am taking a nap, I am exhausted, but call me when you need me for anything. Pam."

Asey hesitated, and then thought, as he carefully locked the door and pocketed the key, the Lord knew she needed a nap, and if she could take one at that point, more power to her.

Outdoors he found Timothy standing beside a small coupé parked in the driveway.

"My grandmother, Mrs. Carr," he said. "With Emma."

The white haired woman inside was too absurdly young looking to be anyone's grandmother. Asey said so, to Mrs. Carr's outspoken delight.

"There, Tim," she said, "that's the sort of gallantry I miss in your contemporaries. I—watch Emma, she's getting out."

The largest Persian cat Asey had ever seen jumped with dignity from the seat down to the grass.

"She's still ruffled," Mrs. Carr said. "Just the sight of brass buttons annoys her, and there were so many over there—and that bird—has Timmy told you how we yearned to kill Marina, and that we're both left handed? And what's to be done about Pam Frye—of course she didn't kill Marina, she's much too nice a child. But everyone seems to think so. That Aunt Nettie person—do you know that Nettie?"

Asey found it hard to maintain his prejudices against Tim Carr and his grandmother. Perhaps, he decided, they were just naturally expansive and chatty. Perhaps they just couldn't help it. On the other hand, under the circumstances, their very natural and matter of fact attitude was in itself suspicious.

"Aunt Nettie Hobbs," Asey said, "has been a pain in folkses' necks as long as I can remember. An' it's kind of hard to sum her up, too."

Mrs. Carr announced tartly that she personally could sum up Aunt Nettie in several words, and that nothing but modesty prevented her from doing so.

"But the funny part of it is," Asey said, "I think she means well. She—"

"She takes jelly and custards to the sick," Mrs. Carr said, "and she makes layettes for the county's wayward girls. And after she departs, the sick promptly die, and the wayward girls, suddenly realizing with a start that they *are* wayward, go out and become utterly depraved. Yes, I know the Aunt Nettie type. But the stinker—dear me, Timmy, you do add such foul words to my vocabulary! But the stinker was identifying the knife that killed Marina as Pam Frye's—"

"She—uh. Was she?" Asey caught himself just in time to keep from adding that Pam had admitted that the knife was hers.

"Yes, I knew it was. I recognized it. But listen here. Pam was away, this afternoon when we all decided to go to this clambake, and we left a note for her, and I personally stuck it on the back door with that knife—it was just sitting there, that knife, on the railing. Tonight I noticed that the note was still on the door, but it was held up by a pin. A common pin. And—"

"And obviously," Timothy chimed in, "Pam Frye wouldn't remove the knife and then pin the note back again! That's just silly. What we think is, someone passing by grabbed the knife, and the same person used the knife to kill Marina with, knowing that it would implicate Pam. Doesn't that seem likely?"

Asey admitted that it did.

"And that Nettie!" Mrs. Carr said indignantly. "There she stood, when we left, telling hordes of police and all those reporters that Pam *must* have had the knife on her belt this evening, because she had on the belt! That woman is a menace, she should be forcibly restrained! And so should the police. Did Tim tell you they're simply combing Octagon House?"

"Combing—what for?" Asey demanded, thinking instantly of the ambergris. That was hidden there, somewhere, And if Hanson's men found it—

"This Nettie saw Pam run out of the garage, and she saw Jack Lorne stumble—"

"What was Nettie doin' back there—or," he amended hastily, "hadn't she gone, or what?"

"She'd come back for her pocketbook, she said. She is," Mrs. Carr said, "one of those women who always strews things so she can have a legitimate excuse to return and stand outside the door and find out what's being said about her after she went—don't interrupt, Timmy, maybe the grammar is involved, but I know what I mean. Anyway, Nettie started for home, but returned in time to see Pam dashing off, and Nettie wasn't sure that Pam hadn't dashed into Octagon House. What did you say?"

"I said," Asey told her, "I ain't sure but what Nettie shouldn't be forcibly restrained. Go on."

"Well, that floor plan—it's simply fascinating the police. All those odd closets, all alike, and everything. I had to shoo two troopers from my bedroom wardrobe. They were banging the wall for monk's holes or—don't let Emma catch that bug, Tim. They make her sick. Or hideaways, or secret panels, or something. Timmy had to go down and stop them from moving the coal in the cellar."

Asey drew a deep breath. Pam hadn't told him exactly where she had put the ambergris, but he felt sure it must be in the cellar. She couldn't have carried it upstairs.

"They thought," Tim said, "she was under the briquets. I tried to point out the impossibility of anyone's hiding in a coal bin, and then pulling the coal over 'em, but they took a lot of convincing. This is my first actual contact with the police, you know, and it amazes me to find that they think the way they do in movies and books. I suppose it's like stupidity in housemaids. If they had brains, they wouldn't be housemaids. Or police. Anyway, Police Were Combing the Vicinity, Setting Dragnets, and all."

"But they found," Asey said, "no trace of Pam?"

"No. Where is she?" Mrs. Carr asked. "Where can she be? And what can we do for her? And poor old Mr. Frye—we've got to do something, for his sake. Did you ask him about charges, Tim? My dear boy, *what* have you been doing in there? Mr. Mayo, how much do you charge for solving things? Because if you have a special rate for widows and orphans, Tim and I would like you to clear Pam Frye. You will, won't you?" she added briskly, as though the whole matter were settled.

"I don't do things for prices," Asey said, "an'—why are you two so set on helpin'? You never met the Fryes till you landed here, did you?"

"No," Mrs. Carr said, "but we like Pam, and her father—and I feel a sort of sympathy with them. And to be brutally frank, I am glad that Marina Lorne finally met up with someone who gave her what she richly deserved. Even if I thought Pam killed her, I should still ask you to prove she didn't. And proving that she didn't won't be hard. I shouldn't think it would take you a day."

Asey grinned. "How so?"

"Why, it's Jack Lorne, of course. Aaron Frye told us he'd

been over there today, trying to borrow money—Marina was in some sort of scrape. Frye refused, and I suppose everyone else refused, and in desperation, Jack Lorne killed her. I can't see why he didn't do it long before. He is a—what's that expression, Tim? A summer guy?"

"A fall guy," Tim said gravely.

"And of course he's left handed—"

"He is!" Asey said. "Are you sure about that?"

"Timmy," Mrs. Carr said plaintively, "what *did* you talk about so long in there in the house? Didn't you tell him anything at all? Jack Lorne paints with his left hand, but he's right handed in everything else. He—Mr. Mayo, this seems rather a personal question, but is there anyone upstairs in your house? I can see a light and it's acting so queerly, going off and on—Tim! Timmy, give me that leash before you go dashing after him!"

5. IN one motion, Asey twisted the key and swung open the door of the upstairs bedroom.

"Pam!"

He groped for the switch and flicked on the light.

Pam was not on the bed—Pam was not there!

Asey jerked at the closet door. A strong odor of mothballs filled the room. Inside, as he had left them, were his old suits, forlorn looking in their cloth coverings.

Pam was not in the cupboard under the eaves. The window screens were firmly hooked in place. There was no connection with any other room.

Asey was peering under the bed when Tim Carr bounded in. His white linen suit was streaked with grass stains, caused when Emma Goldman's leash had tripped him and sent him sprawling.

"What's the matter?" he demanded breathlessly.

"That," Asey said briefly, "is what I'd like to know. She's gone."

"She—who? Say, did you have Pam Frye here all the time?"

"Yup," Asey said. "Come on. We'll do some huntin'—"

Hastily he looked through the house. Then, equipped with flashlights, he and Timothy set out to explore outside.

"I *know* this place," Asey said after half an hour's frantic searching. "I know it! There's no road except the one out front. No one can come or go without using that road, right where we was. It'd take an army to cart that girl off against her will! And how'd anyone get in? How'd they get out? Them screens was in place. That door was locked. I never heard of a human bein' evaporatin' into thin air, but she has! She certainly has!"

Mrs. Carr and Emma joined the hunt.

It was Emma, shying and hissing at something that fluttered in the underbrush, who found the only trace of Pam.

"Her handkerchief," Asey said, picking it up. "Least, it's mine. One I tossed on the pile of clothes I give her tonight. It's the last clean one of that batch of monogrammed handkerchiefs."

"What does it all mean?" Mrs. Carr demanded. "Did someone take her away? Did she just go?"

Asey shrugged. "Presumably she was in that bedroom, takin' a nap. That's what her note said. I locked her in, because it seemed to me I'd been awful careless. If she was in the room, how'd she get out? If she wasn't, where'd she gone, and what'd she leave that note for? It don't seem possible she'd go rompin' off without tellin' me—she knows perfectly well that she's in danger."

"But the police don't know she's here," Timothy said. "They're all over Quanomet, combing and scouring vicinities."

"The danger," Asey said, "ain't from the police. She *must*

have understood—we didn't talk about it, but I thought she knew. I know she knew. And that note!"

"Gran," Tim said, "have you got that receipt she gave you for the board money? She insisted on giving it to us, though we protested that it wasn't necessary—where is it, Gran? She wrote it out, all very formally. You might compare the writing on the receipt with that on the note. Perhaps someone else wrote the note."

Mrs. Carr finally produced the receipt from the depths of her capacious pocketbook. Asey marveled, as he invariably did, at the amount of miscellaneous objects that a woman could pack into a handbag of given dimensions. Mrs. Carr's was unusual only in that it contained besides the usual truck a quantity of puppy biscuit and three chewed catnip mice.

"Emma's," she explained. "We always carry cans of evaporated milk, and paper cups in the car for her, too. You might as well get used to it. We've done it so long that we never think anything about it, but it startles other people. Particularly gas station attendants. They all jump when they see Emma peering at them from the rear window. After they come to, they always tell us about their aunt's cat. All gas station men have aunts with cats, and they seem to feel that because you have a cat yourself, you really care about—"

"Gran," Timothy said, "give him the receipt."

"Here you are," Mrs. Carr passed it to Asey. "Now, where's the note?"

Indoors, in the living room, they compared the handwriting.

"If the note isn't genuine," Timothy said, "then it's the most reasonable fascimile I ever saw. Even to that little squiggle under her name. What d'you think, Asey?"

"I think," Asey said, "that she wrote the note. Mind if I keep the receipt? I'll give it back to you later on."

"What'll we do now?" Mrs. Carr asked.

"You might's well go 'long back to Octagon House," Asey said, "an' get some sleep. If Hanson asks, say that you tried and tried but you can't move me, I just don't seem to care. Say you cried, but that didn't work. But tell Aaron Frye that she's all right, and I'll do what I can, but not to mind what other people say about me or Pam or anything. Tell Frye that I'll take care of Pam. I will, somehow."

Emma Goldman allowed herself to be torn away from the mantelpiece, where she had been peacefully sleeping between two mercury goblets.

"You have a way with cats," Mrs. Carr informed him as she put Emma up behind the seat of the coupé. "Emma likes you. You've been so nice, Mr. Mayo—you're just as splendid as the papers say."

Asey stared thoughtfully up the road as the little coupé whizzed off.

He wanted to like those two. They honestly seemed desirous of helping Pam Frye out of this business. They were candid, they were human, they were pleasant. They liked their cat, and their cat liked them. And Asey had a certain respect for people whom cats liked. This great red beast did not belong to the Carrs; they belonged to her.

On the other hand, their very candidness was against

them. Had they come to pump him, to find out where Pam
was? Had Timothy Carr unearthed the ambergris—say, in
the cellar, or the coal bin, or wherever Pam had hidden it?
Could Tim Carr have been the prowler? Could Mrs. Carr
somehow have whisked Pam away, while Tim chatted in-
consequentially about Marina and his life in the quadratic
surd business? And his story about Marina—there was a
certain glib quality about that yarn, about the key-maker and
the rest of it, that made one wonder.

Asey shook his head. He wished that he knew the answers.
If the Carrs turned out to be perfectly all right, he would feel
a little foolish for having entertained any suspicions. But in
the sort of mess that this gave every indication of becoming,
you never knew.

There was one place where he had purposely not hunted
while Tim and his grandmother were around, and he
strolled there now, along the path to the landing. Pam didn't
know the first thing about automobiles, but she did know
about boats. If she had gone off on her own, she would have
instinctively made for the water.

Why should she have gone? There wasn't an earthly reason, unless she had some quixotic notion that her presence
in his house was dangerous to Asey. That was the only explanation he could think of. If she had been whisked away
—but she couldn't have. People couldn't be whisked as
quietly as all that. Pam was a strong, healthy girl. She
wouldn't have allowed anyone to snatch her, not without
raising a rumpus first.

Unless—the simplicity of the solution brought him to a

standstill. Unless someone whom she knew and trusted had come. And what was it Pam has said, something about intending to tell her male boarder about the ambergris before she set out to Boston, because he seemed such a decent sort?

She'd had no chance to tell him, of course. But just supposing that Timothy had climbed up on the roof and talked to her through the window, while Asey was downstairs in the kitchen. He might have lured her away by some yarn about the ambergris. Then Pam wrote the note, slipped into another room, slipped out while Asey and Tim were talking downstairs, or while they were out by the coupé in the driveway.

Pam might, for all Asey knew, have been in the rumble seat all that time!

But if she had gone on her own, she would have made for the water. There was no harm in looking into the situation.

The sharpie, however, was there by the landing, and the *Mary B* rode her mooring. The canvas cockpit cover was in place. She hadn't been touched.

On sudden impulse, Asey unlocked the shanty at the foot of the landing, and hunted up a padlock.

Then, with the short jerky stroke of the Cape Codder, he rowed out to the *Mary B* and firmly locked her chain to the mooring. If any professional boat thief really wanted to steal the craft, that padlock would not stop him. It would hardly annoy him. But if Pam Frye had any fancy notions of making off in the *Mary B*, that padlock would effectively put a damper on the excursion.

The first red streaks of dawn showed over the outer beach as he returned to the landing. As he tied up the sharpie, the tide turned with a roar, and the red streaks darkened. The air was damp as the great fog banks hanging off shore started to creep in.

Asey turned up the collar of his shirt and started back for the house.

"Huh," he said aloud, "my hat's off to whoever got her, that's what. Or to her, if she sneaked off by herself. It ain't human!"

The sound of a car drawing up in his driveway completely drowned out the slight crackle in the bushes just beyond him.

Dr. Cummings got out of his old sedan.

"Asey," he said, "this has been a night!"

"You," Asey returned, "think you're tellin' me anything? Pooh."

"Roughly speaking, Hanson has his entire command hunting Pam Frye," Cummings said. "I see no particular reason to think she'll stay outside the dragnet very much longer. And Nettie—Asey, you've got to squelch her. Someone's got to. She's talked all night. To the police, to the reporters, to anyone who'd listen. And as she talks, she decorates. She now says that Pam spent the entire evening nervously fingering the knife at her belt, occasionally pausing to snarl viciously, like a spotted leopard in a peeve. She says that Pam dashed out at nine, she saw Pam dash toward the Lornes' garage, and that when Pam returned, there was no knife at her belt. And her expression was that of a leopard after a dinner. Now, you know, that's not going to do Pam Frye any good!"

Asey agreed. "Has she made any statements?"

"Hanson's been too busy to get one from her, but the reporters—wouldn't it be the only time in the life of Quanomet that reporters were there in droves? They've got Nettie's life story, and Pam's life story from Nettie—and both will be greeting John Public over his orange juice and toast, very shortly. And the fact that it's the mural's artist's wife who was killed—that's not going to be any soft pedal."

"What about Lorne?"

"He's in a frenzy. I'm beginning to think he loved that trollop."

"He's left handed," Asey said.

"No, I noticed particularly that he wasn't," Cummings said.

"But he is when he paints," Asey informed him. "An'—"

"Are you sure?"

"I got told that tonight. You might check up on it, if you can. Does Hanson know where he was—an' by the way, was Marina killed at nine?"

"Wouldn't know for sure, I'd say between nine and ten. No, Hanson hasn't delved into Lorne. Lorne's acting just the way a bereaved and outraged husband should, and Hanson is deeply moved by it. I think he'd sooner suspect his own mother than Jack Lorne. Look—what about Pam? Where can she be?"

"I had her here," Asey said. "She was under the wharf

while you an' Hanson strode around over her head—"

"No wonder you pinched my rear end! Where is she now? There are a couple of things I'd like to clear up—is she asleep?"

"She's gone," Asey said, and told him the whole story.

Cummings whistled.

"Did she fall—or was she pushed. Asey, that's awful. And ambergris—look, we'll have to get that out of the way of the police—where is it?"

"Search me," Asey said. "If the cops didn't find it in Octagon House, I'd say it wasn't there. Pam never did tell me where it really was."

"Ambergris—look, we'll have to do something about that!" Cummings said. "We'll have to get it away, and sold, and fixed for Pam. If Marina told anyone about it—why, for all we know, a dozen people might be hunting it!"

"It," Asey said, "and Pam, too. And if the cops find it, well—we could blot Nettie Hobbs out, and all she's said. Once the cops find out about that ambergris incident, and Pam's takin' it from the garage, with the sister dead, well, we just won't think about that part."

Cummings sighed. "It's a mess. I wouldn't know where to start."

"Are you sure about that left handedness," Asey asked, "or were you impressin' Hanson?"

"I'm quite certain that whoever killed Marina thrust that knife with his left hand, and is a reasonably husky sort. Of course, I won't say it isn't possible that someone didn't stand on his head and stab with the right hand—Asey, I'm so tired

I can't think. This story of yours makes me feel I'm home in bed, after eating a large and indigestible dinner topped off with whipped cream cake and pink lemonade. I'm going. Call me when you want me, and when you've figured out some plan or other. I think you'll do well to continue letting Hanson think you won't help him. Otherwise the police'll be around your neck, and they'll curtail you considerably. I'll fume at you, to make it seem genuine. I'll also pass along anything that happens. And look—see if you can't squelch Nettie. She's gone too far."

"Okay," Asey said. "I'll see if somethin' can't get started."

He noticed, as he returned to the house, that the fog was going out and that the wind had shifted again.

If it hadn't, he might possibly have caught another whiff of that Turkish tobacco he had smelled earlier, down by the landing.

6. IT was quarter to nine that same morning, just as Asey poured himself a third cup of coffee, that the side gate clicked and the ample figure of his cousin Syl Mayo's wife hove in view.

Asey sighed. Jennie was a dear, kind thing, and while few women could equal her cooking, few also could equal her curiosity.

"My, ain't it awful!" Asey murmured to himself. "Who done it, Asey, who done it! Huh. Come in!" he raised his voice. "Come in, Jennie."

He would, at least, hear all the details. Jennie was on the twenty-one telephone line, and if Jennie was up to par, she should have at least twenty-one versions of Marina Lorne's murder.

"My, my!" Jennie ran true to form. "My, Asey, ain't it awful! Who done it, do you know? I'd like to ring their necks, that's what I'd like to do!"

"You're the first person," Asey remarked, "who's felt the slightest bit of sympathy for Marina Lorne, or the least drop of anger toward the feller that killed her. Why do—"

"Marina?" Jennie sniffed. "I'm not talkin' about Marina Lorne. Marina! Huh. Plain Mary, that's what she is. Mary Hosannah. And she was a—well, she was a bad woman,

Asey. Just plain bad. Deserved what she got. Who done it?"

Asey was puzzled. "Done what, the murder?"

"Bother the murder. I'm talkin' about them petunias out by your kitchen window here! Who trampled 'em down? I spent all day before yesterday mornin' in the hot sun," Jennie said, "settin' in petunias like you always have, and Syl forgot about while you was off. An' now they're trampled flat as your shoe! Little Gem, they was, the nice kind that spreads so, an' I went way up to the greenhouse to get 'em, an' now they're all trampled up. It's—well, I'd like to find the wretch that did it! I'd give them a good piece of my mind—"

"Trampled?" Asey got up. "I didn't know it, Jennie. I seen the petunias yesterday, an' thought how fine they looked. I was goin' to tell you how I liked 'em—let me take a look, now, at this. This is sort of interestin'."

Jennie's ire was considerably mollified by Asey's solicitude for the trampled plants.

. "I thought myself, they looked pretty nice," she said. "Come on—here, see? Of course I can get the car when Syl come in from quohoggin' an' drive up an' get more. They was dear—"

"I'll pay for the next lot," Asey said, "an' while you're up there, you get some cut flowers for yourself. Well, well. That's tramplin' that *is* tramplin', ain't it? I think—yes, I think I begin to see. Jennie, I was just as dummed a fool last night as I thought I was. Somebody stood out here an' watched me—"

He figured it out. Somebody was watching him there in

the kitchen. Pam, coming into the bedroom after her bath, must have peeked down and seen the person there. She would have been able to, from the far window.

She didn't dash downstairs, or scream out, which on the whole was sensible of her. To let the person know for sure that she was there would not have been so good.

Asey knelt down.

"I wish," he said, "that he hadn't milled around—this earth is so soft, you couldn't get one good print out of the lot. But here's—oho. He ducked at somethin'—say—I wonder! I bet it was my knife comin'—"

Jennie stared at him. "You feel all right?" she asked anxiously. "You ain't goin' to come down with that malaria again, are you, like last time you come back from Jamaica—"

"I'm fine," Asey said. "Fine. An' then he left. An' Pam wrote that note—"

"Pam Frye? Asey Mayo, you *are* mixed up in this, aren't you? Syl said you was. He said that he didn't care a bit what folks said, he knew that you was up to some trick or other."

"Pam left that note for me," Asey said, "an' then she hid. I just locked up the empty room. Then she slid out, probably while Carr was here. Chances are pretty good that she gave the watcher the slip, see? Because she knew about him, an' he didn't know about her. She figured that she'd told me all she could, an' that her bein' here was dangerous to me, as well as curtailin' my comin's and goin's. Without her around, I'd be a lot freer an' a lot safer. She probably rounded out her thinkin' by feelin' that she had nothin' to lose. An' I guess she's right. I guess, Jennie, she can look out for herself."

"You mean Pam Frye?" Jennie said. "She's a mighty nice girl. Clever, too. She give the women's club a talk on art last year, an' did drawin's with chalk on a board. She drew everyone. Clark Gable and Robert Taylor—she did an awful good one of him. And Garbo, and Joan Crawford. Just's nice as she can be, Pam is."

"Jennie, what about flashlights?" Asey said. "How many do I have around the house? Are they all in the chest?"

"All eight," she told him promptly. "I put 'em all eight in the blue sea chest when I cleaned."

"Then let's see," Asey said, "how many we got now. I know she didn't have a light with her. I think we had three last night, Carr and I."

The eight flashlights were duly accounted for, and Jennie promptly wanted to know why they mattered.

"To prove that a light that flicked off an' on," Asey said, "presumably in the spare bedroom, was really a flashlight that our fancy watcher was flickin' to see if he could draw Pam to the window. Probably he was havin' doubts if she was there. We seen the light from the front, an' he was aimin' in the back. It come straight through the dormer, see? Well, if he wanted action, he sure got it. An' certainly, subsequent events ought to of proved to him that I didn't know where she was or where she'd gone. Jennie, your petunias've been pretty helpful—"

"Maybe they have," Jennie said. "I can't make head nor tail of it, myself. But I do know one thing. I know you ought to go straight over to Quanomet and shut Nettie Hobbs's mouth, tight. Why, the way she's been talkin'! It's awful, Asey."

"What do folks think of the things Nettie says?"

"Those that know Pam, they don't believe Nettie," Jennie said. "But those that don't—well, they ain't got anything else to go by than what Nettie says. It's a shame. My mother used to say that Nettie Hobbs was weaned on sour milk and pickle juice, an' she's right. She's a dour, sour old thing, just the same as the pickle limes in her store window, and now she's got her chance to get back at Pam, she's doin' everything she can. An' you'd ought to stop her."

"To get back at Pam? What for?" Asey asked. "What'd Pam ever do to her?"

"Aaron Frye," Jennie said meaningly, rolling her eyes.

"What about Aaron Frye?"

"Nettie," Jennie said, "she set her cap for him. Of course, they're about of an age, an' Silas Hobbs's been dead for years—poor man, what a life he must have led! Did you know his tombstone says 'At rest—At last'? Well, it does. I've seen it. An' of course Aaron Frye's been a widower for nearly nine years. He's a nice refined man—used to be a professor—an' he's a nice lookin' man, an' Pam keeps things up—"

"Do you mean," Asey said, "that on the strength of Pam Frye's meager earnin's, Nettie was aimin' to marry into the family?"

Jennie nodded. "She don't make much with the Woman's Exchange. I suppose she figured if she could get into the family, Pam or the son-in-law or someone'd keep her, if anything happened to Aaron. Well of course it was silly, the whole thing was silly. I said so, the minute I heard about it last winter. But Aaron Frye's sort of a gentle soul, the kind that can be led into things. *You* know. No," she added, looking at Asey's jaw, "I don't s'pose you do. Anyway, he's sort of easy goin' an' absent minded, an' if Pam hadn't caught on about all the pie an' cake an' jelly bringin', maybe Nettie might have got him. I wouldn't go so far as to say Pam and Nettie had words, but I guess Pam let her understand she was wastin' her time, an' her cookin', too."

"So Nettie's down on Pam for that. Maybe that accounts for things," Asey said.

"That's not all," Jennie answered. "At least, that isn't the part that matters so much. The important part is that Nettie kind of let on to folks that she was goin' to marry Aaron, and one night at a church supper, someone—I think it was your cousin Liz Chase—anyway, she asked Pam about it. An' Pam, she choked over her baked beans so hard they had to bring her water an' bang her on the back. An' when she got her breath, she laughed and laughed and laughed so hard she cried, an' they had to bring her more water. Well, Nettie heard about it, of course. I guess that was the part that—"

"That griped," Asey said with a grin. "I see. No more powerful weapon than ridicule—say, that reminds me. You got anythin' on Nettie? Like—well, I don't know what, exactly. But if you could rout up somethin' I could use as a club, I might be able to stop her talk."

Jennie sat down at the kitchen table and casually ate two cold muffins before she answered.

"There's two things," she said, "but neither of 'em'll be much good. There was always talk about the church accounts the year she had 'em, but I don't know how you'd prove it. Mostly I keep thinkin', Nettie and Pam are related, an' it's a mean skinny way to treat your own flesh and brood, talkin' like Nettie is."

Asey wanted to know how they were related. The minute he asked, he knew he was in for it. Jennie began with the first settler with the name of Sparrow who came to Quanomet, and in an offhand manner, as though she were giving her receipt for sponge cake, she traced the Sparrow family down through the centuries.

"Now this Mary Ann Cass," she said, "an' don't get her mixed with Mary Anna—she had a cousin Hester. An' it was Hester's mother—I never knew her myself, but they say she made awful good elderberry wine—she was own cousin to Henry Sparrow. Henry B., the one they called Barney for short, not Henry B., the one they didn't call Barney. There was," she explained, *"two* Henry B.'s. Well, he was Pam's grandfather on her mother's side. See?"

Asey drew a deep breath. "Pam an' Nettie," he said, "they're sort of cousins. Is that it? Jennie, how in the world do you happen to know all that? You reeled it off like you'd been sayin' it every day for thirty years."

"It'd be peculiar if I didn't know," Jennie said, "considerin' that phone's rung steady since six this mornin'. Oh— an' did you hear about Roddy? Roddy Strutt?"

"What's that fellow done now? Smashed up another car or another boat, or just got someone else's daughter into trouble?"

"It's a plane this time. He got a new one yesterday. Seems some friends of his had their plane down, too, an' they was goin' back to New York in theirs, an' nothin' would do but Roddy had to trail 'em in his. Went as far as Providence, to some airport or somethin'. Comin' home, he insisted on flyin' the plane himself—wouldn't let *him* land. He landed. He landed it bang down in Quanomet Depot Square in the middle of the night, they say, an' I don't know how many cars he hurt, or folks either. Seems's if everybody was hurt but Roddy—ain't that always the way? Oh, an' did you hear about the mural?"

"I seen it," Asey said succinctly.

"Did you hear about the minister bein' in it—his face? Folks say they're pretty mad about that in Quanomet. He does have a mole on his nose, but no one thinks anything about it, an' he's a real good man. In the mural, it's awful. Seems they got all sorts of folks in it. An' horrid, too. Horrid drawings stuck onto horrid people doing horrid things. They're pretty mad in Quanomet. I—well, you mustn't tell, because I didn't hear this on the phone, but I *did* hear, Asey, that some of the folks was so mad, they was goin' to do somethin' to that mural. Hurt it."

"You can't blame anyone," Asey said, "for a perfectly natural human reaction; on the other hand, you want to sort of point out that it's gov'ment property, an' the gov'-ment ain't had no sense of humor for a long time."

"You mean they'd send people," Jennie demanded, "like G-men?"

"They might, if it happened to strike 'em that way. Myself, I'd think it sort of funny, but the people that matter might consider it the defacin' of gov'ment property."

"D'you really think it's true what they say about the murder?" Jennie asked. "About what really happened?"

Asey admitted that he didn't know what they said.

"Well, they say someone that was pictured in that mural got mad, an' went for Jack Lorne."

"But they didn't kill him. They killed Marina."

Jennie nodded. "That's just it. Jack Lorne's a good painter, leastaways he was when he first come to town. You could tell what he meant to paint, in those days. After Marina married him, he begun to paint this horrid stuff where folks's faces were the same size as their stomachs, or their heads like pins. He did the nicest picture of the lily pond. I remember that. Last summer I saw his things in the exhibition, an' they was all mud flats an' dung heaps. Stuff like that."

"An' you think Marina made the change in him?" Asey asked.

"It's not that so much, but—well, people did some thinkin', an' they thought about Jack Lorne. Nobody likes him, but he ain't what you'd call Bad. He isn't so horrid, Asey, just sort of slow thinkin', if you know what I mean. Not stupid, but slow. Folks wonder if he thought up them cartoons like—all by himself, see? An' the way some folks figger is this. Suppose someone who's been painted in that mural got mad at Jack Lorne, an' then thought it out, an' decided Marina put Jack up to it—you see what I mean?"

Asey nodded. It was exactly the same sort of thing that Pam Frye had brought up during their conversation on those pink granite post office steps the day before.

"There's also another side," he remarked, "now I consider it. S'posen Jack Lorne begins to realize what a hornet's nest he's stirred up with his mural. An' how the caricatures Marina put him up to are the things that are the most hornety. I wonder if he'd be mad enough—it don't seem so."

"If he thought that, Marina'd of talked him out of it right away," Jennie said. "She's talked him out of lots and lots of things. Why, he loved her, they say. He even thought she was faithful to him, think of that! An' her gallivantin' and traipsing around with every Tom, Dick and Harry. This year it's been that boob Roddy Strutt. They say that's how Jack got to do that mural."

Asey had to confess that the connection escaped him entirely.

"Why, it's simple, Asey. Roddy's uncle is somethin' in Washington. He had the—what would you call it? the letting out of this painting. Lots of people tried for the job in a sort of competition, but Jack Lorne won. An' they say that his wasn't anywhere near the best—from what I hear, I guess it was the worst! Anyway, Roddy spoke to his uncle, and Jack won. An' you can guess why Roddy spoke to his uncle! An' now, Asey Mayo, you go straight over to Nettie Hobbs an' shut her mouth up! Perhaps if you stop her talk, the police won't think so much about Pam Frye, an' then she can come back. Poor Aaron, he must be awful upset! You hurry along, an' I'll finish up my cleanin'."

Out in his garage, Asey surveyed his long, gleaming Porter roadster. Yesterday that car had caused no commotion in the town of Quanomet, but today it undeniably would. Any number of people who didn't actually know him, would recognize him by the car, and by his familiar hat and jacket. Once he was recognized, he'd be surrounded, and then Hanson would come. On the whole, it seemed wiser not to be Asey Mayo.

He walked back to the kitchen door and yelled for Jennie.

"Where's Syl's truck?"

"That old thing? Down in the back garden. He was gettin' loam for—"

"He won't need it today if he's quohoggin'." Asey said. "I'm goin' to take it. An' where's my old paintin' overalls an' coat?"

"Asey Mayo," Jennie said in desperation, "you can't wear them in public! They're all torn, so torn I didn't even mend 'em. You, with all those nice suits upstairs, an' all your nice white flannels, why you dress so badly I don't know! It's disgraceful, a man with your money—an' Bill Porter's tailor made you such lovely clothes—"

"Jennie," Asey said, "you roust out my paintin' overalls, an' my coat. An' that cap."

"Not the cap! Oh, Asey, you can't go out wearin' that cap! It makes you look like Uncle Corny!"

Asey shouted. Uncle Corny, one of the family's blackest sheep, had died in the drunkards' home.

"Go 'long, Jennie," he said. "I'm supposedly not workin' on this case—an' don't you *dare* tell a soul I am, hear me? Less you want Pam Frye in jail! An' if I go in my car, with my ev'ryday clothes, they'll bother the life out of me."

"You're goin' to disguise yourself!" Jennie said. "Oh, I see. I didn't understand."

"I'm goin' disguised as Uncle Corny," Asey told her with a grin, "an' if you don't hustle, I'll get real props, like a bottle of gin for my hip pocket. I sort of think that people won't pay much attention to me, in that outfit, an' with Syl's truck."

When he reappeared in ten minutes, Jennie freely admitted that she had never seen the like in all her born days, never.

"Them overalls don't exactly make you look like a hick, but sort of—"

"Rustic. I know—look here, woman," Asey picked up a cap from the table, "this ain't the one I mean. This is my nice clean new one. I want the old dirty one that says in red letters 'I USE PLINY'S PAINT—DO YOU?' "

"Asey, please!"

Asey roared in his quarterdeck bellow until Jennie, to stop the noise, reluctantly produced the old cap.

"It'll make you look just like a convict, with that funny visor. You use Pliny's Paint—you know right well that you do no such thing!"

Asey laughed. "Then that makes it more of a disguise

than meets the eye, don't it? Anyone that knows me knows I don't use Pliny's Paint, an'—oh, let it pass," he added hurriedly, noticing her expression of bewilderment. "Let it pass."

Jennie eyed the Colt he inserted in a shoulder holster under his painting coat.

"If you was settin' out to see anyone but Nettie Hobbs," she remarked, "I'd say for you to leave that thing behind. But she deserves a gun poked at her! What're you waiting for, whyn't you get started?"

"Glasses," Asey said. "Isn't there an old pair with gold rims around somewhere? They belonged to someone or other. You find 'em while I get me the rest of my trappin's—"

"Not a gin bottle!" Jennie said anxiously.

"Nope, just some paint an' brushes. What would you say was the predominatin' color in Quanomet, white an' green?"

"An' yellow. Lots of yellow houses there."

"I forgot 'em," Asey said, "entirely. Well, if they need paintin', it'll have to be with the punkin I got left over from the kitchen floor. I ain't got any yellow—"

Jennie protested later when he put on the old glasses she had found in the sewing machine drawer.

"Now," she said, "you look like a deacon. An' if you try to drive Syl's truck with 'em on, Asey, you'll kill yourself. They was Aunt Phrone's, an' she got 'em from a mail order house with a test-your-own-eyes card, an' the only time she wore 'em, she walked plumb into the cistern!"

After a brief interlude in Syl's potato patch, during which

the truck barely escaped overturning, Asey came to the conclusion that perhaps Jennie was right about the glasses. Regretfully, he put them in his pocket for future use.

He sailed by his friend the state policeman, on duty at the
Quanomet four corners, without even getting a second
glance. Quanomet's Main Street ignored him, except for two
slick haired and sunburned salesmen who made loud in-
quiries about the price of hay.

Asey paused long enough to ask them sweetly if they
really cared, and went on.

At the entrance to Depot Square stood a local traffic cop,
whose relationship to Asey was about the same as that of
Pam Frye to Nettie Hobbs.

As Syl's truck approached, he put up his hand and blew
his whistle importantly; Asey did his best to obey, but the
brakes of Syl's truck were unaccustomed to quick stops, and
Asey coasted on, up to the rope barriers that were keeping
the throng of people off what was left of Roddy Strutt's
plane.

The cop marched up to him.

"Where's your inspection tag? What's the matter with
your brakes? Gimme your license and registration—"

"I haven't any registration," Asey said honestly. "An' my
license is in my other coat. The trouble is, Jerry, I ain't used
to these brakes of Syl's. They work all right, but they're
sort of fractious, like. Now—"

Jerry's face grew red. In a loud, penetrating voice, he ex-
pressed his opinion of Asey, Asey's car, Asey's brakes, Asey's
general character and ancestry.

In the middle of a particularly pungent sentence, he stopped short.

"Go on," Asey said. "An' I was drivin' on the wrong side, too. I guess, Jerry, if you didn't recognize me without the car an' the Stetson, no one will. Can I park this crate an' slink off about my business, or do you jail me?"

"Asey, have you got into this mess at last? Thank God. We're all goin' crazy. That state cop Hanson is off his nut. I heard that the selectmen were intendin' to ask you over. It's not Pam that killed her sister, it's someone here that was sore about the faces in the mural—"

"Jerry," Asey said, "I come to Quanomet to bring a load of loom an' to do some paintin'. That's all. An' you'd better yell at me some more—"

Jerry winked elaborately and raised his voice.

They spent the next quarter hour putting on an act that charmed the tourist trade. Finally, after promising never to ignore another stop signal, Asey took his paint cans and brushes out of the rear of the truck, and joined the crowd that swarmed the streets.

The space in front of Nettie Hobbs's store was teeming with people. Obviously the Woman's Exchange was doing a land office business.

Asey edged his way to the windows and stared at the display. It reminded him, somehow, of all the church fairs he had ever attended.

There were fancy calico pan holders, crocheted lettuce bags, aprons of every style and color—all apparently designed for the oversize figure, Asey thought. Any one of them would have made a fine pup tent. There were huge quantities of luncheon sets, embroidered dish towels, beribboned cushions bristling with pins, and lines of doll-like door stops made from milk bottles. There were pies, cakes, rolls, dishes of homemade fudge. There was a jar—it was almost a tank —of pickle limes. And the tourist trade was buying just left and right.

"Now I wonder," Asey murmured, "I wonder if maybe the ladies ain't pullin' a fast one."

It was the wife of the minister with the wart, who darted out to talk to a woman standing near Asey, who confirmed his suspicions that the ladies were augmenting Nettie's stock with church fair material.

"Jane, you've got to help! The Baptists have more aprons —go get 'em from Minnie. And a quilt from the Methodist Chapel. And tell Sally to hurry up those quohog ash trays she's decorating—we're getting fifty cents apiece for them. I've got all the children at the shore getting shells—they're paying ten cents apiece just for undecorated ones! And for mercy's sakes, ask Harry where you get pickle limes! We're selling those in there for a quarter each. We—what? Oh, Nettie can't remember where she got these. She's had 'em for years, she says. Jane, you hurry up—we can rebuild every church in town and repave Main Street—if only we can find things to sell!"

"Where's Nettie?" the other woman asked. "What's she got to say about this selling?"

"I don't know, and I don't care," the minister's wife returned. "All she's thinking of is the money she's getting for articles and statements. She doesn't give a fig for the churches! She's out back now, talking to someone—more reporters, I shouldn't wonder!"

Asey edged his way out of the crowd and along the sidewalk to the narrow alley that separated the Exchange from Red Men's Hall. Swinging his paint cans, he marched up the alley and through the gate into the yard at the rear.

Voices—heated voices—issued from the open window in the ell.

"The whole thing's absurd, and you know it's absurd, an you know you're lying like a bloody trooper!" The woman who was speaking accented her words with a good hearty thump on something that resounded emphatically and woodenly.

"What!" It was Nettie Hobbs whose voice rose to a shrill scream. "What do you mean? I saw Pam Frye kill her, I tell you, I saw it with my own eyes."

7.

"YOU lie!" the woman said angrily.

"I lie? You mean, *you* lie!" Nettie embarked on a shrill tirade.

"So," Asey said softly. "So!"

He put down his paint cans and looked critically at the ell.

Its original brown had faded through the years to a particularly unpleasant shade of greyish-red, with which Asey was not prepared to cope. But whoever owned the building, Asey decided, should be glad to have anyone touch up those bare spots. And his green paint was a nice cheerful green.

Before Nettie finished her speech, Asey was standing on an empty packing case just beyond the window, energetically painting the ell with his nice green paint.

"Are you quite through?" the woman asked rather wearily. "I should think you would be. Now, before you get second wind, let me sum things up. I've appealed to your family pride. After all, you're a relation of Pam's. I've appealed to your common decency. I've appealed to everything anyone can appeal to, and you're adamant. Now, I'm going to point out several items. In the first place, if you were actually in any position to view this murder—if you really were in, or near, or outside the garage last night, and if you didn't stop Pam from killing Marina—does it occur to you that you're an accessory after the fact?"

"How did I know she was going to? I just followed her—"

"So you're following her now, are you?" the woman interrupted. "In the original version, you simply sat in Octagon House and peered through the window and saw her run toward Lornes' garage. Little item there, by the way. The only window from which you might possibly have seen in that direction, from the living room, is that awful thing of colored purple glass. And no one ever saw through that. Did that occur to you, Nettie? Because the police are shortly going to have it pointed out to them."

"You're trying to shield a murderer!" Nettie yelled. "That's what! I wouldn't wonder if you weren't hiding Pam Frye! And what if I am a cousin of hers? I'm only a fifth cousin!"

"Oyster Bay," Asey murmured, "versus Hyde Park."

"And besides," Nettie went on, "I have a higher duty, I have. It's my duty to expose a murderer, even if she is a relation! Some laws is higher than others. Blood may be thicker than water—"

"But not when you can pan gold out of the water? Isn't that it, Nettie? Oh, how you must have counted on marrying Aaron Frye!"

Whoever this woman was, Asey thought, she was playing Nettie like a banjo.

"What about you?" Nettie returned. "Didn't *you* expect to marry Jack Lorne, until Marina took him away from you? Didn't you want to paint that mural in the post office, Peggy Boone?"

Boone. Asey thought. Pam had said something about modeling for someone named Boone.

"Of course I wanted to paint that mural, Nettie. So did several hundred other people. But you're wandering from the point again. The point is, you *didn't* see Pam Frye last night, because you didn't even look out of the window; or if you looked out of the regular windows, you couldn't possibly have seen the Lorne garage. Or if you looked out of the purple glass window, you just plain couldn't have seen. That's the point. You suspected nothing at the time, you suspected nothing when you left. By sheer chance you left your pocketbook—and it's the consensus that you never forgot your pocketbook before. You usually have it gripped tightly to your capacious bosom. And when you realized what you'd popped into, you saw your chance to take a whack at Pam, and then you realized the gold in them thar hills. All right, Nettie. But you've got your last nugget."

"What do you mean? Where are you going?" Nettie sounded more annoyed than alarmed. As Jennie Mayo had remarked that morning, there was nothing Nettie enjoyed much more than a good wordy fight.

"I'm going, my little pickle lime, to the cops. And to see some reporters I know. You actually don't know a single thing about this murder, and very shortly the world will know just what sort of filthy hoax you are. Whom the press makes, they can also break. I thought even the stupidest of fools had figured that out. And you, Nettie, are going to be broken. And I'm going to wield the first axe—"

"You vindictive thing, you!"

"Yes, vindictive is the word for Peggy," came the prompt retort. "I'm one of the most viciously and violently vindictive people I happen to know. And I happen also to cherish Pam Frye. And for two cents I'd slap out your teeth and jump heavily on them—except I'm afraid that I wouldn't stop there. Goodbye!"

"Goodbye yourself!" Nettie yelled. "And you wait till I tell the reporters what you've said and how you've threatened me! Threatened! Wait'll they hear that, and then see how much good your lies'll do to shield Pam Frye!"

When Peggy Boone came out to the yard, Asey was innocently stirring paint in the far corner.

"So she's having the store beautified, is she?" Peggy Boone's cheeks were flaming and her eyes shot sparks. "Beautified by the application of a coat of paint. That's the way the *News* will report it this week. 'Our esteemed citizen, Nettie Hobbs, alias the Pickle Lime Lady, is beautifying her store by the application of a coat of paint!' By God, it sickens me!"

"Wa-el," Asey rather overdid his Cape drawl, "wa-el, it needs paint."

"So does my house, and so, probably, does yours. But we don't yap packs of lies to the newspapers to get it done!"

"You seem sort of sore," Asey remarked, stirring expertly.

"Sore? Do you think you ever saw a mad woman? Well, the maddest woman you ever knew was a cooing dove compared to me. I could kill that stinker!"

She strode off down the alley.

Asey felt for his pipe, but that was home in his other

coat, along with his driving license. Feeling a little thwarted, he sat down and considered the situation.

No appeals to Nettie Hobbs were going to get anyone anywhere, he decided. Peggy Boone might point out the discrepancies in Nettie's story till the cows came home. But Nettie had her story in first. And Hanson would take as little notice of the window item as he had taken of Dr. Cummings' point about the murderer's left handedness.

He personally might go in and see what he could do, but Peggy Boone had deftly and thoroughly covered every angle he could think of. Unless he were to go in and wave guns at Nettie, which would give her the unsurpassed opportunity to call for the press, and display Asey Mayo in the very act of intimidating and coercing a star witness.

In brief, Asey thought it might be simpler to move Gibraltar than to sway Aunt Nettie Hobbs at that point.

He picked up his brushes and his paint cans. But before he left, another visitor dropped in on Nettie.

"Why, Mis-ter Strutt!" Nettie said, neatly identifying her caller. "Mis-ter Strutt! Were you hurt last night when your plane crashed?"

"Just banged a bit, that's all. The other fellow took the beating. He's got a broken leg and things. Look, you're all mixed up in this business of Marina, aren't you? Saw it happen, and things like that?"

"I was right on the scene," Nettie said. "Right on the scene. Do you want to read about it? Here are the papers, right here, and—"

"I've read 'em," Roddy Strutt said. "That's just it, you know. You've been pretty decent about me, and I want to do the right thing. Always thought you were a good sort, and all. Look, will this be all right? More where it came from, if it isn't."

"Oh, oh!" Nettie squealed.

"Ain't it enough?"

"Oh, but it's—why, yes." Nettie's voice changed suddenly. Realizing, no doubt, Asey thought, that there was more gold in the hills than she had ever dreamed of. "Why, yes, I guess so."

"All I can spare right now," Roddy said. "But you know me. I make things right. Just you keep up your story and keep me out of it, that's all. Well, so long."

"So long," Nettie said.

"Oh—if anyone gets curious about the check," Roddy hesitated, "just you say it's for your pasture that I want for a landing field. I can give you cash—"

"This'll be all right," Nettie said. "Goodbye, Mr. Strutt."

A door banged.

"Well," he heard Nettie's dazed murmur. "Well, well. Keep you out of it? I should say I would! I guess so!"

Asey nodded. He guessed so, too.

Picking up the can of green paint, he mounted the packing box again. A little beautification, he felt, was a small price to pay for the enlightening details that were being wafted out of that ell room.

He was brought to earth by Nettie's voice at his elbow.

"What do you think you're doing?"

"What's that?" Asey hastily put on the gold rimmed glasses before turning around. "What's that?"

"What do you think you're doing?" Nettie raised her voice, and Asey promptly took his cue from it.

"What say?"

"What are you doing?" Nettie bellowed.

"Paintin'," Asey said, gently.

"Who told you to paint here? What do you mean, trespassing and defacing my property—get away, before I call the constable!'"

"What say?" Asey asked. "What's that? I'm a mite hard of hearin', marm."

He made her repeat it five times, and then he assumed an injured expression.

"You mean, this ain't the Red Men's Hall?"

"It's the Woman's Exchange!" Nettie yelled. "The Woman's Exchange! Woman's Exchange!"

"They do?" Asey said. "I want to know, now!"

"You deaf old fool, this isn't the Red Men's Hall, this is—"

"Then if it ain't the Red Men's Hall," Asey peered down at her, "then you owe me fifty cents for time, an' a quarter for paint. I'll make it sixty cents cash money."

Finally, from sheer exhaustion, she gave him the sixty cents. Asey pocketed it gravely, and removed himself and his cans from the yard.

It was no task to mingle with the crowd until Nettie emerged from the alley, and he could hardly have helped joining in with the young mob that followed her up the street to the bank.

Parking his paint cans on the back doorstep, Asey strolled in the bank's rear door and knocked on the glass of the president's little cubby hole. He had always wondered why he had allowed himself to be made an honorary director of the bank's main branch, and now, he thought as he waited, he knew.

The amount of Roddy Strutt's check, which he had in his hands almost as soon as Nettie deposited it, startled him considerably.

Five thousand dollars, he thought as he picked up his paint cans outside, five thousand dollars meant that Roddy wasn't just trying to keep his name out of this affair. It meant that Roddy was seriously involved. Roddy had no reputation for open-handedness. It had taken a court battle to make him pay for smashing up Bill Porter's car in that accident the year before. And yet he'd given Nettie a check for five thousand, just like that! A check, too. That made Roddy dumber than he'd thought.

But, he remembered suddenly, how could Roddy Strutt possibly be involved in this mess? Presumably he was flying around in his new airplane and wrecking it in Depot Square.

Pam knew nothing about the crash, and she would have been told by Nettie if it had occurred before Nettie left Octagon House at ten-thirty. Jennie Mayo said that Roddy had wrecked the plane on his way home from tagging his friend's plane. Marina Lorne had dashed away from the garage, leaving the ambergris, in order to see some artist, some friend of Roddy's, who was shortly leaving for New York in a plane, presumably via Providence.

Sorted out, that meant that the artist friend had left between six and seven. Roddy's plane had crashed after ten-thirty. It would not have taken all the intervening time for Roddy to trail the other plane to the airport, and to return to Quanomet. Roddy might, of course, have stopped over en route, but if he had crashed on his return late at night, why on earth was he presenting Nettie with checks, and lavishly promising her more to keep him out of her murder story?

Asey strolled back to the square and to his remote cousin Jerry Chase, sitting dejectedly on the running board of a parked car.

"I've given up," he said. "I've given up. You might as well try to stop Niag'ra, as these tourists. They don't give a damn how many cars they jam into this place, or how many they bump. They've busted down the ropes, and they're carting off that plane in handfuls. You'd think they never seen a plane before. Well, I don't care. I tried to do my duty, but now I've given up. Asey, what in the name of God makes people act this way? What's that plane *mean* to 'em anyhow? It ain't got a thing to do with the murder or the mural, and those are the things they supposedly come to town for, ain't they?"

"Well," Asey sat down beside him, "what's pickle limes got to do with things? Or flower holders made out of old coffee tins? But people are buyin' pickle limes an' cut-up coffee cans over at the Exchange, like this was the last chance they had to buy 'em in this world. Jerry, what time last night did this plane crash, do you know?"

"Between one and two," Jerry said. "It busted up a couple of cars, and bruised up Earl Jennings and some others. It was Roddy that did it, but the pilot feller got hurt the worst."

"Where is he, in the hospital?"

Jerry nodded. "Someone got an ambulance and took him over to Pochet. I just heard someone say that Roddy wouldn't even pay the ambulance bill. Said he hadn't ordered it. You know, Asey, I keep hopin' there's a special little corner of Hell all set apart for people like Roddy. Sometimes he's so dumb, you wouldn't believe it. Sometimes he just scatters money. Then again he's so tight with five cents, you'd like to sock him. And sly—say, he's so—oh, damn those tourists! Look, they're pullin' that other wing apart!"

Asey suggested that Jerry might be able to stop them, if he really tried.

"I s'pose so," Jerry said. "I s'pose I could, if I put my mind to it. I would, if it was anyone else's plane. Somehow I don't care about Roddy's. I can't see how the town's liable for any damage people do. We never asked him to land his plane here. We—say, I wonder if we could sue him for obstructin' town highways an' maintainin' a nuisance?"

"You could always try," Asey said. "While you're at it, collect parkin' fees from him, too. You got signs up sayin' that more'n one hour parkin' is illegal, an' that plane's been there for hours. Nick him. So the pilot's in Pochet?"

"Yes, poor feller," Jerry said. "He'll prob'ly rot there before Roddy takes any notice. He—are you goin'?"

"Yup." Asey picked up his paint cans. "You ain't any idea, Jerry, how many spots there is in this town that needs a little slappin' up with paint. By the way, how's the crowd over to Octagon House gettin' along?"

"Hanson's got 'em in order now, I guess. But they ripped up the flower beds, though, and a couple was tryin' to make off with that iron deer before he got 'em under control. There's some still around the garage at Lornes'. Someone went by a while ago with a load of barbed wire, an' there was a state cop on the truck. I guess they're settin' up a barrier. Where you bound?"

"Hither an' yon. Oh, if you know where pickle limes come from, Jerry, go tell the minister's wife over at the Exchange. Tell her I think she could prob'ly palm off lemons dipped in brine, if she got hard up. Oh—an' tell 'em they're missin' a good bet in taffy apples. They'd ought to fetch half a dollar, an' the prime expense is sticks."

He extracted Syl's truck from the maze of parked cars, and bounced over to the little Pochet hospital.

The nurse in charge was the daughter of a neighbor of his.

She hesitated a moment when Asey addressed her by name, and then she laughed.

"Why, Asey," she said, "I hardly recognized you in that outfit. I don't think I'd have known you if I hadn't seen Syl's truck. That truck used to belong to Father, you know. It's a family legend. Isn't this business over in Quanomet simply hideous? And is it true that you're not helping with the case?"

"What do you think?" Asey asked.

"You can't fool your neighbors," she said. "Of course you are. You're up to something, dressed this way, and driving that truck. I suppose you want to see Earl Jennings, don't you?"

"Who's he?"

"That Quanomet selectman who got bumped in Roddy Strutt's plane crash last night."

"As a matter of fact," Asey said, "I'd like to see Roddy Strutt's pilot. Can I?"

She shook her head. "I'm afraid not," she said. "He's in pretty bad shape. We hoped Roddy would agree to sending for Dr. Carter, but Roddy wasn't interested. Roddy isn't even interested enough to notify the fellow's family, if he's got any. We telegraphed all the people whose names and addresses we found in his wallet, but no one's answered, and two wires came back. Unknown, or something."

"Get Carter," Asey said, "and charge him to me, will you? And—"

"Asey, that's swell of you!"

"Not a bit," Asey said. "And when he gets so that he can be asked questions, let me know. Be sure. And—just for fun, if Roddy should take it into his head to see the fellow— what's his name? Brigham? Well, if Roddy asks to see Brigham, cause him to be thwarted, will you?"

"I will, and I'll tell the rest. We're all so mad at him, and anyway, you'll be taking charge. That'll make it all right.

You know," she added, "I shouldn't say this, but there's something queer about this crash. Brigham's sleeping now, but he's been unconscious, and he kept muttering about the plane, and Roddy, and calling him names, and telling him to keep off. It was sort of bloodcurdling."

"Could you say, Susan, if all Brigham's injuries come from the crash?"

"Where else—oh. Oh, I see what you mean. That someone might have hurt him before it. I couldn't say, Asey. Carter might be able to tell you, and Brigham can, certainly, when he's better. It was quite a crash, enough to bang up those cars in the square, and shake up Earl Jennings—look, won't you take pity on him and see him? He's simply raving about this Quanomet business, and everyone in town's so busy making money out of the tourists, they haven't time to do more than send consoling messages by phone. His wife has been over twice, for ten seconds. She's making doughnuts by the hundred thousands, and she says if she can live through another day, they'll have a new car."

"Is this Jennings hurt bad?" Asey asked.

"No, he's sort of an indestructible man. He's just bruised, but his doctor wants him to stay for a couple of days, and rest. He's got a bad heart. Won't you see him?"

"Sure, for a minute," Asey said. "But I don't know the man from Adam."

"That won't matter. He knows you, and he's so eager to talk with someone."

Mr. Jennings, a burly six-footer who seemed far too big for his bed, smiled at Asey and extended his hand.

"Boy," he said feelingly, "am I glad to see a human face!"

Asey laughed. "I hear you're sort of marooned an' deserted."

"Oh, lots of folks phoned, but as soon as they find out I'm all right, and just being kept in cold storage, they send their regards and say they'll drop over when I get back home. You can't blame 'em. There hasn't been so much money loose in town for years. My boy—he's fifteen—he's had trouble this summer, selling little wooden windmills for a dime apiece. Today, he and his friend got the idea of making little octagon houses out of two by fours, and painting 'em up, and they're getting a dollar apiece for just as many as they can make. Think of it! If only the doctor—but I suppose he's right. I wouldn't keep quiet, if I got out. I'd be out hawking with the rest. Say, what do you think about this murder?"

"There's more to it than meets the eye," Asey said, "if that's what you mean."

"Sure there is," Jennings agreed. "After I heard about it, I went up town—I was going to rout out the other selectmen, and have 'em send for you. But they told me you was away, and then that fool crashed his plane, and I landed over here. But you know what I think—and what everyone else in town thinks? We think it's someone that was sore about being pictured in that mural thing. You don't know how mad people in Quanomet are about that!"

"By degrees," Asey said, "I'm gatherin' that there's been consid'rable indignation. But the point is, is there any one person that's madder than any other? And why should

Marina be killed, and not Lorne, who painted the picture?"

"Oh, Marina put him up to it," Jennings said. "Lorne's a fool. The only way that fellow can think is with a paint brush in his hand, and then he isn't too bright. Everyone knows she put him up to painting in the faces. He couldn't have thought of it by himself."

"Then you think it's a local person, who knew enough to figger that Marina was to blame?"

"I do," Jennings said emphatically. "And I thought right off the bat about Aaron Frye. He's in the mural. Father Time, or something. I don't know. But he's had more than that from that daughter of his in the past. So has Pam. The way I figure, if they haven't killed Marina before, that picture wouldn't move 'em to kill her now. Then—you'll laugh at this. But I thought of Nettie."

"Is she in the paintin'?" Asey asked. "I seen it, but I got to laughin' so, I had to go out before I took in more than the main panel."

"The other panels are the ones with Quanomet faces," Jennings said. "Nettie's an old hag gutting a fish."

"A fish wife, huh? Well, that's apt," Asey said.

"Uh-huh. And beside her are two pickle limes. She's had a jar of pickle limes in that window of her store for years. Then I decided it couldn't be Nettie, because the time they said she left Octagon House and the time Pam found her sister, they didn't hitch up. And besides, I had a better idea. And you'll think I'm crazy, for sure. I thought of Roddy Strutt."

"Is he in the mural, too?"

"He sure is. With two girls on his lap, and his face—well, it's Roddy all right," Jennings said bitterly. "Anyway, last night when he crawled out of that plane, he was laughing like it was a big joke. I hate him anyway, but that made me sore, with Brigham lying there. I limped over, and lousy as I felt, I kicked him square in the seat of his pants. Knocked him down, too. And while he was down, I give him a couple more kicks for luck."

"That," Asey said approvingly, "was the proper gesture."

"And you know what I noticed when I kicked him? A couple of streaks on his pants. I thought they were blood at first, but later I seen they weren't. They were red lead paint. And I'm a plumber by trade. And yesterday morning I spent up to Lornes', fixing up that pump, and painting their water tanks with red lead. And the old water tank that I painted, the big one, that's out in the garage where Marina was killed. See what I mean?"

8.

IT was the middle of the afternoon before Asey set about the tedious task of coaxing Syl's truck back to Wellfleet.

That excursion to Roddy Strutt's house after he left Jennings and the hospital had turned out to be a complete bust, as well as a total waste of time.

The Strutt place was surrounded by a tall, iron spiked fence, and the driveway gates were locked. A Filipino with a squint had ordered him off the entrance, and another Filipino with cauliflower ears had chased him away from the wharf. Both men belonged to the general classification of undesirable companions for dark nights in narrow alleys. Even in broad daylight they were slightly repulsive.

"Oh, he may be a brother of William H. Taft," Asey hummed the old Filipino song of insurrection days, "but he ain't no brother of mine."

A dogged series of questionings in the neighborhood of the Strutt house had netted him almost nothing. He learned that Roddy's plane was an amphibian, which he hadn't guessed from the wreckage, and he learned that Roddy had spent practically the entire previous day buzzing around in his new toy. By noontime, people had almost ceased to pay any attention to its comings and goings, other than to hope as they heard it pass overhead, that if Roddy was going to crash it in his characteristic fashion, he would mercifully crash out to sea.

One man said very definitely that Roddy's plane had left at six-thirty with the plane that was going to New York. He was sure about the time, because the noise of the two planes setting off had interrupted his favorite radio program. And everyone was positive that Roddy was returning from that jaunt when he crashed in the square.

Asey eased the truck around a reverse curve.

If Roddy left at six-thirty, and had not returned until the crash late that night, hours after the murder, why was he paying that hush money to Nettie Hobbs?

And how in the name of common sense could Roddy have landed that plane in the square, anyway, without causing more damage? Roddy was just learning to fly. He had never touched the controls of a plane until the day before. And the descriptions of his first flight were nerve shattering.

But if Roddy Strutt wanted to advertise his homecoming, and to set the time in everyone's mind, he had picked the right place. Everyone Asey had talked with knew of the crash in the square, and the time.

Of course it had been a fine moonlight night. There were cars in the square, and possibly some had headlights on. There was an all night lunch cart there which had a couple of flood lights. Even so, it would have taken a far better pilot than Roddy to bring that plane down there without more of a mess. And would Roddy have thought to turn off his engines?

The more he thought about it, the more apparent it became to Asey that Brigham, and not Roddy, had brought the plane down, no matter what Roddy said. Brigham must have brought the plane down. And probably with Roddy standing over him, brandishing a monkey wrench. And probably Roddy had returned hours before to Quanomet. And the plane landing was an act, a part of a brain wave of Roddy's to alibi himself.

Brigham would clear that up.

At home, Asey was greeted by Jennie Mayo and Dr. Cummings, both of whom talked loudly and steadily in unison on widely separated subjects.

Asey sorted out the information.

A delegation of Quanomet's leading citizens had called on him to request his aid in their misfortunes—they put it in the plural, apparently feeling that the murder was not their only problem. They had left a petition, signed by a hundred voters, and a flowery statement which made him an honorary citizen, honorary chief of police and honorary selectman.

"Ain't they nice," Jennie commented.

"Peachy," Asey said. "Me an' the Major. What you got to report, Doc, from Octagon House?"

It seemed that Hanson was still hunting Pam. The police had found no fingerprints on the knife. Or anywhere else. The crowd was still bothersome.

"You don't mean," Asey said, "that Hanson is still after her? Still?"

"He's a peculiarly one-track-minded soul. Asey, more than

anything, I wish you'd insert yourself into Octagon House and find—"

"That stuff," Asey said swiftly, before the doctor could present any information. He trusted Jennie implicitly, but even Jennie had her limitations.

"Exactly. For the love of God, will you, Asey? It means so much to the kid. If she does get into hot water, it very conceivably might pay for her extraction."

"I was going to try this afternoon," Asey said, "but I got lost on side issues. After all, it's not goin' to be easy to slide into that house, an' as for removin' things, I'd say it was near onto impossible. But I'd feel better if I knew it was there. It's goin' to be a job, Doc. It ain't something you can slip out in your hip pocket, in any offhand manner."

"There must be some way," Cummings said.

"I think I can get into the place all right." Asey told about his painting the ell of the Woman's Exchange. "A man that putters around with paint brushes or a hammer an' nails, he ain't a suspicious person. But someone that just loiters, he's spotted right away. I can get to Octagon House, but—"

"Oh, before I forget," Jennie said. "Besides the delegation, there was Elliott the Congressman to see you. He said he'd come back. And there was a girl that waited a couple of hours, I guess. She said her name was Boone. About twenty-five or so."

"Dark and quiet, isn't she?" Cummings said. "I know her. She was over at Lornes' and at Octagon House, too. She's an illustrator, and she keeps a goat. I treated it once after an overdose of hair mattress. Boone tried to get Hanson to stop long enough to look at the living room windows in Octagon House, to prove to him that Nettie was lying, but Hanson wouldn't pay any attention to her. They nearly came to blows—both of 'em were in a violent rage. And what do you think, Asey? This slays me. Roddy Strutt's offered a reward for the arrest and conviction of the murderer. What do you think of that?"

"He has? Well," Asey said, "I think that Roddy is overdoin' things a mite. How much, do you know?"

"The sum varies, depending on who's telling the story. I've heard one thousand, I've heard five. Personally, I don't understand it. I don't understand Roddy's sudden wealth, either. I heard that his father had cut his allowance to the bone—and here he is, crashing up new planes in a carefree fashion, and offering rewards—"

"An' scatterin' largesse besides," Asey said. "Have you seen him today?"

"Yes, I saw him while he was talking with Hanson. Jack Lorne was weeping with gratitude at the lovely gesture, and Roddy was being Prince Bountiful with a smirk. It was maudlin. Too bad that a really good looking boy like that has to be such a punk. His mother wasn't so bad, but of course the rest of the family are just so much mildew. Hanson said that Roddy said that if nothing happened, he'd raise the reward. I gathered he's about to come into money, but from what source, I couldn't even guess."

"Jennie," Asey said, "if you'll rustle me some food, I think I'll heave that old crate back to Quanomet. This is gettin' interestin', this is."

"D'you think you need to keep up this painting costume and the load of loam?" Cummings asked.

"I've discovered," Asey told him, "that it's easier to listen than to ask questions. Particularly when you ain't got much idea of the questions to ask. Jennie, make me a sandwich while I get some putty. I think I'll putty windows for a livin'—an' say, Doc, what men has Hanson got over there, anyway?"

"Virtually the entire force," Cummings said. "I know only a couple of 'em. The last shakeup scattered most of the bunch we knew. Asey, I'm worried about Pam, and her—er—stuff."

"So'm I," Asey said, "but I don't know what to do about her. As for the stuff, I'll see if I can't ferret it out."

The difference between Quanomet, when he saw it on his return, and Quanomet as he had seen it that morning, was startling enough to make Asey blink.

It had been crowded then, but now it was packed like Times Square on election night. No self-respecting sardine would have attempted even to wriggle across the main street.

The regular Saturday afternoon stream of tourists and sightseers and weekenders piled into Quanomet and stayed there, instead of proceeding down the Cape to Provincetown. And the stream showed no signs of abating. If anything, it was growing wider, increased by everyone in the surrounding towns who had a vehicle that was capable of moving.

The place had taken on the general aspect of a five ring

circus, with all the added attractions of carnivals, side shows and midways. Professional pitchmen fought tooth and nail for sidewalk space, in violent competition with hot dog and tonic hawkers. A tent village had suddenly mushroomed in the field beyond the baseball diamond.

In short, Quanomet lacked only fan dancers.

Asey backed his truck into a driveway, and finally managed to maneuver along to a lane leading to the network of back roads. After plowing interminably through sandy ruts, he at last turned off on a road which eventually wound past Octagon House and the Lorne cottage.

An amazingly small group, a mere handful, waited outside the barbed wire barrier. For the most part, they looked like local people.

Asey leaned out and inquired what had become of the tourists.

The man shrugged. "I don't know, I guess they're up town. They don't seem to care much about the murder, or the mural either. They're just out for a good time."

"Then I guess," Asey said, "I can get this loom dumped. I been tryin' all day to dump it here, an' they wouldn't let me."

The policeman at the barrier, overhearing Asey's remark, announced that he couldn't dump it now, either.

"I'd like to know why," Asey said crossly. "Pam Frye ordered this loom, an' I've brought it, an' I can't waste any more time cartin' it around, an' I need my truck. I can't see how I'm goin' to hurt anyone, just dumpin' a little loom, an' doin' some work I been paid to do!"

He spoke loudly enough for everyone to hear, and the group promptly took his side. What harm was a little loam, if a man needed his truck?

They discussed the situation with gusto until the officer bowed to public opinion and let Asey through.

Asey shoveled half the loam into a neat pile by the back porch, while another trooper watched him suspiciously.

"Now," Asey put down his shovel, "now, mister, I want to see Aaron Frye. Ask him—"

"You can't."

"Well, then, you go ask him what windows he wants me to begin puttin' putty on first, mister. I got work to do."

"You can't see Frye, and you can't. do any work around here," the trooper said. "Beat it."

Asey took a can of putty and a knife from the front seat of the truck.

"Pam Frye hired me last week to fix these windows," he said, "an' I'm a-goin' to fix windows. An' who do you bunch of Cossacks think you are? Go get your boss an' tell him to arrest a man that's goin' about his business, doin' his work he's paid to do. Go on—well, whyn't you go?"

"Listen," the trooper said, "do you have to make trouble?"

"Who's makin' trouble?" Asey said. "I ain't makin' trouble. I'm just goin' to putty up some windows, like Pam Frye hired me to do last week. Want you to putty the windows, says she. All right, says I. I'll putty 'em Sat'-day aftnoon, when I bring you the loom for the back flower bed. What trouble is there in puttyin' windows, I'd like to know? Who's makin' trouble? If a feller's promised to putty windows, an' he's got just so much time to putty windows in, then he's got to putty the windows when—"

"For Christ's sake," the trooper said wearily, "go putty your damned windows and shut your face! Hey—hey, Ding!" He yelled to still another trooper who was just entering the house. "This guy's going to putty the windows. He's all right. He's harmless."

"Huh," Asey said, trying to sound badly ruffled, "it sure takes you fellers a long time to make your minds up!"

Swinging the putty pail and gripping the putty knife, he made a slow and searching circuit of the house.

The cellar windows were large four-paned things, and they needed putty just about as badly as he thought they would. He could putty practically till doomsday, or until someone got suspicious and sent him away.

From what he could gather by peering through the windows, the cellar floor plan was a strange and wonderful thing.

The hall apparently ran diagonally through the place, slicing the octagon and leaving visible two triangular small rooms, two rectangles—slightly bashed—and two hybrid rooms that seemed to have at least six walls apiece. He rather hated to contemplate what happened in the middle of the place, beyond his line of vision. He strongly suspected that there was a circular staircase to the first floor, at the very least.

The trooper stopped him as he started a second trip about the outside.

"If you're going to putty, brother," he said, "you putty. Hear me? Putty!"

Asey sighed plaintively. "Looky here," he said, "some of these windows needs putty more'n others does. How can I tell which needs it most, if you keep stoppin' an' interruptin' an' botherin' me so?"

"Get going!"

"All right," Asey said. "All right. I'll get going. No respect for a man's work, that's what's the matter with this world. Honest man tries to do a day's work, an' what happens to him? He gets harried to death by you Cossacks. I s'pose if I was an unemployed r'liefer, you'd ask me inside for a nice cool glass of beer—"

He made his way to the triangular furnace room window and removed all the putty from one pane with such deft celerity as to remove also whatever suspicions the trooper might have been entertaining.

Then he proceeded to putty, with infinite care.

A slight noise in the first floor window above temporarily disconcerted him. He looked up to find the greenest parrot he had ever seen staring down at him fixedly from a perch in a cage. On the window sill lay Emma Goldman, surveying him with a skeptical eye.

"Emma," he heard Mrs. Carr's voice as she entered the room, "Emma, must you park under that bird? Must you, for mercy's sakes? Can't you just be a good cat, and sit, and relax, and breathe the nice air? I've never seen such a predatory beast! You cannot get that parrot, and don't you try.

She'll snap at you. Toots, you're the worst parrot I ever saw
—if you don't like Emma, why don't you let her know it?"

"They enjoy this refined skirmishing," Tim said, and
closed the door. "Well, on the whole, what do you think of
things, Gran?"

"I think, on the whole," she said, "that we have been sufficiently open and garrulous to allay suspicions. It was a lovely
idea of yours, Timmy, and I give you full credit. You're
masterly with details. I always thought so. The only real
point is, where did she put it? Where, in God's name, did
the girl put it?"

9.

ASEY felt as though someone had hit him sharply between the eyes.

"Where did she put it?" Mrs. Carr asked again.

"Where?" Timothy sighed. "I don't know, Gran. All I'm sure of is that she hid it somewhere. No one's brought it to light yet, so it still must be here. It's got to be. And by God, I'm going to find it!"

There was something rather grim about the determination in his voice.

"You will, Timmy. You will. I know you will. And I hope that you don't let grass grow under your feet when you do."

Timothy laughed. "When I find it," he said. "When— well, I'll act, all right."

"But there's still the chance," Mrs. Carr said, "that it'll come to light some other way, even if you do manage to find it first. You can't guess how many people she might have told. And then there's Asey Mayo to consider."

"Don't you think I know it?"

"He believed us last night. But if he finds one break in our story, Tim, he'll turn those blue eyes on us—oh, dear, I don't like to think about it. Get along, and keep hunting. Hanson doesn't suspect you, does he?"

"Hanson," Tim said, "thinks I'm a perfect fool. It's the old Harold Lloyd influence, he thinks anyone with glasses like mine is a fool. Of course, he might have a brain wave. Very shortly it ought to occur to him that Pam Frye did not kill her sister, and then you can't predict where his fancy may turn. I've asked a lot of questions. And of course there's Aaron."

"Frye won't talk," Mrs. Carr spoke with assurance. "He wouldn't dream of talking. Why should he? Everything was so beautifully timed. We saved *his* skin, too."

"How about driving over and chatting with Comrade Mayo?" Tim suggested. "Shouldn't we continue this intense interest of ours in Right and Justice, and all?"

Mrs. Carr hesitated.

"I don't know. Too much, and he *will* suspect something. I wish he didn't seem to look at you as though he could read your private thoughts as well as your public utterances. That sort of calmly piercing gaze disorganizes me so. It's so bland. Like Emma Goldman watching that parrot, or waiting for her fish to cool. Yes, Tim, I should feel far more at home with Asey Mayo if our relations were on a more honest foundation. If he finds out about the movies—"

"Cool!" Timothy said.

"He might."

"Gran, what drab ideas you have! We implanted that movie idea firmly, and after all, we went to the movies, didn't we?"

"We implanted the movie idea," Mrs. Carr admitted, "at least, you did. And we went to the movies. But that will hardly matter if Asey Mayo happens to find out that we left the movies long before the time Marina was killed. And I wouldn't put it past him to find out. Get Emma—she's itching to jump up to that cage. Such an inhuman parrot! Just beadily staring and staring. I wish it would talk."

"Perhaps," Timothy said, "it's a mercy that it doesn't."

"Perhaps so. Let's go out and take a walk. All these police around make me so nervous."

Before Timothy picked up the cat, Asey ducked away and walked rapidly to the rear of the house.

"Say, mister," he said to the trooper, "I got to get into the cellar an' find—"

"You can't go in the cellar."

"Mister," the note of desperation in Asey's voice was not entirely assumed. He could hear Timothy and Mrs. Carr approaching the rear porch. "Mister, Pam said she'd leave the sprigs in a box for me, an' I need 'em for this pane—"

"The whats in a box?"

"Sprigs," Asey said. "Flat headed nails, like. Ain't you ever reset glass? One of them panes's half out. I got to get sprigs."

"All right, get 'em. Do you know where they are?"

"In the furnace room," Asey said. "At least, that's where Pam said she'd leave 'em. Can I go in this door?"

He was through it before the trooper had time to answer.

The door opened directly into the hallway that diagonally sliced the octagonal cellar. He paused by the circular staircase that led to the first floor, and removed from his hip pocket a battered tin box of sprigs. He had about eight or ten minutes, he decided, before the trooper would wander in. When he did come, Asey would have the box of sprigs at hand, ready to wave triumphantly under his nose.

In the meantime, he might see if Pam Frye had really hidden her ambergris in the cellar.

There was an inside, built-in chute for coal attached to the window on which he had been working. Probably Pam had wheeled her barrow over from the Lornes' garage and dumped her ambergris, still covered with the tarpaulin, down the chute. Then, somehow, she had got it into the coal bin and covered it with coal.

He was so positive that the ambergris would be in under the coal that it came as a shock to find that it wasn't.

Pam might, of course, have wheeled the barrow directly in the back door. The abnormally high door sill would have presented a problem, but if she solved it, she might have left the ambergris in any one of the other rooms.

Asey began a cautious investigation.

One of the rectangles was a laundry, with old-fashioned soapstone tubs. There was no trace of the ambergris there. The other odd rectangular room was fitted up as a workshop. Everything was in plain sight, and there were no closets or cubby holes in which to hide anything. The other triangle which matched the furnace room was empty except for an old churn and a dust mop. The two largest rooms, the peculiar six-sided things, were both jammed full of dusty furniture.

Nothing was big enough to hold the ambergris. The old trunks were far too small, and the lids were still opened from the frenzied search of Hanson's men for Pam Frye, the night before.

"You—oh, you in there!"

"Yup," Asey put on his gold rimmed glasses. "I found my sprigs. They—where are you? They was—oho. I thought you was that cop," he added as Aaron Frye walked up to him.

"Yes," Mr. Frye said. "Yes."

He stared searchingly at Asey, and Asey stared back at him.

He had almost forgotten what a distinguished looking man Aaron was, with his massive head and white hair that somehow canceled his slight stoop. His grey flannel suit was old, but neat and well cut.

"Yes," Mr. Frye said, obviously puzzled as to what Asey was doing and who he was anyway, "what *is* going on? I'm sure Pam never mentioned anything about having the windows fixed, although the dear Lord knows they need it. I should have got to it myself—see here, if you're more reporters—"

He stopped uncertainly. If, Asey thought, he had happened to be more reporters, he could get an interview from Aaron Frye without half trying. He could almost feel the man trying to decide whether to dig to the root of the situation himself, or to call in the trooper.

"The last time you seen me," Asey said, "was at your wife's mother's house. A fourth of July back—oh, ten years ago, easy. I was teachin' your daughter to sail, around that time."

"Oh," Frye was obviously relieved, "you're—"

"Yup, but I'm incog.," Asey told him. "Right now, I'm the man Pam hired to fix windows. I can't see why she didn't tell you. She made a point of my comin' here this afternoon. Name of Nickerson."

"Why, I do remember now, Nickerson," Frye played up nobly, once he had been given his cue. "Yes, indeed. Nickerson. I wonder if you could fix my study window? The latch is very bothersome. In fact," he added as they walked down the hall to the door, "it's really beyond repair, but Pam said she was certain you could fix it if anyone could. Ah, Shorty," he spoke to the trooper, "it's Nickerson, you know. Quite all right, really. My daughter did tell me that he was coming, but I forgot. I'm forgetful. Shorty knows how forgetful I am, too. He had to save the house from flames today when I absent mindedly filled the oil stove tank with water. I can't think why. I never did before—it's all right if he fixes the latch on my window, isn't it, Shorty?"

"Sure, I guess so, Mr. Frye. Sure, all right. Go ahead. Hanson said no one was to come see you, but he's gone till midnight, and what the hell?"

In the book lined study at the front of the house, Aaron pulled up an old Morris chair and sat down heavily.

"Where is she?"

Asey shook his head. "She was all right with me last night. Then she lit out. But I'm not worryin' about her, because I think she's one girl that can take care of herself. I'm not worryin' a bit about her. Now look—how absent minded are you?"

Frye smiled. "Terribly, sometimes. As I was today about that stove. More often, as Pam knows, it's a matter of policy. A very polite method of ignoring things I don't want to be bothered with. Particularly town affairs. But if there's something you wish to tell me, and you're afraid I'll blurt it out —well, I think you may safely trust me."

"Have you any idea what Pam found on the beach yesterday afternoon?" Asey asked.

Aaron Frye drew in his breath sharply.

"There is only one thing," he said, "that Pam hunts on a beach. Did she—ah. I think I see. Yes. I see. And somehow Marina entered into it."

He took the information, Asey thought, with superhuman calm.

"You don't need to tell me any more," Frye said. "Pam found the—"

"Stuff," Asey interrupted swiftly.

"That might be best. Stuff. I've always hoped that Pam might find some, she wanted to so badly. But I feared the consequences. I've a notion, which time has never disproved to my entire satisfaction, that sudden wealth is a rather awful thing. Legacies, for example, always seem to bring nothing but bitterness. Sweepstakes winners—this is a variety of sweeps, isn't it? But you see what I mean."

Asey nodded. "What's goin' on in Quanomet right now is a swell example of quick money," he said. "Look—what I want to know is, where can the stuff be? Where could Pam have put it? Here, I mean."

"Nowhere in this house," Frye said promptly. "The police combed this place last night, hunting for Pam. They would have been sure to have uncovered it. And—"

"An' these boarders of yours," Asey said. "Where were they last night, an' yesterday evenin'? I thought that you three went to a clambake an' the movies."

"We did go to a clambake, and then Tim parked the car up in the square, and we set off for the theater," Frye said. "But I got sidetracked. Main Street was dotted with anti-mural groups, and some of the discussions interested me. I told the Carrs I'd drop into the movies later, but I never got there. Some of the talk was violent. Pam and I had already talked over this ugly undercurrent—"

"She told me."

"Did she? Well, I listened, and when I heard one eager handful planning to burn the post office, and to tar and feather Jack Lorne as a side issue, I decided to stroll rapidly home and warn Jack. In fact, I thought of suggesting that he and Marina might possibly be happier if they took a brief vacation elsewhere. I foresaw difficulties, for I knew they were broke again. Jack had been around in the morning, trying to borrow from me. He—"

"Any special problems?" Asey asked. "Or was it more in the line of general brokeness?"

"Marina's bills, as usual. She had a talent for bills. Anyway, as I came out of the woods behind the house here, I saw the crowd, and the Carrs. I joined them, and the police assumed I'd been with them to the movies. The Carrs—they're very quick witted—they rather led the police to believe that—what did you say, something about the Carrs?"

"Go on," Asey told him.

"Well, I saw no reason for disillusioning the police, under the circumstances. I had nothing to do with the murder, but if it hadn't been for the Carrs, I should have been dragged into it, I know. I'm really very grateful to our boarders for giving me that alibi, although I suppose it's quite wrong on my part. They're charming people, Timothy and his grandmother."

"Uh-huh," Asey said. "Now, you come home by way of the woods, out back. I don't suppose you happened to bump into anyone lurkin' around there? I'm sure you didn't, because if anyone was lurkin', they'd take care not to be bumped. But did you notice anythin' that didn't seem to be quite as usual?"

"Nothing but that elaborate roadster of Roddy Strutt's, parked near the entrance to the old foot path. But I didn't see Roddy." Aaron got up and walked over to the window. "I don't suppose you *could* fix that window lock, could you?" he asked. "I spent last night sitting beside the phone here, hoping that Pam might call, and—oh, probably it was my nerves, but I thought I heard someone outside. It wasn't the police, and I couldn't see anyone—"

"Have they tapped your phone?" Asey asked.

"I wouldn't know. They apparently haven't given up the hope of getting Pam, through me. But they're not as adhesive about the idea as they were last night. Oh—here are Mrs. Carr and Tim. I'm sure they'll want to see you. They thought you were so splendid, last night."

"I want," Asey said truthfully, "to see them, too. But you let me choose the time. An' while I dally with this window lock, will you keep your eyes on the Carr family, an' tell me where they walk to?"

"They're just strolling around," Frye said. "Why are you interested in—"

"It's their intense charm," Asey said. "It's got me. Will you watch 'em, while I fix your window lock?"

He was a little annoyed when Aaron Frye, a few minutes later, went out and joined the Carrs in their walk. That was, of course, one way to find out the Carr family's destination, but he doubted if it would be the same destination they originally had in mind.

In one sense, Asey thought, it didn't matter very much. If the Carrs were contemplating any dirty work, their plans were due for a rude shock. Timothy and his grandmother were very shortly going to be put through a wringer, and he intended to apply the handle with considerable force.

And Aaron Frye was going to come in for a bit of wringing, too. That pose of indecisive absent mindedness was going to be chased right square out of the picture. He could be decisive enough when he wanted to, like the way he had acted up to the Nickerson idea.

Frye must have known, Asey thought, about the ambergris. He must have known. He did know. Any man whose nervous system reacted to loose window catches would have reacted with considerable violence to news like Pam's finding her long-sought-for ambergris. But Frye hadn't even asked how much she found. He hadn't even displayed ordinary curiosity. He'd taken the information as casually as though ambergris grew luxuriantly on the trees outside Octagon House, and it was his custom to pluck great hunks of it every morning before breakfast.

Frye was an odd duck anyway, Asey thought as he finished with the window. He'd once been some sort of college professor—Bill Porter always called him "Doctor," and so did lots of other people. But why a college professor should choose to bury himself in a place like Quanomet, Asey couldn't imagine. People said he had come for his health, which was very possibly true. And Pam had attributed his lack of interest in breadwinning to her sister's actions. Perhaps Marina's goings-on *had* done something to Frye's pride and ambition.

Perhaps. Asey thrust the screw driver back in his pocket. Perhaps. Anyway, Frye was odd, and he wasn't the only odd thing in this mess, either. And it was high time, Asey decided, that he personally got down to work. Whatever painting, puttying and tinkering around he did in the future, he would do as Asey Mayo. He'd diddled long enough.

Squaring his shoulders, Asey started for the back porch.

When he came through the strange circular hallway with Aaron Frye, he had not noticed anything but its shape, in the dim light. But now as he stepped out of the study, he stopped short and stared at the clocks lining the walls, and wondered how he had missed them before.

There were twelve angular sides to that hall, not counting the doors to the kitchen, the dining room, the study, and the parlor, and every available inch was covered with clocks, or shelves with clocks on them. Asey had never seen so many clocks in such a limited space—and no one, he thought, ever saw so many queer clocks anywhere, outside of a bad dream. There were clocks like cats whose eyes moved, clocks like cats whose eyes didn't move. There were clocks like dogs whose tails moved. Clocks with ship pendulums that swooped groggily over painted waves. Clocks with moon faces, clocks with human faces. Cuckoo clocks—any number of them. And one whole wall was devoted to a collection of frying pan clocks, of all sizes.

Asey blinked. They were enough to make a man blink. They were enough to drive a man crazy.

"Huh," he murmured. "I wonder how many cartons of soap an' oatmeal was bought to get them things originally. It's certain sure that no one bought 'em for themselves alone—ow!"

The hour struck, and for the next five minutes there was pandemonium in the hallway.

Asey gritted his teeth. No wonder things happened in Octagon House. It just wasn't sane.

He found the back porch deserted. The trooper with the tired voice had gone. There was no sign of Aaron Frye, or of the Carr family.

He walked around to the front of the house. To his surprise, not a single person lingered behind the barbed wire barricade. A lone trooper, sitting on an overturned bucket, munched a hot dog and sipped orangeade from a paper container.

"What happened?" Asey asked.

"Supper time, for one thing, and fan dancers."

"What!"

"Yeah. I hear they got a regular midway going full blast up town. Streets of Paris, or something. The town's gone nuts, if you ask me. Getting hot, ain't it?"

Asey took off his cap and mopped his forehead.

"Hot," he agreed, "on all sides."

The trooper grinned. "You'd ought to keep that cap on," he said. "Once you get out from under that visor, you're you."

Asey thrust his cap into his pocket. "Between you an' me," he said, "it binds me, anyway. Where's Hanson gone?"

"Out after you, I think. He's got a new idea, and I think it's good. I think the boy's got something. Of course he claims he had it all along, and this girl business was just a blind. I wouldn't know."

"Jack Lorne, huh?" Asey asked.

"That was my idea," the trooper admitted, "but Lorne's got the hell of an alibi. A couple of summer folks picked him up at a garage in Chatham last night, around eight-thirty. His car'd gone on the blink. They had a few drinks on the way home, and then they dumped him off here around a quarter of eleven. People across the street seen 'em. Pam Frye had already phoned for someone to come to Octagon House. We checked up on everything. The couple's okay. The garage time's okay. The guy at the road house remembers 'em. So Lorne's out of it. He—there he is, see? Going along in that convertible? Whee," he added, as brakes squealed. "I guess he's changed his mind and is coming here."

Asey watched curiously as Jack Lorne got out of his car and crawled through the barricade.

He wore sloppy, paint stained dungarees and a faded red polo shirt on which two gold safety pins served for buttons. He was amazingly young looking, in spite of the day's growth of beard on his face. And even the beard couldn't hide the weakness of that mouth and chin.

"Where's Hanson?" he demanded petulantly. "Where is the man? Away? Well, when's he coming back?"

"I don't know," the trooper said. "Tonight, later, probably. If this mob up in the village doesn't take up his time."

"What does he think this is, a mardi gras or a murder case?" Lorne turned and looked at Asey. "You're Jennings's helper, aren't you? Thank God. That water system's all haywire again. He didn't begin to fix it yesterday. The bathroom's overflowing all over the place, and the tank in the cellar is leaking in all the places he said he fixed. You *are* Jennings's helper, aren't you?"

"No," Asey said, "that's just my incognito. I'm Asey Mayo."

"Well, thank God for that," Lorne said. "I want you almost more than I want Jennings. Peggy Boone and I've been hunting for you in relays all afternoon. Where's Pam, do you know?"

Asey shook his head. "Doesn't Peggy Boone know? Somehow I thought she would."

"She doesn't. I don't. We've been to all the people she might have gone to, and no one's seen her. We've got to find her. We must!"

"To hand her over to the cops, you mean?"

"No!" Lorne said. "Of course not. What a crazy idea!"

Asey looked at him. "But I heard tell that you said she killed your wife, an'—"

"Yes, I know. I did. I thought so. You'd have thought so too, last night. Look, sit down here and let me talk. I've got to talk with someone. If I don't, I'll go mad. I want—"

"Say," the trooper said, "if you two're going to talk, just guard the place here for me, will you, for a few minutes? I want to see where Shorty went. He ought to be out back there, and I haven't seen him for a long while. Just because things look quiet isn't any reason for him to take a nap—"

"Okay," Asey said. "We'll sit here. Now, Lorne, what's come over you to change your mind so?"

"Peg Boone, for one thing," Lorne said. "She sat me down in a chair and talked to me like a Dutch uncle—and she can, too. She's got a horrid temper. She's tried to talk to me before, of course. Lots of people have. But I never believed 'em. I—" he choked, and turned his head away.

"You mean," Asey said, "you loved your wife. Is that it?"

He nodded. "I loved her," he said. "I—well, I believed in her. I didn't believe the others, and what they said, and the wisecracks, and the things they insinuated, and all the rest. I wouldn't have believed Peggy today, except—well, I'd found out lots of things. When I saw Marina lying there in the garage last night, I nearly went crazy. I was a little tight, too. And I recognized Pam's knife. And then Pam came in, looking like the wrath of God—well, I just went off my head. I thought Pam had killed her. Just as I thought Roddy was doing a big favor to offer that reward. And then I found things out for myself. I—oh, I can't talk about them! I can't do it! I don't want to believe them even now! I hate them—here, take these and read—"

He pulled an envelope from inside the faded red shirt and thrust it out to Asey.

"Read what's inside!" he said bitterly. "Read them! Read them and see how I feel! See why I'd have done some murdering on my own account this afternoon, if Peggy hadn't taken the gun away from me!"

10.
ASEY read through the two papers, and then he read them through again.

Then he looked beside him at Jack Lorne, face down in the grass, unashamedly and uncontrollably weeping his heart out.

The contents of those two sheets of paper were, Asey thought, sufficient to cause far stronger men than Lorne to weep.

"If," Asey said, "they're genuine—"

Jack Lorne sat up and wiped his eyes with the back of his hand.

"They're genuine enough! Don't you see? Marina was never really married to me! Our marriage never meant a thing. She was married all the time to Timothy Carr! That marriage certificate is genuine enough. It's all about it, in her diary—" he couldn't control his voice.

"And this other. This note," Asey picked it up. "Twenty-five thousand dollars, payable to Marina Carr. On demand. Signed by Timothy Carr, and witnessed by two people. Where, Lorne, in the name of God, did you find these two chunks of dynamite?"

"I found them this morning, in a tin box in the bottom drawer of a wardrobe trunk of hers. I never knew she had such a box. I was hunting for a will and insurance policies —I told her to put 'em in the bank box, but they weren't there. So I hunted, and I found this box. There were lots of other trophies there. Diaries. Everything. You—want me to tell you about those diaries?"

Asey nodded. "Or you could let me see them."

"No one'll ever see those!" Lorne said savagely. "I burned them, page by page!"

"Was that wise?" Asey asked. "I see how you might have wanted to, but this note and this marriage certificate'll put Tim Carr in a hole—"

"The diaries," Lorne said, "would have hanged him. That's one of the minor reasons I burned them. The real reason was me. Me, and Aaron, and Pam. I decided that the three of us had taken enough. We—" he gulped. "We took plenty, we did."

"I'm inclined to think," Asey said, "that maybe perhaps you all have. Now, she married Tim before she went through the motions of marryin' you. That right?"

Lorne closed his eyes and leaned on his elbows.

"Today," he spoke as if he were quoting, "today I hooked Tim Carr."

In the same voice, he sketched the story.

"Hooked Tim Carr. Found today he's all front. No money. Tightwad. Everything for that grandmother, the old bitch. I hate her. Today I swiped his prize money and the old lady's jewelry. Going abroad with Lorne, the sap. He'll be famous some day. Got Carr fixed. The sample note he wrote for his math class, when they learned about making out checks and notes and accounts. Grabbed it from waste basket and ironed it out last week. Got Sammy and Peter to sign. They'd sign anything if I asked them. Let Carr try to divorce me—"

Asey whistled softly. "I get it. If Tim tried to divorce her, she'd raise hell with that note. But her witnesses—"

"She thought of them," Lorne said. "She thought of everything. They witnessed it in the apartment, while Carr was there, just after he'd written something at the desk. She shifted the paper. The diary had all the details. She had him cold. For Carr to divorce her would have cost him twenty-five thousand, and I guess it might as well have been a million as far as he was concerned. Marina hated the grandmother. That's why she did it. The grandmother told her where she got off, and she was going to make the Carrs suffer for it. She had them, don't you see? If they tried to do anything about her, or her and me, all she had to do was to wave that note. She had them. And she also had some pretty rabid letters from Carr. I burned those."

"Threatening her?"

Lorne nodded. "I started to give them to Hanson, and then I burned them up. They would have hanged him."

"And you don't want him to hang, even though you think he killed your wife?"

"All of us, Pam and Aaron and Carr and I," Lorne said, "we've suffered enough. I don't know—I'm not supposed to be very bright, and I'm not. I don't catch on to things quickly—God knows I don't!" he laughed bitterly. "But people who do things like Marina did, some time or other, things catch up with them. They caught up with her. I don't know how to explain what I feel. I'm not angry with Carr now, though I was at first. Before I read the diaries. I'm sorry for him now. I'm sorry for myself. For all of us. We trusted her—and she tore us into strips! I'm dumb. I didn't know what was going on. The others did."

He lighted a cigarette, and Asey noticed his hands. They were long slender feminine hands, sensitive and expressive.

"The diaries had the whole story," Lorne went on. "What she did to the family, and before she met me, and afterwards, and who she did, and everything. Everyone. Roddy. She was playing him for a sucker. Anyway, it's all over with now. Carr did it, not Roddy, as Peg thought. And I hope that you and Hanson can't get him."

"Know anythin' about ambergris, Lorne?" Asey asked.

"That's what Pam's always talking about," Lorne said. "What she's always hunting. I never understood much about it. It's used for making perfumes, isn't it, or something like that? It's a whale's chin, or tail. I never could see why she made such a fuss over it."

"It's a sort of greyish stuff," Asey said, "that grows in the intestines of a whale. Fatty, an' a little smelly, an' sort of streaked like marble. You can probably get around thirty-five dollars an ounce for it."

"An ounce," Lorne said. "An ounce?"

"Yup. An' yesterday, Pam found a lump of about a hundred pounds out on the point. And Marina found Pam. After a squabble, Marina brought it back in Roddy's beach wagon, to your garage. And—"

"Where is it now?"

Asey shrugged. "Pam went over there later, and found Marina dead, and she removed it. I thought she brought it to Octagon House. It's not in the cellar, an' the cops didn't uncover it. I don't know where it is."

"That's swell for Pam, isn't it?" Lorne said. "She—oh. But if someone found it and took it—gee, you've got to find it for her, haven't you?"

Asey looked at him curiously. There was no doubt that the fellow was perfectly sincere.

"Yes, I got to find it before someone else does," Asey said, "an' someone else is huntin' it. Now—you don't breathe a word of this, you know. Not to anyone. But can you think of any part of the house where it might be?"

"No," Lorne said. "You'd think from the outside that the place was awfully queer, but it isn't, except for the shape of some of the rooms, and the arrangement. I'll get a pencil, though, and see if I can think it out."

"Think hard," Asey said as he got up, "while I investigate Brother Carr. You know, it's just possible that this marriage certificate an' note was what he meant, an' not the ambergris—come on."

"All right," Lorne said. "You know, I—I keep wondering what this is going to do to my work."

"Huh?" Asey didn't quite understand.

"My work," Lorne said. "Of course this publicity has got me dozens of offers—but what will this *do*—to my work, you see?"

Asey nodded, and suppressed a smile. If Lorne had got to

the point where he could gauge his reactions to the murder in terms of his work, then there was little sense in worrying about him, or feeling sorry for him.

"I see," Asey said. "Yes, I see."

He wanted to ask Lorne if he knew the part Marina had played in helping him—with other people's work—but he decided that this was not the time to find out about that.

As they walked up past the house, Asey paused by the cellar window on which he had been working.

"Might's well take two seconds," he said, "to finish up this pane here."

"Now my work," Lorne said importantly. "My work—"

"It won't suffer," Asey said cryptically.

Before he finished with the pane, Peggy Boone came up the road, vaulted the barbed wire barrier, and strolled up the driveway.

"Ah," she said. "Mr. Fix-it. You get around, don't you?"

"He's Asey Mayo, Peg," Jack said. "I've told him everything."

"I began to suspect that he was," she said, "after I left Nettie's. Your eyes give you away, you know. Do you know where Pam is?"

"I've got a lot of faith in her," Asey said. "She can take care of herself."

"I hope so—and have you heard about the town? Nettie has joined the midway, and between her and the fan dancers, it's bedlam. There's a nickel-a-dance joint been set up— Why, the whole place looks like a gold rush camp. Forty-niners on a bust. My car's jammed up there somewhere. I just gave up and left it."

"How are the local boys taking it?" Asey asked.

"The invasion? Oh, they're trying to stop the riot. So is Hanson, with some of his cops. But you might as well turn back a cyclone with a bean blower. Honestly, it's awful! I haven't seen the like since the last bootleggers dumped their last loads on the clam flats, and the town was knee deep with bottles for days. It's the same sort of thing, only they've got something to do besides drink. And it's not the local folk. The natives are furiously trying to get the National Guard out, or something. They'll have to. The crowd's got to the stage here it thinks it's fun to start fires."

"You're makin' it up," Asey said, "as you go along!"

"I'm not!" Peg protested. "I'm not, I tell you it's an orgy! There were three brush fires when I was up there, and a small tent went up in flames. And they've tipped the fire engine over on its side. Of course, it's a silly old engine, and it looks funny, and that siren sounds funny, but still there's no reason—oh, well. I suppose Hanson will solve the problem somehow."

"It's as bad as you say? You ain't kiddin'?"

"It's as bad as that. I've never seen anything like it. Just a mob—what are you going to do?"

"Phonin'," Asey said, and went indoors.

He looked worried when he returned.

"I can't even get the office," he said. "The line sounds dead. They ain't touched the wires, have they?"

"I wouldn't know, but I wouldn't put it past them. Roddy was there, having the swellest time—he'd think of phone wires. He thinks of so many things—"

"Say," the trooper who had been at the front of the house walked up to them. "Say, I can't find Shorty or O'Malley— you seen 'em?"

"They've probably gone to see the fan dancers," Asey said.

"Like hell—they ought to be around. The car's here. But I can't find 'em. I've yelled my head off."

"Been back in the woods?"

"Say, I been all over. I can't see why they didn't tell me if they was going some place."

"Probably they're after the Carrs and Aaron Frye," Asey said. "I wouldn't worry. Now listen, they're having a real riot up town. I want you to get your car and go find Hanson, and tell him to get fire trucks from other towns, and use the hose—and if he hasn't already, to call Captain Andrell. He—"

"But Shorty and O'Malley—I got to find them. And I can't leave this place!"

"We'll look after things here," Asey said. "You go get Hanson. I'll find your friends. You trot along. That's an order. If it makes you feel better, I outrank Hanson in an hon'rary way, an' I'm an hon'rary officer of the law of this town, accordin' to a piece of paper I got to home. You go on. I'll take the r'sponsibility—"

"Well, okay. But I'd like to know where Shorty and O'Malley are," the trooper said. "I don't see where they could be. You find 'em, will you? I'm worried—"

Asey promised, and the trooper went off reluctantly to his car.

"Much," Peg Boone said, "against his better judgment, I know. I—well, well, look at precious!"

She pointed to Emma Goldman, stalking majestically out of the woods, her leash trailing behind her.

"Run away, huh?" Asey said. "Hi, Emma. Where's your folks? Come here 'fore you get caught up with that leash—"

The cat walked up to him and rubbed her head against his trouser leg.

"You," Asey tied the leash to a trellis, "should know better, Emma, than to beat it like this. You'll get whacked."

"Funny," Peg Boone leaned down and stroked the cat's head. "She seemed frightened. Isn't this odd, everyone missing? Shouldn't we yell, in chorus? O'Malley!" she yelled at the top of her voice. "Shorty! Aaron Frye! Carrs!"

Asey laughed. "You raised someone," he said. "I hear— oh, Mrs. Carr."

She panted up to them. "Have you seen Emma—oh, thank goodness! Something frightened her, and she ran like a streak. Pulled the leash square out of my hand. I never knew her to—"

"Where's Tim?" Asey asked. "And Aaron?"

"Aren't they here?" Mrs. Carr asked in some surprise. "They aren't? Aaron wandered off, and Tim went after him —long ago. Emma's been acting so strangely—"

"Have you seen two cops, named O'Malley and Shorty?"

"No, I haven't seen anyone. Except a skunk, after Emma left. And two squirrels. All the animal life seems to be in a perfectly terrible rush this evening. I don't know whether Emma got her fright from them, or they got it from her—stop tugging, Emma! Look at her ears! She—"

"Listen," Asey said. "Listen—"

"I don't hear anything," Peg said. "Do you, Mrs. Carr? I—"

Asey motioned for her to be still.

"Somethin' queer," he said. "It's a rushin' sound, seems like. I'll walk around back by the barn, an' see what I can see—"

"Emma!" Mrs. Carr said in exasperation as Asey hurried off, "take that tail from between your legs, and come—she won't stir! Emma, what in the world is the matter—"

"My God!" Jack Lorne said. "My God, look—look at that barn!"

11.

11. PEGGY BOONE raced after him around to the back of the house.

The scene before her brought her to a standstill.

Some hundred and fifty feet from the Octagon House, the old octagonal barn was flaming like a piece of cotton wool dipped in gasoline. She had never seen anything so completely and so furiously on fire.

Asey and Jack Lorne, both choking, ran up to where she stood.

"Phew!" Asey said. "Phe-ew! I was just goin' to shove that side door open when the whole thing went—phut! I kind of wonder that I got a face."

"Don't tell me!" Jack said. "I saw you. One minute the barn was all right—the next split second it was a torch! Can't we do something? What'll we do? We've got to do something—"

"Like what?" Asey inquired.

"Put it out! Call help—hurry, come on, we've got to do something!" Jack said excitedly. "Hurry—"

"This house," Asey pointed out, "has only got a pump. The water system at your house is on the blink. The fire truck's out of commission up with the town riot. So's the phone. What can you do?"

"We can't just sit!" Peggy protested.

"Maybe you can't," Asey returned, "but that's what I'm goin' to do. That barn's tinder, pure an' simple. It'll be down in five minutes. It's even hot here. We better move up onto the porch."

"But the house!" Jack said. "Suppose the house should catch?"

"S'posin' it does?" Asey said.

Jack Lorne looked at him in amazement. Had Asey Mayo forgotten that Pam's ambergris was in the Octagon House somewhere? For a man who was supposed to be so clever, Jack decided Asey Mayo was pretty dumb. Stupid.

He started to say so, but Asey's wide-mouthed yawn shocked him into silence.

"Heat," he remarked, "always makes me awful sleepy. You see now why the cat was in such a fidget."

"How could that cat know about this?"

"She seen skunks an' squirrels runnin'," Asey said. "Prob'ly there was dozens of animals livin' in that old ark. When the fire started, they beat it. Emma seen 'em, an' city cat that she is, she knew enough to run. Don't ask me why she should run home. I ain't up on the mental processes of city cats. Just give her credit for gettin' the idea that runnin' was in order."

"I don't believe it!" Peg insisted.

"Didn't you ever see a forest fire, with all the animals runnin' from it?" Asey asked. "Fire panics 'em. Say, you know I wouldn't wonder if maybe perhaps this house didn't catch, at that. It's kind of warmin' up in sympathy, sort of."

"Aren't you going to *do* anything?" Peg demanded. "Are

you just going to sit there? We must do something—something! They always drape wet blankets around when there are fires like this, over my way. Shouldn't we?"

"If this was a proper an' logical Cape house," Asey said, pulling out his pipe, "we could dabble an' dribble around with wet blankets on the far roof. But it ain't a logical house. An' did you ever notice the size of that hand pump in the kitchen? Well, then. Just sit an' calm yourself—"

"But we ought to save things!" Jack said.

"If worse comes to worse," Asey said, "we'll salvage silver an' books an' things. It's the heck of a pity that Aaron Frye can't be around to tell us what he treasures the most. You know, I remember once in Wellfleet nearly scorchin' my hide off to save some old pewter plates an' a couple of fiddleback chairs, an' a stack of silver, all for an old aunt of mine when her house burned. An' that woman, she laid me out in lavender. She tongue lashed me to a pulp, afterwards. What'd she care for pewter an' fiddleback chairs an' silver? What she wanted, an' what I didn't save, was the old wooden spoon she stirred batter with. There goes the roof—watch! An' an inkwell her brother'd carved out of a root. It didn't hold ink very good, but she liked it. An' then again—"

Leaning back against the porch railing, he chatted on casually about fires he had entered into, while the octagonal barn swiftly reduced itself to a mass of charred embers. Without quite understanding why, Peg and Jack found themselves assuming his matter-of-fact and philosophical attitude. Neither of them noticed his preoccupation with the woods around the barn.

"There," Asey said at last, "that's the end of that. Sun's gone down—maybe them embers'll glow up tomorrow mornin' when the sun comes up, but I think that'll matter very little. Wonder if Frye had insurance?"

"Probably not," Peggy said, "unless Pam thought about it. Asey, why didn't anyone come to see this fire? Quanomet's a great old fire town. They come in droves to see fires."

"The other shows is givin' us too much competition," Asey said. "Neighbors is either up watchin' or deplorin' the fan dancers, I guess. Or else they figger this is another visitin' reveller fire. Well, I guess this concludes the performance—"

"Performance is right!" Peggy interrupted. "Do you realize that we sat—sat, and never lifted a finger? And Asey, how did it start? Was it set?"

"What a horrid thought!" Asey said, the shadow of a smile playing around the corners of his mouth. "Set? Tch, tach! Why, barns—includin' octagonal barns—they burn down every day. Set? My, my. An' there we never lifted a finger, never did a thing we was s'posed to do. Just twiddled our thumbs. Someone is probably writhin' with disappointment out there. In fact, someone is there, I'm sure. But I'm guessin' about the writhin' part."

"What are you talking about?" Lorne demanded. "What do you mean, someone set the barn on fire? Why? Who? What for?"

"It was a questionin' fire," Asey said. "But it didn't get answered, 'cause there ain't no answer. Now, if you two'll be good enough to hold the fort—"

"Where are you going" Peg asked.

"I'm goin' to rec'noitre," Asey said. "You an' Jack are herewith pro tem deputies, or somethin'. Anyway, you stay here, you stay put right here, no matter what you think, or feel inspired to do. Both of you. See?"

The pair nodded. There was somethin' in Asey's voice that forbade any questioning.

"Okay," Asey said, "an' hang onto the Carrs, please, if you have to hang on to their shirt tails to do it."

He strolled out past the smoldering barn to the woods beyond.

Once in the deepening shadow of the pines, he dropped his mantle of carefree indifference.

He had not actually seen anyone lurking around, but he felt sure that someone was lurking. There had to be.

Someone had fired the barn, all right, and Asey was the first to admit that it was an excellent piece of work. Not just as a complete bit of demolishing, either. Someone had done a neat bit of thinking. There was no better way for someone to find out where Pam's ambergris was than to start a fire in the general vicinity, and then sit back and watch to see who ran where.

And that person, Asey thought, would never know how he personally suffered, sitting there on the porch and spinning yarns, while he fairly itched to be hunting the Octagon House from attic to cellar.

The woods were thicker than he had supposed existed any more, what with all the reforesting and deforesting that had taken place in the neighboring towns. The air was damp, and the tops of the tall pines cut out what twilight there was left.

Not the sort of place, definitely, where Asey would care to meet up with those two muscle-bound servants that belonged to Roddy Strutt.

He stopped for a moment to tie a shoestring, and for the first time it occurred to him that he was being trailed. He couldn't hear anyone—the carpet of pine needles was too thick to carry the sound of footsteps—but he knew. He could almost feel the presence of someone behind him.

"Ho-hum," he said aloud, and started back the way he had come.

He couldn't see anyone hiding in the dense growth.

And then suddenly someone to his left started to run.

Asey set off in pursuit.

Within ten yards, he knew that he would never catch the figure that twisted and turned and sidestepped so nimbly ahead of him.

It wasn't so much a question of speed. It was the combination of the slippery pine needles and his leather soled shoes. Those were the things that were going to lick him.

The sneakers which he'd worn out in the boat the day before were still wet that morning; not wanting to unpack, he'd put on the smart brown brogues in which he'd journeyed home. And then, when he changed to his painting clothes, he'd climbed into an old pair of work shoes from the back shed. Each shoe weighed five pounds, he decided as he stumbled along, and the soles were so dry and brittle that they might have been made of wood.

Grabbing at a tree to save himself from a fall, Asey yanked the shoes off, and then dashed to catch up with the figure ahead.

An unexpected patch of blackberry vines made him wince and wish that he had kept the old clodhoppers on. But he was gaining on the figure. If he could keep up, he'd get the fellow before he reached the edge of the clearing.

The man sidestepped, swung around suddenly and started off on a right angle course.

Asey started to follow, and then stopped short.

Before him on the ground lay Timothy Carr.

He blinked as Asey leaned over him, and put a hand vaguely toward the lump on his forehead.

"Be back," Asey said briefly, and started off again.

"Back what?" Tim said, and struggled into a sitting position.

The woods and the pines and the branches all danced dizzily inside his head, and he groped around for his glasses. But even after he found them and cleaned them twice, everything continued to spin.

Finally the scenery slipped back into its normal place, and Timothy got shakily to his feet.

"Cool!" he said with deep feeling. "Cool! Hey, Aaron. Aaron, where are you? For the love of God, where's everybody gone? Hey—Asey! Asey, where'd you—oh, there you are—here, Asey. Here—"

But the man whose face he saw for the fraction of a second was not Asey.

"Hey, you!" Tim said. "Come back here—all right, then, I'll go after you! Hey, where'd you go? What's the big idea, anyway?"

The man slid away into the shadows. Tim couldn't even tell what direction he had taken.

"The hell," Tim muttered, "with the whole lot of you! All right, I *won't* go after you. I'll sit and wait. Hide and seek in the woods, or fun for the boarders! Come to Octagon House. No modern improvements, but plenty of old-fashioned action. Coo!"

But after sitting and waiting for nearly a quarter of an hour, Tim marched off toward where Asey had disappeared.

He found Asey, too. Lying under a scrubby pine.

He blinked as Timothy leaned over him, and put a hand toward the lump that was beginning to rise on his forehead.

"So you got tagged too, did you?" Tim said. "I didn't even understand you were in the game."

"Neither did I," Asey said. "My, my!"

"It's best not to open your eyes right away," Tim advised. "I speak with authority. Too many things move too much. Quote, the very trees whirl. Unquote. Asey, who is this stranger with homicidal tendencies? I don't like him."

"I didn't see him," Asey said, "but he's a near relation to Joe Louis. Did you catch sight of the lad?"

"I had a glimpse of someone," Tim said, "shortly after

you left. I suppose it was our pal. Look, when you feel up to it, we'd better seek out the bush where Aaron's probably stretched out. Or did you happen to find him?"

Asey sat up.

"Aaron? Look, what's been going on here, anyway?"

"There are bad mans in the woods," Tim told him, as he lighted a cigarette. "They hit folks over the head. I don't quite understand the game, Asey. Aaron wandered away from Gran and me, just the way he kept wandering at that clambake. I went after him—my God, I forgot Gran and Emma! I do hope no one's beaned them!"

"They're back at the house."

"That's a relief. Emma's pretty resilient, but I don't think Gran would take a beaning very well. Anyway, I went after Aaron. I heard him call me. That's all I can tell you. En route to the noise, I got tagged. Then you peered at me—d'you know you were quintuplets? You were. And then I came here and found you. I think," he rubbed his forehead reflectively, "that the curtain has been lowered to denote a lapse of considerable time. It wasn't nearly as dark as this, when I got biffed. Look, we'll have to find Aaron before this trickle of grey light disappears. He ought to be in the vicinity. Let's scour."

But Aaron was not in the vicinity, nor could they find any trace of him.

"I don't like this," Tim said. "To me this smacks of foul play. What do you think?"

"We'll go back to the house," Asey said. "Most likely he's there, safe an' sound with your grandmother an' Emma. If he ain't here, he must be there. It's my idea that the troopers followed you two, and prob'ly they escorted Aaron back. Look, while we're on the topic of foul play, what were you hunting so hard in the Lorne house, an' roundabouts? An' why did I get told so much folderol last night?"

"A little bird," Tim did his best to maintain his flippant tone, "tells me you already know. You do, don't you? Timothy's Error, or The Blighted Life. Who found the marriage lines and that pretty note, you or Hanson?"

"Lorne."

"Poor Gran," Timothy said. "It may sound like Galahad, or that man with that hair shirt, but I'd hoped it wouldn't happen, for her sake. That's why you got that yarn. There was a chance the stuff wouldn't turn up. I hoped I'd find it first. But if Lorne found it, well—that's that. We didn't discover until the clambake that Marina was Frye's daughter, living virtually next door. We left the movies early and drove around, wondering what to do. Then we came back and found she'd been killed. I don't know where we drove. No one can alibi us. I'm left handed. If Marina happened to hang onto some letters I wrote her—well, I'm as good as electrocuted right now."

"Lorne burned your letters," Asey said.

"He did?"

"Yes," Asey said, "after readin' Marina's diaries, he felt a burnin' sympathy for a fellow sucker. This has sort of hit him, you see. You caught on pretty quick that Marina was the sort of person she was. Lorne didn't realize until he read them diaries. He ain't suffered as long as you have, but he got a big dose all at once. Of course," he added, "it's wearin' off. He's beginnin' now to wonder what effect this sufferin' will have on his art."

"That lovely haze," Tim said, "of artistic unreality. It always charms me. What Will It Do To My Art? Dear me, if I'd been able to think that way, I might be an artist now instead of just a person in the quadratic surd business. A sense of humor makes life easier, but it's not awfully good for art."

Asey admitted that he could see where a sense of humor might well be a handicap. "Look," he said, "did you or your grandmother kill Marina?"

"On my word of honor," Timothy said, "I didn't, and she didn't."

Asey nodded.

"You don't mean that you believe me, do you?" Tim sounded incredulous.

"Yup," Asey said. "For one thing, I don't think you're the sort of person who'd swipe Pam's knife to do your murderin' with. An' for another thing, you're not the person who biffed me, the one I played hide an' seek with. An' I don't think you biffed yourself. So—"

"You feel that our pal the biffer," Tim said, "our palsy-walsy with the left—he's the murderer?"

"If he ain't," Asey said grimly, "then this little game has got more compl'cations than I like to c'nsider. Lorne," he added as they came to the clearing behind the ruins of the barn, "has your two papers, but I shouldn't ask him for 'em for a while, if I was you. I'd wait—"

"The barn!" Tim said. "My God, where'd it go?"

"Bad mans," Asey told him with a chuckle. "Burney-burn, zzst, like that."

"Did, did he?" Tim said. "The scoundrelly pyromaniac. Demolishing a relic like that! Thank God, I took pictures of it the minute I came. That's something. It's the first octagonal barn I've actually seen—you know, octagonal barns were very sensible thoughts, Asey. You could drive your wagon in, and turn around. Didn't have to back. And you had different bays for things. Every bin in its own bay— Asey, where is Pam?"

Asey shrugged.

"For obvious reasons," Tim said, "I've been soured on all females except Gran, for some time. But I liked Pam. I think she's a pretty swell girl. In fact, I'll go so far as to say that she interests me vastly. And I'm worried about her."

"Pam," Asey began, "can take care—"

"Of herself," Tim interrupted. "Yes, I know. Gran's been singing that refrain at intervals all day long. On the order of a Greek chorus. But you and I got smacked down, didn't we? And just suppose, Comrade Mayo, that Pam *can't* take care of herself. Suppose she can't, and you don't find it out until later. Or too late. Shan't you feel just a wee bit silly?"

"Uh-huh," Asey said serenely, "I should. But I'm bettin' my money on Pam."

"You seem strangely convinced," Tim said.

"I am," Asey told him.

And he was.

The squirt of a match in the skylight window of the Octagon House attic, and the cigarette tip glowing up there now —both made him feel considerably happier about Pam Frye. Like a sensible girl, she had probably come back in the cover of darkness, knowing that Hanson's attention was distracted by the mob up in the village. And there wasn't a much safer place for her. The Octagon House had already been searched. And someone had already tried to have the ambergris pointed out to him by the barn burning.

And it would, Asey thought feelingly, be a relief to find out where that confounded ambergris was anyway, and to take steps about disposing of it.

"Well," Tim said, "perhaps you *are* convinced about Pam. I'm not. If X can biff A and T, then X can biff anyone, including P, a mere slip of a girl. You know, they seem reasonably worked up, whoever's howling there in the house."

Asey chuckled. "Doc Cummings," he said. "That's his extra de luxe bellow, for special occasions of what he calls profound irritation. He's goin' to be so speechless with rage that he can't talk. That is, not more'n three hundred words a minute. I wonder who he's mad at—"

Asey walked over to the doctor's old sedan, and played a tune on the asthmatic horn.

"Cummings," he said, "will be out directly."

The doctor's stocky figure bounded out of the house.

"Well," he said, "it's about time! Where have you been? I never was so furious in all my life. Never so thoroughly— where have you been, man? It's disgusting," he went on, without giving Asey a chance to answer, "it's revolting. It's doing things to my stomach. You know who's in there, waiting for you? Roddy's uncle, the feeble minded toad! That's just what he looks like, a feeble minded toad, and that's just the way he thinks. In brief hops. In brief, aimless and undirected hops. He—"

"What's he want me for?" Asey asked.

"Roddy," Cummings said in tones of great restraint. "Roddy's being menaced."

Asey clucked his tongue. "Bad mans," he said. "Who is menacing him?"

"Oh, they don't know, but they want you to save Roddy's little skin. Brought the Strutt checkbooks with him, and for all I know, the best gold tea set as an added incentive. Asey, if you sully your hands with that toad and that slug of a nephew of his—that spot of mildew! If you sully your hands with 'em, I'll never speak to you again."

Asey grinned. "Send the toad out—no, wait. I'll go in."

Carveth Strutt did look like a toad, Asey thought as he entered the kitchen behind the doctor. Carveth was also a dead ringer for the sick capitalist up in the post office mural. Bloated and pink and puffy.

"My nephew," he informed Asey excitedly, "is being menaced! It's his legacy. His grandmother's legacy. He's just got it this week, and now he's being menaced! You must help—"

"He is, is he?" Asey said. "Last I heard of Roddy, he was gambolin' with the mob up town. Kind of sudden, this menace, ain't it?"

"He's kept it a secret till just now. You must help!" Carveth squeaked. "You must, you must!"

"Where's Roddy now?"

"Home," Dr. Cummings answered before Carveth could. "Home, with Filipinos on either side of him, all heavily armed. The place is a beehive of walking arsenals with passwords. They are taking every precaution, every single precaution. Carveth has told us all about it, twice. Sounds like the Treasury, awaiting the revolution. You can almost hear the rabble—"

"How long you been here, Strutt?" Asey asked.

"Fifteen or twenty minutes. See here, you've got to come and—"

"I thought so," Asey said. "Roddy probably figgers this is a swift bit of brain work. Only it ain't. If he's bein' menaced, then of course he can't be menacin'—uh-huh."

"Roddy is in danger of his life!" Carveth said. "We must have your aid. We are prepared to pay any sum—"

"Sp'cifically," Asey said, "what is the danger? Who's the menace?"

"A man prowling around yesterday," Carveth said, "pretending to be a workman. Asking questions. And then to-day—why, the poor boy's out of his mind with fear!"

"Yeah," Asey said. "Now, you run along home an' you tell Roddy that I'll be over to see him later. Then he'll learn just what menacin' is. Got that?"

Carveth nodded. "You'll be over later and tell him who the menace is. Oh, I'm glad you'll help—"

"Not who the menace is," Asey said. "What menacin' is. There is a dif'rence. Run along—"

Cummings smiled as Strutt left.

"To hear you menace the toad and the slug," he said happily, "I'll forego sleep I badly need. Where is he, Asey?"

"Who?" Asey said, looking at the cashmere sweater cas-ually tossed over a chair back. That was the sweater he had bought as a present for Betsey Porter, the sweater he had given to Pam the night before. And it was a very clever way of letting him know that she had come home, since no one else would recognize it as hers.

"Where's Aaron?" Cummings asked again.

"Aaron?" Asey stared at him. "Ain't he here? Didn't he come back with the troopers?"

Cummings let out a shrill yell.

"Haven't you got him? Isn't he with you? Aren't those troopers with you?"

Asey shook his head.

"My God," Cummings said, "where are they?"

12. "WHERE *are* they?"

Cummings' lusty bellow brought the trooper rushing into the kitchen from the front of the house, and behind him rushed Jack Lorne, Peggy Boone and Mrs. Carr.

They were followed, rather disdainfully, by Emma Goldman. Something in the arch of her plume-like tail explained clearly that she thought the whole business was pretty silly, but she was conforming.

"Hanson said that Aaron Frye and the troopers were with you. Didn't he, Ding?" Cummings said.

"That's right," the trooper answered. "That's what Hanson said. He said they were all of them with Asey. That's just what he said. And now—say, where are they?"

"What inspired that brain ripple of Hanson's?" Asey demanded in tones that were crisper than usual. "How'd he get that idea?"

"Why, I told him," the trooper said, "that O'Malley and Shorty had gone, and Frye and the Carrs, too. I told him when I went up to tell him about the fire hose, like you ordered me to. He asked how things was, and I told him they was all gone. And Hanson said if you was here, all right, not to worry. You'd get 'em. You got one, anyway," he pointed to Timothy. "You got one. Where's the rest?"

Timothy muttered under his breath something about the part and the whole.

"And Hanson said," the trooper continued, "for God's sake will you carry on while he looks after the town. Where are O'Mall—"

"How's the town?" Asey asked.

"Oh, they'd got those hoses from Pochet and around, before I got there. That stopped things. They're rounding up drunks now, and fixing phone wires, and unjamming the cars and all. It didn't last so awful long, but it's a hell of a mess. I never seen anything like it, even in strikes. Say, where are O'Malley and—"

"They're not in my pocket." Asey was tired of the trooper's refrain. "Lorne, you and Carr and this fellow an' I, we'll have to do some tall huntin'. Got some of those fancy lights in your car, trooper?"

"Yes. I—"

"Get 'em. Help him, Jack. Tim, you go along, too. Doc, you'll have to stay here an' look after this place an' Mrs. Carr."

"Can't I hunt, too?" Peggy Boone asked.

"You better hadn't," Asey said. "The lad we met up with was a great old basher. Say, maybe you want to get home—do you?"

"Go home, with all this going on, don't be silly! Not unless you send me—"

"Tell you what," Asey said, "you go down the street an' drop in on the neighbors, an' tell 'em we'd like some help in a man hunt. Mrs. Carr, you go along with her, will you?"

"To second the invitation? I'd love to. Come along, Emma," she picked up the cat, "you're going to get tied up. I don't trust you alone with that parrot. How many people would you want, Asey?"

"As many as you can inveigle," Asey said. "But get natives, please. No outlanders—"

As soon as the group scattered, Asey slipped upstairs to the attic.

"Hi," Pam Frye greeted him genially. "You don't mind if I don't welcome you with a light, do you?"

"Hi yourself," Asey said. "I'm certainly glad to know you're safe an' sound—how'd you get here, an' when?"

"Oh, I walked in the front door," Pam told him, "while the rest were on the back porch. And if you had a can opener, I could enjoy a light repast of cold beans."

Asey presented her with a jack knife.

"Golly, what gadgets!" Pam said. "I'll have to take a match to see this. What a—what a *thing*, Asey!"

"It was sent me by an unknown lady admirer," Asey said. "I'm sure there's a can opener on it—there's everything else, includin' a microscope that don't work. Pam, where in time is your father?"

"Is he missing?" she said. "Oh, I wouldn't worry, Asey. He often wanders. Probably in his present mental state, he had to wander or bust. Who burned up the barn?"

"God A'mighty," Asey said, "is the only one that knows that. Pam, where does your father wander to?"

"I've known him to walk to Hyannis," Pam said, "without meaning to go any farther than the store when he set out. Probably he's gone up town—have you seen the mess?"

"An' we're shy two troopers," Asey said.

"Then I certainly shouldn't worry about Aaron," Pam remarked, struggling with the can of beans. "He wandered off to town, and they went after him, and probably they're all up there now. Didn't you see the to-do? I spent some time viewing it this afternoon, and apparently my tourist face is convincing—no one noticed me."

"Where did you go last night?"

"Someone," Pam said, "was prowling around your house. I don't know who it was, but I saw the figure beneath the window. There didn't seem to be any sense in exposing you to danger, so I upped and left. Went to your garage, as a matter of fact, very stealthy-like. Through the shed—"

"I looked in the garage an' the shed too."

"Oh, I climbed a tree until after you'd gone to bed," Pam remarked. "Then I sneaked into the garage and curled up in your Porter. And if Jennie's mad about a pie she missed from the shed this afternoon, don't blame tramps. Asey, the can opener works—what's that noise outside? Hordes of people—"

"My man hunt," Asey said. "Look, you stay here quiet for the night, will you? Don't go rushin' off again. I'll be up later an' bring you some food. Cummings an' Mrs. Carr'll be downstairs. I've got to go an' make sure your father an' them fellers didn't meet up with my biffer—"

"Okay," Pam said with her mouth full.

It occurred to Asey as he ran down the stairs to the kitchen that he had not, in his relief at finding the girl, asked a single thing about the question uppermost in his mind.

He still didn't know where that infernal lump of ambergris was!

"We've got around two dozen for you," Mrs. Carr said with a touch of quiet pride. "All natives, and for all I know, all of impeccable Mayflower ancestry. And the trooper says he has his lights all set, and we told our two dozen to bring flashes with them."

"A triumph," Asey said, "of organization. Thanks. We'll see if we can't get somewheres."

At two o'clock that morning, they gave up the search.

Not a single trace of Aaron Frye or of the two troopers could be found in the woods or the vicinity.

"An' that," Asey said wearily, after dismissing his searching party, "is that!"

Cummings agreed. "What are you going to do now? What—say, here's Hanson in his car. Maybe he's got some news."

Hanson regarded them sleepily through glazed eyes.

"News?" he said. "The town's in order, if that's what you mean."

"But Frye, and your two men, they're still missing," the doctor said. "Missing!"

"Don't shout. I believe you," Hanson said. "I believe anything, after that mess up town. My God!"

"Wake up for a second," Asey said. "Have you seen Shorty an' O'Malley up town? They're still missin'. I'm beginnin' to believe they must have joined your crowd in the village."

"They didn't." Hanson yawned widely. "Just finished a roll call. One was missing. He got locked up in someone's garage when he was chasing a drunk. Someone thought he was the drunk."

His eyes closed, and he pried them open.

"I went on duty," he said, "at six o'clock yesterday evening. Way back there. I came over here at eleven. When is it now, half-past-two?"

"Half-past-two tonight," Asey said. "The next day. Go grab some sleep, Hanson. You need it. There's a hammock on the front porch. Tumble into it. You can sleep and be on guard duty at the same time. I'll look after things here. I've got Lorne and Carr to help."

"That's white of you," Hanson said. "I mean it. Usually I can take three or four days without sleep, but this mob in the town got me."

Asey led him to the hammock. Before Cummings finished draping a blanket over him, Hanson was dead to the world.

"I'll get another blanket," Cummings said. "He's dripping perspiration—ought to have a bath and clean clothes, but I don't think we could wake him up enough—want me here, Asey?"

"Nope, just tend to Hanson, an' we'll settle things in the house. I'll call if I want you."

"You probably will," Cummings said philosophically. "And look, what about Roddy?"

"He could menace me," Asey said, "more'n I could menace him, at this point. If there was another hammock, I'd flip into it myself. Say, what's good for feet?"

"For what?" Cummings looked down. "For the love— what have you *got* on your feet? What are those things?"

"I think they're rubber bathing shoes," Asey said, "an' I think they belong to Aaron. I took 'em off the clothes line. They're most likely fine for bathin', but they ain't the ideal things for man hunts. Things sort of percolate through." He kicked them off. "When you come back over here, bring me some footwear from home, will you? Ask Jennie."

In the kitchen of the Octagon House, Mrs. Carr was bustling around with coffee and sandwiches.

"You have a choice," she said, "of ham with mustard or ham without mustard. Last week I saw an ad of the perfect hostess serving a midnight snack, and she had thirty-four different kinds of cheese and sixteen varieties of cold cuts. By those standards, this is a low-class party. But it's food. Peg, get the butter—"

"I forgot about you," Asey spoke to Peggy Boone. "Want Cummings to take you home?"

"She can't go home," Mrs. Carr said. "She's going to stay and take the bedroom next to mine. I shall feel safer. Did you know that my bedroom has sixteen sides? It has. It's fine for insomnia. Your head gets going round and round, and you sleep quite literally like a top, and in the morning, your neck is like a corkscrew—"

"Gran!" Tim said. "You're running on."

"I'm sure it's true, dear, every word of it. Oh, Emma—
Tim, don't feed her ham, please! You know what the vet
said!"

It was long after three o'clock before Asey got the household straightened out, with Mrs. Carr and Peggy Boone
upstairs, Tim on the front porch beside the snoring Hanson,
and Jack Lorne in the cellar.

"I'm takin' the back porch," Asey said, "an' it seems to be
that between us, we'd ought to discourage any further
prowlin' or firin' or bashin'."

He had just settled himself in a straight-backed chair—
he didn't dare sit in anything comfortable for fear of following Hanson's example—when Mrs. Carr tiptoed out.

"You've found out about Tim," she said, "and us—"

"Yes," Asey said, "you've both had a tough time."

"And you're really not going to arrest him—oh, bless you!"
she said. "He's all I've got, and I know I get simply maudlin
about him, but—"

"I know—"

"But I don't think you do, Asey. He didn't kill her, nor
did I. But you'll never know how much I yearned to—oh,
Emma's followed me! I thought she was asleep in her basket—grab her!"

Asey, with the cat purring in his arms, steered Mrs. Carr
up to her room.

"Now," he said gently, "you go to sleep!"

Gratitude was all very well in its way, and he liked the
Carr family and its cat, but right now he was too exhausted
to cope with them, singly or otherwise.

A more complete mess, he thought as he resumed his seat on the porch, a more peculiar mess, he had never seen. It must have been Roddy Strutt's fellows who were bashing around in the woods. It seemed very likely, in view of Carveth's alibi visit, and even though Tim insisted that the man he had caught sight of was not one of the Filipinos.

On sudden impulse he walked through the house and asked Tim if he knew Roddy Strutt.

"Saw him when he was offering rewards for the murderer," Tim said, "but he wasn't the one I saw in the woods, if that's what you mean."

Asey returned to the back porch.

When you sorted it all out, the essentials of the mess were simple enough.

Someone, between nine-thirty and ten-thirty the night before, had stabbed Marina with Pam's knife.

Almost anyone had access to that knife, holding up Mrs. Carr's note to Pam on the back door. Anyone could have twitched it out. There was very little to be done in the matter of tracing the twitcher.

And the time element didn't mean so much. You could ask questions till the cows came home on the Where-were-you-last-night-from-nine-thirty-to-ten-thirty order. But it was Asey's experience that people, when they set out to commit a murder, usually saw to it that their whereabouts at the time could be explained with great fullness and conviction.

Jack Lorne was lucky enough to be alibied. Tim Carr wasn't, but he believed Tim. Those two were out.

Then you came to the problem of motive.

Practically everyone, he thought, who ever had dealings of any length with Marina wanted to kill her. Just knowing her seemed to be motive enough in itself. All the people in Quanomet vented their wrath about the mural on her. The town was sorry for Jack Lorne, but they blamed and hated Marina.

And then of course there was the ambergris.

Someone might well have killed her for that; but why hadn't they taken it with them?

And before anything else happened, Asey decided as he got to his weary feet, he was going to find out where that ambergris was, and do something about it.

Pam Frye, without any warning, swung up over the porch railing before Asey reached the kitchen door.

"You, huh?" he said, briefly flicking his flashlight at her. "How did you get out?"

"Tree," Pam said. "A leaf from Marina's book. She always used that big maple for sneaking out in her younger days. Asey, I need your help. I've found Father."

"You've found—"

"Yes, all of you kept beating the woods, but no one seemed to think of Jack's house. He's over there."

"Is he—is he all right?"

"He's got a broken ankle, and his face is smashed up. I think his jaw must be broken. He can't talk. He's in the cellar. I gather he'd been thrown there. He couldn't get up, or yell—"

"Just a sec," Asey said, "till I call Tim. He can phone

Cummings an' join us there. An' I want to see Jack. He can stay here."

He found Tim sleeping as heartily as Hanson, on the front porch. It took a good shaking to awaken Lorne.

Asey snorted with disgust. "Guards!" he said. "Some guards! Mrs. Carr an' her cat'd of done better. Now, Pam, let's get over. An' on the way, will you tell me—before these feet of mine make me forget—where *is* that ambergris? Where is it, Pam?"

"Coal bin," she said. "Not a very bright idea, but the best I could think of at the time. Asey, who did this to Father? What's going on?"

Asey swallowed hard.

"I wish I knew," he said.

"But Father is strong!" Pam said. "You mightn't think so to look at him, but he is. Who could have done this?"

"I'm strong," Asey said. "So is Tim. So're those troopers. Tim an' I got knocked out, though. An' I don't think I ever got hit much harder in all my life."

Pam sighed.

"Anyway," she said, "the ambergris is all right. Old Strongarm hasn't got that. That's something to be thankful for."

Asey couldn't bring himself to the point of telling her that the ambergris was not in the coal bin. He tried to, but he couldn't.

Over in the cellar of the Lorne house they found Aaron Frye.

His face and jaw were bruised and swollen, and his face was contorted with pain.

"Don't try to talk," Asey said. "Just wait— Dr. Cummings will be over in a sec, an' then we'll get you up those stairs in a stretcher an' fix you up. I—"

"His ankle looks frightful," Pam said. "Father, don't try to talk! You mustn't—you *mustn't!* Asey, we've got to—"

"Get some paper," Asey said. "He's yearnin' to say somethin'—get some paper and a pencil."

Pam raced up to Jack Lorne's studio.

With difficulty, Aaron scrawled on the block of drawing paper which Pam had brought.

"I found," he wrote, "amb. in coal bin when I got coal for stove—"

"Where is it now?" Asey asked. "Man, *where* is it now?"

Aaron Frye gripped the pencil.

"In barn," he wrote.

13. THE bells of Quanomet's three churches were pealing out their summonses the next morning as Asey and Pam emerged from Aaron Frye's bedroom and slowly descended the stairs.

The instant the bells stopped, Aaron's clocks burst into their tirade—rather, Asey thought, like someone waiting breathlessly with his mouth wide open for the opportunity of climbing into a conversation.

Peggy Boone, who had been waiting with Mrs. Carr in the circular hallway, covered her ears with her hands.

"I hope Aaron's better," she had to yell to make herself heard above the din, "and—my God, I've got to get out! Those clocks!"

"Poor girl," Mrs. Carr said sympathetically as Peggy rushed away. "The clocks nearly drove her crazy last night. They bothered me at first, but I'm used to 'em. She says she woke up on the hour every hour, and just as she got to sleep, the half hour rolled around. She looks exhausted."

"The cumulative effect is shattering," Pam said. "I hate clocks myself. So does Peg. But Father enjoys—"

"How is he? What can I do, Pam? If *only* I'd know about him last night, and could have helped— I'll never forgive

Tim for letting me think all the to-do was over those troopers! Never! Can't I read him the Sunday papers, or something? Is he well enough?"

"You might take him up the funny parts," Pam told her. "He's partial to 'Mr. and Mrs.' and he likes 'Corkey' pretty well. And—"

"But should he laugh?" Mrs. Carr demanded. "Won't it be bad for him to laugh?"

"He won't laugh!" Pam told her with finality. "Don't you worry, he won't laugh! He not only can't laugh, but he doesn't want to. He wouldn't laugh if he were in the best of health, the pinkest of the pink. He wouldn't laugh at anything—look, you might see what you could do about Emma Goldman and Toots. Father wants the bird up there, and I rather think that Emma wants her, too. They're glaring at each other malevolently on the foot of his bed."

"I'll see to Emma," Mrs. Carr promised, "and him, too. The poor man!"

Pam followed Asey into the study and threw herself wearily on the couch.

"In all honesty," she said, "can you find any small vestige of silver lining, Asey?"

"Wa-el," Asey said, "Aaron's jaw isn't broken, an' that tooth can be replaced, an' his ankle'll be all right in a few days. An' when you consider what happened to Marina, it's nice to know nothin' worse happened to him."

"I didn't mean about Father— I know it's a holy wonder he's here. I'm thinking about the ambergris. Oh, Asey, that ambergris! I wasn't going to tell Father until he felt better, but the minute his eyes opened after Cummings' pills wore off, he raised himself up and peered out of the window and saw the ruins of the barn. And then of course I had to tell. I wish the place had been insured. Somehow it would have consoled me just to get fifty dollars out of the mess. I'd settle for ten, cash— Asey, why do you look so enigmatic?"

"Didn't know that I was," Asey returned. "I'm just sort of wrestlin' an' jugglin' things over in my head an' I ain't responsible for what it does to my facial expressions."

"What is there to wrestle about?" Pam asked. "The ambergris is gone. There you are. That's that. I suppose I should be a brave girl and stick out my chin and say I don't care, better luck next time, it's courage to face facts—aren't there lots of worthy sentiments for misfortune and defeat? And all I could think of when I found the ambergris—was it only the day before yesterday? It seems like fifty years. Anyway, all I could think of when I found it was, 'Gee!' Now I can prattle about counting chickens before the're hatched, and fools' paradises, and—oh, damn! Asey! Damn, damn, damn, damn, damn!"

"I dunno," Asey said. "I don't think it's as bad as all that."

"Oh, I still have my health!" Pam retorted savagely. "I know. Father will be well in a few days, and I still have my health. Good old health! Think of all the poor Spaniards and the poor Ethiopians and the unemployed and the distressed areas—sure. We still have our health, and we still have what passes for a roof tree. Untold thousands would consider us heavily endowed. Overburdened with fortune. Dear me, yes!"

Asey grinned at her. "Stop bein' so sorry for yourself," he said, "an' pause an' reflect. Why was the barn burned down?"

"For all I know," Pam said, "someone wanted to toast a marshmallow."

"The barn got burned," Asey said, "because someone wanted me—or anyone at Octagon House who might know about the ambergris—they wanted us to rush to it and save it from possible flames, thus pointin' it out, so that the some-one could get a line on its location."

"Weren't they fooled!" Pam said bitterly. "What's the old adage about the goose and the golden eggs? It'd make a nice headline. Goose burns goose."

"Yup," Asey said. "But would the goose have started the fire an' burned the barn without a nice careful investigation first? Don't be silly."

Pam sat upright on the couch.

"Asey!"

"Well, would they of? Would you? I wouldn't, myself, an' I give this feller credit. If he had brains enough to think of burnin' down the barn to find out where the ambergris was, he had brains enough to make sure he wasn't burnin' up the ambergris in the process."

"But if that's so—no, it won't work out, Asey. Father found it in the coal bin when he went down for coal for the kitchen stove Friday night. The cops were all over the place —whose car is that outside? The cops? And, by the way, if it is, what's Hanson's attitude toward me?"

"He's too upset about them two missin' troopers of his to

have attitudes," Asey said. "Don't worry about him. That's the doc's car, I'd know the sound of that coffee grinder anywhere. I'll bring him in."

Cummings strode into the study and dumped his inevitable little black bag down on the table.

"The recuperative powers of this village," he announced, "are amazing, simply amazing. The litter's cleaned up, the carnival atmosphere has departed, and Quanomet's going to church as sedately as if things had happened in two other towns entirely. If I hadn't seen that riot yesterday with my own eyes, I wouldn't believe it took place. How's Aaron, pretty unhappy?"

"His jaw looks better," Pam said, "and the swelling on his ankle has gone down. I think most of his present suffering is mental. He's seen the barn."

"He had to know sooner or later," Cummings said. "But I'd imagine it would add to his suffering. He thought he was doing such a big thing, to put the ambergris safely away in the barn for you—oh, Asey. We didn't need to use the sea serpent—"

"The what?" Pam demanded. "What sea serpent?"

"Asey's idea," Cummings explained, "for the sidetracking of the press. We didn't need it. One of the Barn Players punched another Barn Player, and Senator Hemmingwell's sons cracked up their roadster, and there's a pogy boat ashore on Black Gull Bar. Between 'em, the reporters are having a field day. I don't think they'll be bothering you for a while. But orders have been given to have the serpent spotted the minute the present attractions die down. You should see Nettie Hobbs, speaking of attractions. Piously going to church, dripping black crepe from every pore."

"All set, no doubt," Pam commented, "to pray for my soul. I know that crepe. It's a part of her Good Woman act, and she's worn it to every funeral since I can remember."

"Well, she had her picture taken with the minister on the steps," Cummings said, "and then dropping a dime into the foreign mission box. I hear it's the first dime she ever dropped on anything— Is Aaron really badly broken up over the ambergris?"

Pam nodded. "He's utterly downcast about it, and he knows I am, too. And even if I could pack my voice with conviction and tell him not to worry, it doesn't matter, he'd still be downcast. And every time he looks toward the window, his eyes get all watery—I wish he'd been willing to stay at the hospital when they had him there last night."

"So do I," Cummings said. "But once he found out, he'd have felt the same way, no matter where he was."

"Were the X-rays all right?" Asey asked.

"Yes, I drove over again just now. Nothing's broken, though I'm sure I don't know why not. I think it was that tooth that messed things up so, and added such a gory touch—have you found out yet what actually happened to him?"

"We've pieced most of it together," Asey said. "When he walked out back in the woods with Tim Carr and his grandmother, he thought he saw someone lurking in the bushes. He slipped off without sayin' anything, an' tried to investigate the matter on his own. He thought he saw some-one sneak into Jack Lorne's house—didn't have on his long distance glasses, so he couldn't be sure, but he followed anyway. He went in, an' someone was waitin' for him by the door, an' give him that belt on the jaw. He didn't see the person, it all happened too quick. In fallin', he went head over heels down the cellar steps that lead off the entry. That accounts for his ankle, an' the gen'ral abrasions an' contusions he's got."

"Did he hear anyone in the house when he came to?" Cummings asked.

"He didn't hear anythin' or anyone," Asey said, "until Pam called him. He didn't have a watch, an' the time element's all confused. He must have been out for a good while, though."

"How'd he get the ambergris into the barn?"

"Believe it or not," Pam said, "he just casually wheeled it there yesterday morning."

"He didn't!" Cummings said.

"He did," Asey assured him. "Same order of things as my paintin' an' puttyin' yesterday. With troopers to the right of him an' troopers to the left of him, he wheeled it out to the barn in an offhand manner—it was still covered up with the tarpaulin—an' dumped it into an old zinc lined feed bin. The cops didn't say a word. Aaron was bein' open an' aboveboard, an' they was sort of losin' interest in doggin' his footsteps by then anyways, an' Hanson was away at the time. That's how that happened."

"And Asey doesn't think that the ambergris was in the

barn when it burned," Pam said. "Of course, that particular bin *was* near the door, and I suppose it would be the first thing anyone would look into—but see here, Asey. If the person who fired the barn actually had looked around beforehand, he'd have found the ambergris right off the bat! And then there wouldn't have been any need of burning the barn at all, unless—"

"No," Asey said. "He looked around, an' couldn't find it so he burned the barn in order to get us to point it out."

"Listen, Asey," Pam said. "Take it slowly. Get the whole picture. I put the stuff in the coal bin. Father finds it, and has a fanciful notion that it'll be safer in the barn. So he takes it there. Someone wants to know where the ambergris is. You claim that they looked around the barn—well, if they did any hunting at all, they certainly found it in the bin. And if they didn't hunt for it, then it just got burned up."

"They looked for it," Asey repeated, "an' they didn't find it, so they set the barn on fire to see if—"

"If they didn't find the ambergris in the bin," Pam interrupted, "where in the name of God *was* it, Asey? You just aren't makin' sense!"

"Sure I am," Asey said. "Your father put it in the bin. But someone moved it from the bin after your father put it there, an' before the person who fired the barn began his huntin'. That's clear, ain't it?"

"Asey Mayo, do you mean that there's more than one person after this ambergris?"

"I'm sort of beginnin' to think," Asey admitted in a characteristic understatement, "that maybe perhaps there possibly might be."

"Two!" Cummings said. "Two? My God, I'm speechless. What do you mean, two?"

"Two people, or two sets," Asey said. "Maybe more. Probably more. I wouldn't know. That's what I been wrestlin' with in my mind. I think the feller that fired the barn ain't the one that biffed Tim Carr and Aaron an' me. The barn burner uses his head. The biffer seems to be a violent sort of lad. The barn burner—"

"You certainly can't call *him* any quiet shrinking violet!" Pam interrupted. "And after all, arson isn't one of the gentler crimes!"

"I know. But I think the person that burned the barn hunted through it first, and then waited around to see if his burnin' theory worked out. N'en I think he called it a day, an' left. N'en I think that someone else carried on the violent part, biffin' your father before the fire, an' Tim an' me after it. An'—"

"And what about those two troopers, O'Malley and what's-his-name?" Cummings asked. "What happened to them?"

Asey shrugged. "No one knows. Hanson's tryin' to solve that one right now. P'raps they landed up with the violent gent, p'raps they didn't. They're not within a mile of this place, anyway. It's been looked over again this morning."

"Listen," Pam said. "I've got another idea. Suppose someone found the ambergris in the bin, removed it, and then fired the barn to make us think the ambergris was burned up in it. What about that side, Asey?"

"I thought of it, but I don't like it," Asey told her. "If he'd have swiped it, he'd have beaten it and not paused for the fire to call attention to things. Firin' the barn then might of lost him too much time, and of course, how an' when could anyone of got the ambergris away, with that mob in the woods, later."

"Perhaps that's why Shorty and O'Malley are missing. Parhaps they saw the man take it away, and perhaps they went after it," Pam said. "Perhaps—"

"Wait an' let me get straightened out," Cummings said. "Aaron put it in the barn. Someone else—call him B, removes it. Someone else—call him C—hunts for it, an' can't find it, an' so he burns the barn. And now you think there's still another person, D, who's responsible for the violent biffings that went on. Well, that leaves you with three people, or one person three times, or—oh, it's beyond me! And suppose the ambergris was taken from the barn—where was it taken to?"

"Not very far," Asey said. "Not—"

"And who did it?" Pam demanded. "Who is this B, and who's C, and who's D? Who are they?"

"Who," Asey returned, "did your sister Marina tell about the ambergris before she was killed?"

"I don't think Marina told a soul," Pam insisted. "I truly don't. She was out to get that for herself. And supposing that she did tell someone. She and the person would have teamed up and whisked it off long before I got over there to the garage at ten-thirty. And—"

"Wait," Cummings said. "Wait another second. Suppose

for the sake of the argument that Marina told someone about the ambergris, and suppose the person decided to get it for himself. And with the ambergris as a motive, suppose they killed Marina, and—"

"You can stop supposing right there," Pam said. "If someone killed her for the ambergris, why in the world didn't they take it after they killed her, Friday night? Why did they leave it for me?"

"How do you know they did leave it for you?" Asey asked. "You left it in the garage because you didn't have any way of removin' it. It's perfectly possible that the person who killed Marina was in the same position. You've hunted ambergris all your life, but you never thought about transportation problems. Marina could have been killed for the ambergris, and the person could of been stumped on the transportation angle just the same way. Now, let's suppose—"

"No," Cummings said, "don't let's suppose. Let's stop supposing. I can suppose up to a certain point beautifully, but from there on into higher mathematics, my mind doesn't function. And my mind's had enough. Except just this— suppose that the person who killed Marina didn't know anything about the ambergris at all, and suppose they killed her because she put Lorne up to doing those caricatures in the mural. That's what everyone in the town of Quanomet firmly believes, anyway. Asey, do you think she was killed for the ambergris, or because of the caricatures?"

Asey shrugged.

"You must have some opinion," Cummings said.

"Seems to me," Asey remarked, "that fifty thousand dollars' worth of ambergris is a sounder motive than just bein' mad at bein' painted into a picture. You could fix the picture up some dark night with a can of paint or a bit of paint remover. In fact, you could chip off a little of the offendin' face each time you went for your mail. But with a person like Marina, I don't think you could put your finger on one special thing an' call that the motive. She seems to have been the sort who inspired people with motives for murder."

Pam sighed. "That's true enough," she said. "Oh, dear, this gets so complicated—Asey, if this person found the ambergris in the bin, what did they do with it, I'd like to know!"

"I don't think they got it away very far," Asey said, "an' I don't think they'll get far with it tryin' to sell it. Because I did some phonin' last night. I'd ought to have, before. There's only a limited number of people who'd buy that stuff. If anyone has managed to get it away, and if they manage to get it to Boston or New York, they're like to find themselves good an' thwarted."

"Asey," Pam said, "this is insane! Consider if they didn't get it away, it's still here, or hereabouts! But you've gone over the whole vicinity, hunting for those troopers—hundreds of people have—and if the ambergris had been around, you or someone would have found it. But you didn't. And if you ask me, the ambergris was burned up last night, and if it got re-stolen before the fire, then it's hundreds of miles away. Must be. As far as I'm concerned, the ambergris is gone—oh, dear, I've just remembered, I forgot weekend groceries! D'you suppose the Carrs' amiability will extend to scrambled eggs for their Sunday dinner?"

"You've got two chickens in the lower part of your ice box," Cummings said. "Didn't you find them? I brought 'em over last night, with the compliments of Jennie Mayo, when I came back to see Aaron. I stopped in for Asey's shoes, and she thrust the chickens at me. Said she didn't wonder a bit if no one'd thought a thing about ordering, and she'd had Syl kill her a couple extra broilers. Always has a thought for the inner man, Jennie has."

"She's a magnificent woman," Pam said, getting up from the couch. "I'll go see to the critters. Let me know what to do about Father after you've been up."

"Well," Cummings said after she had gone, "Well, what do you *make* of things, Asey?"

"I don't, if you want to know the truth," Asey said. "We've got one shrewd an' canny soul, an' we got a violent number. The shrewd one don't know where the ambergris is, an' the violent one—well, I don't know what he's after, unless it's just a series of punchin' bags. Maybe his got broke an' he's huntin' a substitute."

"But what about the third person, the one who took the ambergris?" Cummings asked. "That's what interests me the most. Who took it, providing they did take it before the barn was burned, and how? Why couldn't the burner have taken it before his burning?"

"Your guess," Asey said, "is every bit as good as mine about the whole business. I don't know, an' I don't know how we're goin' to find out. I just hope I get a crack at this biffer, though, before this is over with. I got a sock to repay. I want to meet up with that violent one."

Cummings laughed. "Speaking of violence, you should have seen Earl Jennings over at the hospital this morning. He was being mad with Chase, the traffic cop. There's a man that's sore at that mural—"

"Chase, you mean?"

"No, Jennings. He's a big husk, and Lorne put him in as Industry Mending the Leaking Pipes of Civilization. Jennings is taking it as a personal affront, and an insult to his business. Particularly as an insult to his business—"

"Are you talking about Jennings?" Pam passing through the hall stopped long enough to stick her head in the door. "I thought so. He was simply enraged—I think myself that's why he did such a rotten job on the plumbing over at the cottage, as a sort of revenge. You know, that bathroom overflows copiously and hideously every time it's flushed—"

"An' no one," Asey said sincerely, "could think of a much worse revenge than that. It occurs to me that Lorne ain't goin' to have an easy time gettin' his vine an' figtree repaired."

"Not to speak of his grocery bill," Pam said. "His credit is nil—look, I'm going to yank some carrots and things for dinner. I'll be in the garden if you want me."

"Jerry Chase kidded Jennings about the leaking pipes," Cummings went on with his story, "and they had to be forcibly separated. Asey, what about Roddy, the menaced? I think you ought to see him."

"Yup."

"Well, why don't you, then?" Cummings demanded.

"I'm waitin' to talk with that pilot of his, Brigham, first," Asey explained. "They told me last night at the hospital that I could see him this afternoon. After him, we go to Roddy. In one sense, I don't want to wait one bit. I've got a feelin' Roddy might try beatin' it, though I don't think he'll dare to. An' on the other hand, I don't think I'd ever get the truth from Roddy unless I got somethin' solid on him first. If I get Brigham's story, I think it'll be worth the wait."

"Brigham," Cummings said. "Oh, yes. I'd forgotten that pilot. So you're going to let Roddy slide?"

"I'm goin' let him sizzle," Asey said, "on the theory that the longer he sizzles, the better it'll be when we do get him. You go see Aaron, Doc. I want to run to the village an' find out how Hanson's comin' on with his trooper hunt."

"Where can those fellows be?"

"I wish I knew!" Asey said. "I wish I knew!"

As he went out on the back porch, Tim Carr drove up in his little coupé.

"I've been helping the bloodhounds, but there's no sign of O'Malley and Shorty," he reported. "Hanson is now little better than a psychopath."

"How's the reporters?" Asey asked. "Where are they?"

"Gorging themselves on shore dinners at that roadhouse near the junction. They ought to be logey and waterlogged for hours to come. I mean, you can eat just so many steamed clams and wash them down with just so much beer before —what's the matter with you?"

"Timothy, my son," Asey said, "crawl back into your little low backed car. I just had a brain wave."

"You've had something," Tim agreed. "This rosy glow— look, you don't think you know where the troopers went to, do you?"

"I don't know where they went to," Asey said, "but I bet you ten dollars I know where they are now—let me drive, d'you mind? I'm in sort of a hurry, like. Waterlogged. That's the answer. Waterlogged. Hang on, Timothy."

14. THE coupé backed down the driveway at a speed that made Timothy blink behind his glasses.

Before they reached the corner, he was gripping the door strap with both hands.

"The right rear tire," Tim remarked in what he hoped was a conversational tone, "is quite old and very eccentric."

"Is it?" Asey said. "Handles nice, for a little car, don't she? We had one at the Porter testin' grounds, an' it run circles around our sixteen. If only they'd stand up—"

"That's exactly my point about the rear tire," Tim interrupted quickly. "If only it'd stand up when you go over fifty-five. But no matter what tubes you put in, it always seems to blow—"

"Don't seem to be blowin' now," Asey said.

Tim watched the speedometer needle swing around the dial.

At least, he thought, if the tire stood up, he could truthfully report to his grandmother that those last figures were not the fakes they had always imagined.

"What about the troopers?" he asked, suddenly remembering that the speed of the car and the stamina of the rear tire were not, after all, the principal issues.

"Oh," Asey said, "you gimme the idea when you talked

about the reporters bein' waterlogged. It just occurs to me that we done a lot of land searchin', but we sort of ignored the water. Pretty silly of me not to think of it before. There's so much water around."

"So we're going to sea hunt, are we?" Timothy sounded very dubious.

Asey nodded. Without apparently decreasing speed, he turned off on a sand road.

Tim averted his eyes from the ruts. It was simpler not to look ahead, in this particular case, he thought.

"Er—you intend to use the coupé, do you?" he inquired. "To sea hunt, I mean?"

Asey grinned.

"Oh, I know," Tim said hastily. "I know you're a director of Porter's automobile factory, and you're a pioneer automobilist—somehow I'd rather have liked to see you in goggles and a dust coat, scorching along at eleven and a half— yes, Asey, I'm sure you know cars, and you seem to have a way with fate. But this is a city car. It can't swim. Not the teeniest bit. Sissy, I know, but there you are. How do you organize a sea hunt, by the way? What does one do? Stand on the beach and squint to leeward, or something?"

"You know the woods back of Octagon House," Asey began.

"Know them?" Tim said. "My dear man, Robinson Crusoe never knew his damn island the way I know those woods. I can truthfully say that, after last night, I know every nook and cranny, every last bit of poison ivy. I know it by heart. What about the woods?"

"Eventually," Asey said, "the woods come to the river. We didn't hunt that far. A salt river, it is, an' it runs off Wherry Pond. That's a salt pond. An' Wherry River—"

"I know, I know," Tim said excitedly, "even the Wherriest river runs somewhere safe to sea."

Asey sighed. "These folks in the surd business," he said, turning off the road and proceeding over an old cranberry bog, "make the bummest puns."

Timothy stuck his head out the window and watched the wheels squashing gummily through the bog.

"Sorry," he said. "The pond goes to sea. Go on."

"O'Malley an' Shorty," Asey said, "met up with the biffer. Our pal. Our shrewdy was too shrewd to be seen, an' I don't know about the other feller. I'm sure it was the biffer, an' I sort of feel the cops must of got biffed. Cops ain't never so int'rested in a chase as they are in a chase where they got biffed, person'ly. A good smack seems to sort of inspire 'em. I think O'Malley an' Shorty chased our pal the biffer through the woods, an' along to the river, an' then I think they took to a boat."

"All in the same boat?" Tim asked.

"You must," Asey said, "have been an awful irritatin' boy, when young."

"It's my mathematical mind," Tim said. "I have to put every item in its place. The biffer took to a boat in the river, and the cops took to another, and followed. That right?"

"I think so," Asey said.

"You make things so simple and brief," Timothy said. "Like a news reel—no, I'm not being funny, I mean it.

Didn't you ever notice the simplicity and clarity of the news reels? Say some dictator says something that shakes the world and sets international crises going left and right. This Means War. Civilization on Precipice. And just as you think about laying in a lot of canned milk and pemmican, then you go to the movies and see the news reel of the dictator making his statement, and it's just a man waving his arms around at a lot of heads. Simplicity itself—am I boring you?"

"Had much radio experience?" Asey asked drily.

"No, it's just my fluent way," Tim said. "It's—why do we stop?"

"This is where we get out an' walk. Take off your shoes."

Timothy looked at the sedge grass, half submerged in the water, and the shells, and the stones with barnacles that were scattered along the shore.

"I suppose," Tim said, "you really do expect me to take off my shoes, too, and tramp bravely in my bare feet? No. I had some brief experience with that grass and those barnacles, the day we came. My shoes stay on."

"Then head 'em the right way," Asey said. "We're goin' round the point."

"Where are we?" Tim asked. "Roughly, I mean. And where are we bound?"

"We're on the river," Asey said. "Ocean's to the right, beyond the pond an' the channel. The old landin's around the bend. It ain't been used since they built that nice new alphabet wharf up in the cove, but I know Pam keeps her boats here. She said so. Prob'ly others do, too. If you wanted to fly straight like a crow, you'd be able to shoot back to

Octagon House over the tree tops, an' the swamp. We circled around an' got here a lot quicker than we could of on foot. We're also nearer where we want to get to than if we started from the town wharf."

"I see," Tim said. "It was that swamp where I got in before I knew it, during our man hunt. Now, what about the troopers?"

"I think," Asey said, "they went down the river, followin' the biffer, an' then I think they got across the small end of the pond, an' into the channel current. An' then I think the tide intervened, an' took 'em out to sea. At least, as far as Dune Island."

"And what do we do?"

"Oh, we take a boat an' investigate," Asey said casually. "Here—here are Pam's, see 'em? The *Frying Pam I, II,* and *III*. One sailboat an' two sharpies. Chained an' locked to the moorin's, but—uh-huh. There's two other boats that belong here, see? They b'long here an' here."

"The old trapper," Timothy said in a rapid monotone, "pointed dramatically to the oak leaves at the foot of the tree. Flying Cloud and his redskins, he hissed, have been here within the hour. Let's see. One was a tall boat with a black mustache, and the other was a short fat dory with a front tooth missing, and a slight limp—"

"For that," Asey said, smashing the lock on the *Frying Pam III*, "you row. Get in, whippersnapper—bust that chain on the oars—oh, give it to me! Yup, you get in an' row."

"The muscles on Carr's neck and shoulders," Timothy continued imperturbably, "stood out like those of some

ancient Greek athlete about to meet his lion. Row, my boy,
Minnie whispered in his ear—all set, Asey? Row, my boy,
for dear old Quanomet. Quanomet, oh, Quanomet. Labor
Day, oh Labor Day!"

"Yes," Asey said, "you *can* row, can't you? I seem to remember, now I think of it, I seem to r'call seein' you row
before. It was the year Bill Porter got through college.
Single scull champ, wasn't you? Gold cup—"

"Oh," Tim said, suddenly very flustered and pink, "I used
to row when I was a kid—is it your idea that the biffer is
a native?"

Asey nodded. "Port your helm," he said. "Yup, I begun
to think he was a native; last night. I also think he's the
outcome of the mural trouble, an' I know he knows his way
around this region. An' he had sense enough to know that
he was licked on land, but there ain't many troopers you
can't fox in a boat. He cut across here in the dark, see? An'
he made for shore, an' home an' mother. An' he let the tide
take care of the troopers. Now, lean back an' let the current
take you from here. In about ten minutes we'll hit Dune
Island."

Timothy was silent while they drifted along.

"Asey," he said at last, "what's the story that Hanson and
the rest of us don't know? It's something that concerns
Pam, I'm sure, but Gran and I can't dope it out."

"Ord'narily," Asey said, "I'd tell you. In this particular
case, I think it's nicer that you don't know."

"For 'nicer,' " Tim said, "read 'safer.' I see. Is Pam in any
danger?"

"Anyone else might be," Asey said. "But Pam seems to have a happy kind of faculty of treatin' trials an' tribulations an' dangers like they was very ord'nary things. I don't think Pam can be bluffed. An' at this stage of the game, I think the person that's dangerous to her prob'ly realizes that Pam knows no more than he does. Turn around, Tim, an' see what you think of Dune Island."

"I think," Timothy said, looking over his shoulder, "I think you've got something here, Mayo. D'you suppose that blue shirt on a stick is a signal?"

"Must be," Asey said. "The usual run of bathers that come out to Dune Island don't as a rule bother with things like shirts. Put her ashore."

They found the two troopers sleeping at the foot of the center dune.

"A lovely sight," Tim said appreciatively, as he and Asey stared at the two recumbent figures. "A lovely sight. Sleep it is a gentle thing—is this what they call squandering the taxpayer's money? And where's their boat? Shall I wake them, or will you?"

"Seems a pity," Asey said, and let out a bellow that brought both men to their feet.

"Sorry," he continued politely, "to disturb you, but where in God's name have you been, an' how long do you intend to disrupt a murder case by your seaside snoozes?"

"Say," the shorter one said, "you're Asey Mayo, aren't you? Well, say—we got him!"

"You," Asey said, "got who?"

"The guy that was prowling around Octagon House and

the woods, and around there. The guy that knocked the two of us out. Boy, what a night! We're lucky to be here. But we got him, all right!"

"Where?" Asey asked briefly.

"We got a picture. We—"

"A picture!"

"Two pictures, while it was still light. O'Malley had his camera. He's a camera fan, see? And we'll get that guy—"

"Where's the camera?" Asey demanded.

"Where'd you put it, Shorty?" O'Malley asked.

"Me? You've got it."

"I gave it to you. You've got it!"

"Say, I guess—"

"Wait up," Asey said. "Who had it last?"

"When we got out of the boat," O'Malley said, "I had it, and I give it to Shorty to hold while I tried to pull the boat up, but the undertow was too much—"

By degrees, Asey and Tim got a very vivid picture of how their old boat, knee deep with water, refused to be beached.

"So we let the old tub go, but we kept the camera dry," O'Malley said. "Then we walked over here. It was daybreak then, and we went to sleep. Were we ever dead!"

"And you've been sleepin' ever since?"

"No," Shorty said, "we got up and tried to hail a fishing boat to take us off. The engine waked us about nine. But they just waved at us and went on. Thought we was just being friendly, I guess."

"Ever think of swimming back?" Asey inquired.

After a poignant silence, Shorty admitted that whereas they could swim, they were not experts.

"I see," Asey said. "Now, where's the camera?"

It was Timothy who finally found it, buried deep in the soft dry sand of the dune.

"But your pictures have pfft," he said. "See? The film's exposed. One of you gave the camera a good swift kick with a nice heavy boot. It's coming apart—it's dripping parts! Here—"

O'Malley grabbed it from him, and then turned to his companion.

"You—"

"No," Shorty said firmly. "I didn't. That's where you was sleeping last. And you been kicking around a lot. You talked loud enough to wake me up. You done it yourself. Well, there's that bright idea of yours all—"

"Let's just sum it up," Asey said before O'Malley could let himself go, "by admittin' that the pictures was a nice idea that didn't work. Now, let's sort. What happened to you?"

It began, Shorty announced, with him.

He thought he saw someone near the barn. Before setting out to investigate, he called O'Malley, and the two of them went back to the woods together.

"We headed for the barn," Shorty said, "and then I seen something move in the woods to the right, so we went there, and someone made a noise, and I pushed through a bush near that sort of summer house, and wham! That was that. Somebody biffed me."

"And he squeaked," O'Malley said, "and I come running up to where he was—and bam! I got mine. I never was hit so hard in all my life! The guy must of had a billy. When I come to, my head was splitting. And then I found Shorty, and then we heard someone running—boy, was that a chase!"

"You got knocked out before the fire," Asey said. "I see. Then the feller went to Lorne's and accounted for Aaron. Now, what about the fire?"

"What fire?" Shorty said. "After we pulled ourselves together, we seen someone running, beyond Jack Lorne's, and we chased him clear to Chatham—"

"What? Who was it? How?"

"We grabbed a car parked there by the corner. Belonged to some tourist, I guess. Had Indiana plates. And we chased this guy that was running—he got into a sedan with Jersey plates. He turned out to be a tourist, too. Nice guy. He was taking pictures of the scene of the crime for his collection," O'Malley said. "Boy, did he ever have an outfit!"

He went into rapturous detail regarding the camera and the outfit of the tourist from New Jersey until Asey brought him back to the point.

"Then what?"

"We started back in this Indiana car," Shorty said, "and we left it where we found it, and then we seen this other guy running out of the woods—that place was lousy with people! So, we run after him—"

"By then," Tim said, "the biffer having laid me and you out, I suppose. I'm—"

"Let 'em go on," Asey said, "an' see if it turns out like I think."

They had chased the man to the river, where he grabbed a boat, and they followed him in their leaky tub. Pam's boats had caught their eye, but the chains had thwarted them in their haste.

"Then," Shorty said, "all of a sudden we got into a current, and the oars we found in the boat wasn't much, and one got lost overboard, and while we tried to get that—"

"You lost the other," Asey said.

"How'd you know?"

Asey sighed. "People always do. I don't know why. If they lose one oar, they always lose the other. Seems like a law, almost. Well, I guess it happened about the way I thought. He got you, Tim, an' then he got these two, and then he got Aaron. Shorty an' O'Malley got sidetracked to Chatham, an' durin' that time the biffer got me. Then, as he left the woods, he run into the troopers comin' back, an' they all had their little boat trip—when'd you take your pictures?"

"When we came back from Chatham, as he was on the edge of the woods. You see, I had my camera ready to take a shot—"

"What did he look like?"

"He was big."

"An' strong," Asey said. "Yes, I know all that. But what did he look like? How tall was he? What size?"

Fifteen minutes of questioning brought forth only the information that the man was big and dark.

"You followed him all that time, an' that's all you can tell?" Asey demanded.

"It was dark in the woods," Shorty said. "And he was big and dark—"

"Big and dark," Tim said, "and doubtless about to start on a long, long journey, overseas. Why, I saw more of him in a tenth of a second than you two did in all your chase! I know that he had a horrid scowl—what did you say, Asey?"

"I said, the next time these fellers went off on chases," Asey wagged a forefinger toward the troopers, "they better remember all the things they got taught in school, about how to place an' describe people. Just leave your cameras for your lighter moments—"

"Happy Days on Dune Island," Tim suggested. "Our Night on the Beach. Boating Time on Old Cape Cod."

"Just so," Asey said. "Big, an' dark, an' mad! A woman would of been able to do better than that. Least she could say what he wore."

"Dungarees and a dark shirt," Shorty said. "I know that much. No hat. And listen—this'll make you kid us more than ever, but this fellow that knocked us out, I don't think he was the first person I saw, before I called O'Malley. The first one wasn't so big."

"Perhaps," Tim said, "he got bigger the more you saw of him. There are people like that. There's a master at school who grows more darkly looming every year."

"It was different people," Shorty insisted.

"It should have been," Asey told him. "The first one you

seen was the one that fired the barn. Then the biffer got you, and you chased him again after your interlude with the tourist that took the nice pictures. Now, there's a few more little d'tails I want to get settled before we go back. Did either of you see Aaron Frye wheelin' somethin' into the barn, yesterday?"

The troopers stared at him.

"Why, he carried some coal out," Shorty said, after a pause. "I asked if I could help, the first trip. I helped him dump it. He told me he could manage the rest."

"I see," Asey said.

Apparently Aaron had first carried a load of coal out in the barrow, and thus lessened any suspicions anyone might have had. Once having implanted the idea that he was carrying out coal, he could carry out the ambergris. "I see," Asey said again. "Now, did you spot anyone carryin' anythin' *out* of the barn?"

Shorty shook his head. "I don't think so. There was such a mob around, of our fellows, and Hanson yelling something every minute. But I don't think anyone carried anything out. You see anyone, O'Malley?"

"I don't know, it seems to me—who helped Frye later? Someone was doing some carting. That woman, the one with the cat."

"Oh, not Gran," Tim said. "She's not much of a one for carting. She's better at telling people where *to* cart, if you know what I mean."

"No, she was the one," O'Malley said. "I know, because the cat was sitting in the wheelbarrow, big as life—I used to have an aunt that had a cat that liked to be carried around."

"Did you," Timothy asked instantly, "ever sell gas? Like at a gas station?"

"Yeah, once. Why? What's that got to do with it?"

"It's the Carr survey," Tim explained, "of gas station attendants who have aunts with cats."

Asey chuckled, recalling his grandmother's comment about the excitement that Emma usually caused when filling station men saw her peering at them from the car.

"Well," O'Malley said, "she had the barrow."

"I do remember, now," Tim said. "It was after they put up the barbed wire, after the crowd had trampled around the flower beds. Gran couldn't stand it, so she went and tried to repair the damage. I was flitting around," he explained to Asey, "with Hanson and over at Lorne's, trying to catch sight of those papers. Gran did do some repair work, on the zinnias, and probably she used the barrow then. What does it all signify?"

"Was that after Aaron did his carting, or before?" Asey wanted to know.

"I don't think I remember," O'Malley said. "After, I guess. I tell you, yesterday was mixed up. It was around the time that Strutt boy was there, too, I think. I," he frowned, "I think he wheeled something, too."

"It sounds," Timothy said, "as though everyone in the vicinity of Octagon House had spent the day playing with barrows, like training for a gymkhana, or a field day, or something. How many things did happen!"

"An' don't they still," Asey said. "Come on, you two. Timothy, the rowing expert, will ferry you back to civ'lization in our boat."

It was a perilous trip in the overloaded boat, and the current and Timothy had a vigorous battle all the way.

Asey tied up the boat, shepherded the troopers to the car, and proceeded to drive the coupé back to Octagon House at the same rapid and nonchalant pace which had distressed Timothy earlier in the day.

"Now," he said, as he got out of the car, "I want you to drive these fellers to Hanson, an' then bring your car back, please, an' leave it here for me. I want to see Jack Lorne, an' then I got an errand to do."

Jack was sitting in his studio before a littered table. He was dressed in crumpled green pajamas, and he hadn't yet bothered to shave off his accumulation of beard.

"Have you discovered," Asey asked him without any preamble, "whether or not anything got taken or disturbed here last evening by the person who socked Aaron?"

"Haven't looked," Jack told him with a yawn. "I wouldn't know, anyway. Marina kept everything in order, in the portfolios. I never bother with stuff like that. Say, come see what I've got planned for Senator Hemmingwell's dining room wall. Marina didn't like my first sketch, but I did another last night while I was in the cellar—"

"Guarding Octagon House," Asey said.

"Yes," the irony didn't even touch Jack Lorne, "yes, and it's a honey. Isn't it swell?"

He held out a sketch, and Asey looked at it.

"Mmmm," Asey said. "What's that in the corner, the fatted calf, or the Senator himself?"

Lorne snatched the drawing from his hand.

"Jesus!" he said. "You hicks make me feel like vomiting! What do you know, anyway? What do you know about art? That's the trouble with this country, people like you—"

"I know," Asey said sadly. "Just an old Philistine. An old, old Philistine—"

"Philistine!" Lorne said, and started off on a shrill tirade that lasted for ten minutes.

Asey listened appreciatively as he wandered around the studio, peeking into portfolios and lifting the lids from the countless cardboard boxes that served as files.

Probably the boy thought that this display was temperament. Dr. Cummings would diagnose it as what happened when a man didn't get enough sleep and plenty of good, hearty food—including a good, hot breakfast. Personally, Asey thought the outburst was temper. Just pettish, ornery bad temper, with a little childish tantrum thrown in.

Asey crossed over to the fireplace and looked into it reflectively, and then he resumed his steady pacing around the room.

There was not, he thought, much sense in telling Jack Lorne.

Lorne would find out soon enough that whoever had biffed Aaron Frye had also removed the contents of all those portfolios and boxes.

Removed them, and neatly burned them up.

15. "THAT'S art!" Jack wound up, thumping the table with his fist. "That's art!"

"Just so," Asey said soothingly. "Just so. I don't doubt it a bit. Tell me, did your wife help you a lot?"

"Well, she helped," Lorne admitted grudgingly. "Not a lot, but she used to have some ideas sometimes that weren't too bad."

Asey remembered that at one point in their conversation the day before, Lorne had wondered how he would go on without Marina's aid.

"Helped with your plans, did she, huh?" Asey suggested.

"Well, yes. Yes, she did. She used to make rough sketches. Funny thing, her style was always so different," Lorne said. "She might have done something if only she hadn't been so variable."

"She never went in seriously for drawing or painting did she?" Asey asked.

Jack laughed. "My God, no. Of course, she did have a certain amount of talent, but she never did anything about it. Never wanted anyone to know about it, either. Always hid away by herself when she worked. She never would let me watch her, even."

"I see," Asey said. "She helped in your early plans with

rough sketches. Always dif'rent. I s'pose all her ideas was original with her?"

"But of course they were!" Lorne said. "Of course!"

"I see," Asey said, sitting on the arm of a chair.

So Jack Lorne didn't know that Marina had swiped Tim Carr's sketches. And if she had swiped Tim's, she might well have swiped others. She probably had, if her suggestions were always in such "different styles." But Lorne didn't know. Apparently he had never even entertained any suspicions.

Asey watched him out of the corner of his eye.

Any fool should have been able to guess what Marina had been up to. Of course, Jack Lorne had always trusted Marina implicitly; if he had thought, up till the time he read her diaries, that her friendship with Roddy, for example, was purely platonic, why should he have suspected that her ideas were not always original? A brighter person would have caught on, but Lorne had admitted that he was not bright. And he certainly was not!

"Where are your sketches of the mural?" Asey asked suddenly. "Got 'em here? I'd like to see 'em."

Lorne waved a hand toward the corner.

"In the portfolios there," he said. "But why not go see the mural itself?"

"Today is Sunday," Asey pointed out. "The post office is closed. Whose idea was it to stick in the natives?"

"Marina's," Jack said. "It was fun. She knew 'em all so well. Some of them are sore, but that doesn't matter. They'll get over it. Some day they'll be proud, as I told the reporters.

I'm not sure that my own plans weren't on the whole better
—Marina has, of course, influenced me," he explained, "but
after working on these Hemmingwell things, I wonder if
my own ideas aren't a lot stronger."

"I suppose you'll miss her help?"

"Oh, I don't know," Jack said. "I don't know. I've thought
it all over, and I think I'd pretty much outgrown her help,
anyway. Such as it was. Oh, Aaron didn't die, or anything,
did he?" he added.

"It's nice of you to be so interested in him," Asey said.

"Oh, I like Aaron. He's been quite decent to me. Of
course, he doesn't know any more about art than you do,
but he's usually willing to fork over cigarette money."

Asey was beginning to understand how Jack Lorne
could infuriate the native population of Quanomet without
even trying.

"All right, is he?" Lorne added. "Aaron, I mean."

"Mercifully, he will be in time. Before I go, can you think
of any one person in town who was more annoyed about
the mural than any other person?"

"I haven't given them a thought. Look, I wish you'd ask
Porter if he doesn't want me to do some work for him. He's
got a splendid living room—"

"Bill Porter," Asey said, "ain't much of a hand for a mural.
Will you get your mind off art long enough to tell me who
was maddest about the picture in the post office?"

Jack laughed. "Oh, Pam was hopping. So was Aaron. And
Peg, and Roddy and Nettie—and the minister, and the
plumber, and—say, I wish he'd get over here and fix that

tank! They were all of them sore. Everyone in it. Some of them even threatened to beat me up!"

"It's just this lack of appreciation for true art," Asey said blandly. "You shouldn't worry."

"Oh, I don't," Jack said airily. "I didn't. I just told them they were too stupid to understand. They think a butcher's calendar is beautiful—even Peggy. She thinks she's so damn hot, but she's not much better than you are. You're not going to Boston tomorrow, are you?"

"I doubt it," Asey said.

"Too bad. I've got to find someone to go to Anderson's and get some stuff for me. If you happen to run up, just let me know. I might go along with you."

"That would be just too peachy," Asey said. "When this murder case involvin' your wife gets settled, maybe I'll take the little drive for you—you haven't forgotten that your wife was murdered, have you? Or has it slipped your mind, in the press of art?"

"No," Lorne said crossly, "no, I haven't—damn it, that's the last sheet I've got of that—look, couldn't you get to Boston tomorrow? It's really quite important that I—"

Asey left the studio before he broke down and laid violent hands on Jack Lorne.

Timothy Carr met him as he strode back to the Fryes'.

"You look mad enough to chew nails," he observed.

"Tall, greying and mad," Asey said. "Yesterday I was sort of sorry for Jack Lorne. Today he's rubbed me so much the wrong way, I could turn him over on my knees and spank him."

Tim nodded. "Yes, I know. We got into a discussion last night. On mature reflection, he's not at all sure that this incident won't help his Art tremendously. Artists should suffer. His Heart Has Been Broken, Of Course," Tim made a vague gesture so much like Lorne's that Asey laughed, "and his Soul is Shattered. His trust in mankind has suffered a severe setback. A blow. But Lorne thinks this may be just what he's been needing. It will make the difference between just An Artist, and A Great Artist. I wonder what Marina would say if she heard him discuss her as an incident in his art."

"He needs," Asey said, "a paddlin'."

"He always has. The car's ready for you, if you want it. I even put in gas. And—er—you won't forget that rear tire, will you?"

Asey grinned. "You changed it, didn't you?"

"How did you know? Oh, I'm smudged, I suppose. Yes, Sherlock, I shifted on the spare, for my own peace of mind. Pam thought it was very funny of me."

"I bet. How's Aaron?"

"I just asked him that," Tim said. "He took up his block of paper and wrote on it—he and Gran have been holding the most bizarre conversation, by the way. She talks, and he writes. They'd been discussing the habits of the night blooming cereus, whatever that is. Anyway, I asked Aaron how he was, and he wrote with exquisite poignancy on his block, 'Did you ever try to suck hot chicken soup through cellophane straws with a bashed jaw?' In other words, he's suffering, but his spirits are better."

"Good," Asey said. "I'm glad of that. If anyone wants me, I'll be over in the Pochet hospital—"

"What's the matter with you, or are you just visiting a sick friend?"

"Visitin'," Asey said. "So long."

Timothy shook his head as he watched the little car scud down the drive.

"Don't look so unhappy," Pam said, coming up behind him. "Asey leads a charmed life, and he probably will bring the car back safely. He always does. Did he tell you all about the great ambergris loss?"

"What are ambergris?" Tim asked. "And tell me, do you like steak and kidney pie?"

"No. Didn't he tell—"

"How about caraway seeds?"

"They make me sick," Pam said. "But what's that got to do with—"

"I never," Tim said, "could think of marrying a woman with a passion for caraway seeds, and steak and kidney pie. Singly or together. It's one of those vital points I like to get settled at the start."

"Oh, you do, do you?" Pam said.

She hated herself for turning red, and not being able to frame a proper retort, with just the proper amount of gay flippancy in it. The sort of easy and successful retort Marina could always make, to Pam's deep envy.

"Oh, you do, do you?" she said again, mentally cursing her inability to say anything else. Compared with what Marina would have said, she sounded like a coy housemaid.

Looked like one, too, Pam thought, suddenly conscious of her kitchen apron. And her hands. Dishpan hands of the first water.

"Pam!" Peg Boone called from the kitchen. "Pam, where are you?"

"I've got to go," Pam said hastily. "She wants—"

"I do," Tim was replying to her housemaidy question. "I do, do I. What nice hands you have, I'm so sick of painted claws. Look, what's this about ambergris? Is it like verdigris, or a variation of ampersand? I'm sure I ought to know, it's probably something I should be teaching the youth of America, but my mind's a blank. What are ambergris? And—oh."

Peg Boone walked over to them and eyed them both rather curiously. Pam felt herself turning red again.

"Something's definitely wrong with the Spanish cream, Pam," she said. "You'd better come and cast spells on it. I can't tell if it's too Spanish, or too creamy, but it's not as it should be."

"I'll be right in," Pam said.

Timothy watched Peg stride back to the house.

"What," he said, "does she do around here?"

"What do you mean, what does she do?"

Tim shrugged. "Every time I manage to haul you off for a nice long chat, up she pops. She reminds me of Aaron's clocks. Just as you forget them, they strike."

"She's nice," Pam said. "She's a friend of ours."

"I suppose she is," Tim said with a sigh. "Well, I'll just have to take the bitter with the sweet, I suppose. You won't like lots of our friends, either. We know a tea taster who wears a coral bracelet around one ankle, and sandals with a thong next his big toe. I'll tell you what—we'll introduce him to Peg. Maybe they'll marry. Isn't it wonderful how problems disappear, if you just put your mind to work? And," he added before Pam had time to speak, "where did Aaron get those clocks, anyway? With shaving soap?"

"Auctions," Pam said. "He got the first ones by accident, and then it got into his blood. He slinks around attics, hunting them. Why don't you like—"

"Gran's that way about elephants," Tim said. "She buys—look, do you really have to see about that Spanish cream? I thought it was one of those things you couldn't alter afterwards. I know you can always beat scurvy custards with an egg beater, but Spanish cream has a certain finality about it, hasn't it? I mean, either you hit it on the head, or you don't."

"I know," Pam said. "You're what they call an extravert. You—"

"The things I draw on phone pads," Tim said, "are as normal and healthy as can be. Well, let's cope with the Spanish cream, but don't let's ask the Boone to stay on indefinitely—"

Pam stopped short. "Why ever not, Tim? What's the matter? Why don't you like her?"

"If I were a woman," Tim dropped his bantering tone, "I'd say it was just my intuition. I don't know why I don't like her. Do you warm up to her much, yourself?"

Pam hesitated.

"There!" Tim said. "See?"

"But I do like her," Pam said. "She's been awfully decent to me. I'm not violently enthusiastic about her. I've known her too long and too well, and besides, I don't often get violently enthusiastic about people. What is it you have against her?"

"Nothing," Tim took her arm. "Come on—"

"You have," Pam said. "I want to know before we go in."

"Well, you asked for it," Tim told her. "It's just that she's so damn hearty, but her eyes don't smile. I feel the same way about your brother-in-law. God knows no one would ever accuse him of being hearty, but his eyes are such fishy things. Like cod on ice in a fish market window. And then every time I get myself up to the pitch of telling you about Marina, she appears on the scene. That's worse than her eyes."

"What about Marina?" Pam said.

"I was married to her," Timothy said. "Before Lorne. I— no, please don't say anything now. Not till you've considered how much we have in common. It isn't Marina that matters. It's what she did—now, tell me about ambergris. Is it either portable or valuable?"

"Both," Pam said in a small voice.

"Really," Tim said. "Tell me all about it—"

He remembered, as they went into the kitchen, all the questions Asey had put to the troopers about the barrow and the cartings that had gone on the day before. And he remembered that Peggy Boone had helped his grandmother repair the flower beds.

"All about it," he continued, still avoiding Pam's eye. "Ambergris One, an Introductory Course."

While Timothy was being told about ambergris, Asey parked his car in front of the Pochet hospital, and went in to see Brigham.

"I was just going to call you," the nurse on duty said. "Susan asked me. Brigham's doing nicely. He really shouldn't have any callers, though, so you won't get him excited, or stay too long, will you? Dr. Carter sent you his regards, by the way, and says he's coming down for a sail before his vacation's over. I'll show you the room."

"How's Earl Jennings?" Asey asked as they walked down the corridor. "I hear he's been actin' up."

"So you heard about that episode, did you?" the nurse sighed. "Thank goodness, he's going tomorrow. We're just about worn out with him. And he was so nice at the beginning, too! It's the mural that's fretted him and got him so obstreperous. Here you are. Mr. Brigham, this is Asey Mayo."

"I hope," Asey said sincerely, "that all them bandages ain't any indication of how you feel. An' what's this contraption for, the busted leg?"

Brigham smiled behind his bandages. "Thanks to you and your doctor," he said, "I feel pretty good. And I'm glad to see you. I've got a lot I want to tell you, and a lot more I want to be told about—"

"Fifteen minutes," the nurse said warningly, and went out.

"Then," Asey said, "we got to work fast. First off, who are you really? They didn't get any response from the wires they sent off about you, to the folks whose names they found in your wallet. That made me wonder if Brigham wasn't a kind of pen name."

"It is. I'm Charles Horn."

Asey whistled. "Horn!"

"The lad himself. And because we haven't a lot of time, I'll tell you that I was sacked from the L. and N. for drinking. So I'm Brigham for a while, till I can work up to being Horn again. And if I hadn't been a little bit tight the other night, Strutt wouldn't have got me into that plane. And if I wasn't one of the best pilots I know, I wouldn't be here now, nor would Strutt. All I ask is that I can get out of here and give that mug a good licking before somebody kills him for me."

"To save a lot of fiddlin' around, an' to save you from talkin'," Asey said, "let me guess, an' you tell me where I'm off my trolley in the story. Go back to Friday. You spent the day takin' Strutt an' his pals on joy rides—"

"God, yes. And how! If I'd known more about that outfit, you couldn't have got me there in irons. What a bunch! What a nestful of lice!"

"Uh-huh. Friday evenin', you an' Roddy trailed a pal of his to Providence, an' then come back here—when?"

"Around eight or so. And I sat down for the first time all day, and had a couple of drinks. I needed 'em, too," he said. "I needed 'em!"

"And Strutt went out, and then he came back," Asey said, "say around eleven, and told you that you had to go up again. That right?"

"Yes. I said he was crazy, and I was tired, and the plane needed some overhauling, and his lighting system was lousy. But nothing would do, after arguing and arguing, but we had to go up. Finally we got things organized—and the way I felt about him and his crowd then, I didn't care if I did smash up his plane, and him, and myself, too. And he went up, and he dared me to land in the town square. For the hell of it, I did. I wouldn't have cracked up if he hadn't got panicky and froze onto me—say, what was going on? What was his idea? It must mean something, or you wouldn't be interested."

Asey explained. "Alibi," he finished up. "No one's asked him just what he was doin' an' where he was, an' why, durin' the time Marina Lorne was killed—you know about that?"

"The nurses don't talk about anything else," Brigham said, "except her, and that plumber that wants to fight anyone his weight for two cents. They've been having a time with him. He roared for a solid hour this morning. Say, was Strutt mixed up in the murder?"

"That," Asey said, "is what I yearn to know. Can't you cast any light?"

"All I know is, he went off after we got back from trailing that guy, all high and happy. When he came back around eleven, he was frightened about something. He hasn't,"

Brigham added, "much guts. So that crash was planned. Didn't care if he killed me."

"He took the chance of killing himself," Asey reminded him.

"Aw, he probably didn't even think of that side. You know, he can't think of more than one thing at once. One thing is hard. Ask me—I tried to teach him to fly! He's not a bad mechanic, but he hasn't any brains—"

The nurse came in without waiting for her knock to be answered.

"The time—" Asey began.

"I know, it's not up, but would you help? It's Earl Jennings. We had some trouble with a pipe in the lavatory, and he thinks someone broke it on purpose, to bring up that mural and the leaking pipes, and make him mad. We can't do a thing with him, and Dr. Ben's too far—"

"I'll come," Asey said. "Try an' remember more, will you, Brigham, while I go calm this feller—"

Two agitated nurses sighed with relief as Asey marched into Jennings' room.

For a moment Asey stared at the man. His face was purple with rage, and the veins on his forehead stood out sharply.

"For a man with a bad heart," Asey said, "you certainly manage to work yourself up, don't you?"

"These women, they busted that pipe!" Jennings shouted. "They heard about the mural, and they busted that pipe to make me mad! Everyone's laughing at me because of that picture—let me up, I'm going to get Jack Lorne and wring his neck! He can't make a fool out of me—"

"No," Asey observed, "he can't. You're doin' that all by yourself. Let him get up, Susan. Let him go kill Jack Lorne. He'll die of apoplexy before he gets there, but when a man wants to make a fool of himself that bad, it's wiser to let him die happy. Go on, get up, go kill Lorne an' get it over with. Don't wait to change your clothes—go right along as you are in your silly night shirt. Go on!"

"Who do you think you are?" Jennings yelled. "Who—"

Asey came over to the bed and looked down at him.

"I'm a man," he said, "with a lot of patience. But you're tryin' it hard. Now, let's get this straight. You're sore because of the mural. So're lots of others, but they don't make matters worse by callin' attention to themselves an' their soreness—"

"They weren't made out as bad as me!"

"Oh, yes, they were. Now, sorehead, you do one of three things. You go over and wring Jack Lorne's neck, or turn over and go to sleep. Or—"

"Or what, Mister Smart Aleck?"

"Or," Asey said, "I shall plant my fist smack on your jaw," he demonstrated, "like that, only harder. Much, much harder. Then I'll pour you into a straitjacket. Now, what are you going to do?"

"No man can hit me and—"

"Which?" Asey said. "Think quick."

"Listen, I'll wring your neck, too! No one can—"

"Susan," Asey said, "go get a straitjacket, please. Nurse,

you move a little to the right. No, the other way—oh, get some iodine an' stuff. When I lose my patience, I lose it. Jennings, look up an' watch for the birdie—"

"Say—"

"Better keep your mouth closed," Asey suggested. "You wouldn't want to lose any teeth or get your tongue bit off. And—"

"All right!" Jennings said sullenly. "All right, all right—"

"Sensible gent," Asey said. "Apologize to the nurses, for bein' a nuisance—"

Jennings muttered an apology.

"There," Asey said. "Susan, we won't need the strait-jacket, but keep one handy. Remember it, Jennings!"

What a splendid biffer, he thought as he went back to Brigham's room, Jennings would have made. Jennings was born to be the biffer of the night before. But Jennings had been in the hospital. If only he hadn't, lots of items could be cleared up.

Asey sighed, and opened the door.

"Thought of anything else?" he asked Brigham.

"Well, no. I was trying to remember if Marina and Strutt had a fight Friday, but they cooed around like a couple of doves. All over each other. Strutt wouldn't have thought up so many funny things, if it hadn't been for her. She thought of everything, she did. Wanted to skim over the waves like a bird, she said, and fly over dunes like a seagull. Thank God she got tired, around four, after she'd had me skimming like a seagull over the beach, and went home. I guess she'd had enough flying. She lost interest in it all of a sudden."

Asey looked at him.

"Brigham," he said, "you've given me an idea I hadn't brains enough to figger out all by myself. Look, you flew over Quanomet Point, didn't you? Where Roddy has his camp?"

"That place? Any number of times."

"An' Marina was with you on some of those trips, includin' one around four in the aft'noon?"

"Marina, and a lot of others. They came and went in droves, all day, having nice rides in the pretty plane."

"Yup. An' right after that four o'clock trip, Marina decided to leave. After one of the beach skimmin' episodes. That is very enlightenin', that is."

"Maybe. I don't see it," Brigham said.

"Very enlightenin'," Asey repeated.

And it was. It brought up a point which had not entered his head before.

Marina, and heaven knew how many others, had seen the ambergris first, from the plane.

16. "AFTER we got back from Providence," Brigham said, "Roddy went tooting off. I'm sure he went to see Marina. He didn't tell me so, then or later. But that's what I think. There was a note waiting for him when we got back. I'm sure it was from her."

"Are you really sure," Asey said, "or do you just hope that Roddy'll get nice an' involved in the murder?"

"He already is, isn't he?" Brigham returned. "What else would he have staged that crash act for? Doesn't that land him smack into the murder without anything else? You don't go rushing around, cracking up planes and taking chances like that for nothing. Not unless it's something pretty big."

Asey agreed.

"I wonder, now," he said. "Aaron Frye saw Roddy's roadster out back by the lane. Prob'ly Marina did write a note an' leave it for him. From what Pam said, Pam don't bear Roddy any love, an' he prob'ly has got things against her—you don't mind if I meander out loud, do you? Pam—"

"That's Marina's sister, isn't it?" Brigham interrupted. "They talked about her. Not very—well—"

"Very pretty?"

"That's about the size of it. I gathered," Brigham said, "that Pam was a very decent sort."

"How did Roddy seem to feel about her?"

"They laughed at him, I remember," Brigham said. "Kidded him that he couldn't make any headway with her at all. He didn't like it."

"I sort of think," Asey said, "that I begin to get the gist of things here. You know what ambergris is?"

Brigham was vague on the subject, so Asey briefly enlightened him.

"I think," he said, "that while you was skimmin' over the beach around by the point, I think that Marina spotted that hunk of ambergris an' got to wonderin' about it. She's heard Pam talk about it all her life, an' she might have been curious enough to go see. That's why she left off flyin' in such a hurry—"

"And why she asked Roddy for his beach wagon," Brigham said excitedly. "I remember now—she said she wanted to get something she left out at the camp. Someone else wanted the beach wagon, but Marina insisted she had to go to the camp. I'd forgot all about it, but now I remember. Sure, that must have been it. She spotted it from the plane, and then she went after it in the beach wagon with the sand tires. Pretty smart—she didn't let on to anyone."

"And when she got out to the point," Asey said, "she finds Pam there. That's a nice point—Marina prob'ly seen it first, but Pam got there first. Marina didn't say she'd seen it. She knew that Pam wouldn't believe her anyway, an' she knew she was in the driver's seat, lit'rally. What she got stuck on was Pam's spirit. That licked her. Yup, I think I begin to see how it went. Then later, Marina left the ambergris while she raced after some artist—"

"He was the one we trailed," Brigham said. "A greasy little pip. Something-stein. Look, Roddy and I didn't see Marina again after she left in the beach wagon. We were busy with the plane. That's why she left the note. We left before she got a chance to speak to Roddy."

"I think so," Asey said. "Now, let's see. What did she write him? Would she have told him about the ambergris?"

"Oh, his grandmother just left him a pile," Brigham said. "He told me all about it. He wouldn't have cared a hoot about the money end of it—"

"Maybe not," Asey said, "but Roddy has his savin' side. He wouldn't pay for the ambulance that brought you over here—now," he added hastily, forestalling the thanks he knew Brigham was going to offer, "now, what was Marina's plans? How's for highjackin'—sure, that's it!"

"I don't get it," Brigham said.

"She tells Roddy here's a nice place for him to play a trick on Pam, an' get even with her for bein' so standoffish," Asey said. "'Dear Roddy, we're going to have a holdup. You're goin' to hold up Pam an' me. See?' That's why he parked his car in the lane. He was goin' to the garage an' stage a fake holdup, an' make off with the car an' the ambergris. Marina was clever enough to stall him off with some explanation—somehow I don't think ambergris would mean anythin' to Roddy even if she did tell him. She'd get her stuff back, all right, an' she could also pull an act to make Pam think it was a genuine holdup. Pam couldn't have any kick comin' then. The stuff was stolen. There you are."

"But Roddy killed Marina," Brigham said. "Didn't he?"

"I wonder," Asey said. "Or did he come there an' find her dead—prob'ly before Pam did? Must have been before. An' he paid Nettie hush money. That means that he seen someone, or someone seen him, either goin' to or comin' from the garage. He thinks it was Nettie Hobbs, but it wasn't. Yes, this begins to fit itself some."

"But there's the time part of it," Brigham said. "I think in terms of schedules. He left after eight o'clock, Roddy did. Marina wasn't killed till long later. If Roddy waited in the lane, or outside the garage all that time, then he must have seen everything, including the murder."

"Suppose that Roddy went somewhere else first," Asey said. "Suppose the note told him where Marina was going to be. They'd have had to lay a few plans. Marina—I think Hanson or Cummings said that she was at a party. Anyway, Roddy didn't have to come there to the garage at once. But I'll soon pry the truth out of him. Brigham, you've been a great help."

"I'd feel more of a help," Brigham returned, "if I could think of something to prove that Roddy killed her. I'm sore at that guy, crashing me—" he broke off as the nurse returned.

Asey got up. "So long," he said, "an' thanks. I'll be seein' you. Have someone phone me if you get any new ideas."

"I will," Brigham said, "and look. About the bills—"

"Goodbye," Asey said.

As he left the hospital, a large black sedan drew up. Elliott, the Congressman from the district, hurried up to him.

"You're one of the hardest men to find, Asey," he said, "that I ever knew. I've been on your trail since yesterday afternoon. Jennie Mayo's fed me two pies, piece by piece."

Asey grinned. "How's things," he inquired, "from the rockbound coasts of Maine to the sunny shores of California?"

"It's fate, I suppose," Elliott said, "that the only time in my life I used that sentence was also the only time you ever heard me speak. Listen, this Quanomet business is getting me hot under the collar. The citizenry is aroused."

"Tch, tch," Asey said. "A lobby, huh?"

"I'm pretty aroused myself," Elliott said. "This post office and this damn mural—do you know how they happened?"

Asey waved toward the coupé. "Come sit down," he said, "and tell me. I been wonderin' just what part you played in that. An' I don't mind sayin', I think you'd ought to be ashamed of yourself, too."

"I am. Look, you know me, and you know I've done as much for this neck of the woods as anyone could do for a solid Republican block crying in the wilderness. And you know how little ice I cut, too."

"I'd almost forgotten," Asey said, "about modest an' honest politicians. It's wonderful."

"I'm a member," Elliott said, "of one of the most feeble and impotent committees existing. Bear that in mind. And

bear in mind that last winter I was sick. I had three opera-
tions, interspersed with pneumonia. And frankly, I didn't
care much about the government at that time. I paid no attention to it. I didn't know that for various and sundry
reasons that committee had suddenly become vastly important, and my vote infinitely so. People came to see me in the
hospital and said, I had a swell new post office, where did
I want it?"

"And you said, Quanomet?" Asey demanded.

"Why, I didn't believe them!" Elliott said. "I thought
they were kidding. I said, kidding back with a straight face,
the one town on the Cape that needed a luxurious post office was Quanomet. They said okay, and asked me how I
spelled it. Then I got sick again, and then in a comparatively
healthy interlude, the boys came back and said, did I want a
mural? I said, sure. I still thought they were kidding."

"An' then you got sick again?"

"Exactly," Elliott said. "And—well, think what I thought
when I saw the pictures of the place! Think!"

"What I really want to know," Asey said, "is, how did
you vote?"

Elliott threw back his head and howled with laughter.

"By special dispensation or something," he said, "I voted
from the hospital, before I saw the pictures. I defeated their
bill! Young Nickerson, my secretary, he suggested names
for the contracts—really, we did this part of the world a lot
of good!—though God knows, I'd have had the building in
my own home town, if I'd only known! Well, Nick's got a
sense of humor, and—"

Elliott's laughter was so infectious that Asey found himself giggling.

"An' what?"

"The biggest contract," Elliott said happily, "they let out to the chairman of our committee. They asked if he was a good party man, and Nick said there was none better! Well, there's the story of that. If ever a Congressman got fooled, I'm it. But look here, Asey, here's what's bothering me. I've been flooded with petitions—before the murder and after—and it's plain that Quanomet is mad. Now, I can settle the thing in time, and get the mural condemned for being unsanitary, or something—God knows it is! But I've got to let the shouting die down first. I can't touch the thing now. And the town—"

"Is impatient?"

"More than that," Elliott said. "Here. Take a look at some of my anonymous mail." He pulled a sheaf of letters from his pocket. "Here are samples. I don't like 'em."

Asey read through half a dozen.

"Pam and the rest all spoke the truth," he said finally. "Quanomet's mad clear through. In a way, you can't blame 'em."

"I don't," Elliott said. "I'm in that mural, too! Didn't you know? I'm in a sort of geyser of hot air, spouting. I'm not sure what the symbolism is, but the meaning is unmistakable. But these threats of what they're going to do if the mural isn't yanked off at once—I don't like them. These people will get into trouble. If only we could persuade 'em to wait—"

"They won't," Asey said.

"I know, they'll do something crazy and get everyone into hot water—sometimes I feel like a clucky hen in this job! Did you know that some of the cranberry pickers wanted to start a march on Washington last year?"

"How'd you solve 'em?" Asey asked.

"Oh, I sent 'em passes to New York on the boat," Elliott said. "Free return, good for three days only. They never got to Washington. But see here, Asey, this murder business. How much of it is due to the mural?"

Asey shook his head.

"I don't honestly know," he said. "I don't know. If the person who killed Marina killed her because she inspired her husband to stick in those caricatures, then it was a native who knew enough about her an' him to know that she'd be responsible. People do odd things when they're mad, particularly when a lot of 'em are all mad about the same thing. But I wonder now," he paused and thought about Earl Jennings, "if anyone could get mad enough by himself to murder —well, I don't know."

"They can get mad enough!" Elliott said. "What should I do? I'm honestly afraid of more bloodshed, though I suppose that riot last night sort of cooled 'em down and took the edge off."

"P'raps," Asey said. "But someone sneaked into Jack Lorne's house yesterday evenin', an' destroyed all of his stuff they could lay their hands on, includin' the sketches of the mural. I think that your best bet is to call in the Quanomet selectmen and tell 'em that you'll get the mural removed, just as soon as you can, what with all the red tape and all."

"Meantime—"

"Meantime," Asey said, "you might find that the paints ain't proper paints. Non-union. Or that the dampness is eatin' into Myles Standish's hair. Get the D.A.R. to pass a resolution—"

"Oh, they have. They have!"

"Well, fix things so that the mural has to have a cloth hung over it. But get the selectmen to handle the town crowd. You put on a good Maine-to-California bit about do they want the fair name of Quanomet bandied about in the gutter an' hiccupped over bars? Impress on 'em that they got to keep cool an' calm, so's publicity'll die down. An' when that goes, you'll take steps about removin' the mural. An' I sort of have a feelin', Elliott, that with your defeatin' vote, you may have a kind of a hard time."

"I wish," Elliott said, "that I dared to subsidize a couple of good bums, and have them take the chance of getting caught, just to cover that mural with tar for me. A good defacing would solve everything. Well, you're probably in a hurry—you seemed to be when you came out. I won't detain you. I'll go and chat with the selectmen and see what can be done. Oh—there is one thing more. Carveth Strutt has been after me, yelping about that stinker Roddy. Says he's being menaced—would you know about it?"

"Somehow," Asey said, "Roddy is mixed up in this Marina business. He's bein' menaced because it's such a nice alibi, like. If you're bein' menaced, then no one'll believe for an instant that *you* had anything to do with the murder."

Elliott whistled.

"Does Roddy—oh, I don't like this! His other uncle in Washington—oh, Asey, I don't like this! I'm having enough trouble as it is, with the hot-headed citizens of Quanomet. I definitely don't want the Strutts to ride into battle. God knows they're bums, but their money's handy. Not just for politics, either. I expect to work a park out of Carveth, over home, and I'm banking on Dighton to get the Milk Fund out of the red. Is Roddy really involved?"

"I think so."

"There is no justice," Elliott said. "None at all. If Roddy's involved, can't you wait till I get the park and the fund money? I tell you what, I'll run over and see Carveth and tell him I'm taking steps, and not to worry about Roddy— let me get my innings first. Can't you wait?"

Asey grinned at Elliott's anguished tones.

"I've already waited too long on Roddy," he said. "I had to hear the story of that pilot of his before I could do anythin'. But you don't need to worry now. Just stick all the blame on me, an' in the end, who knows but what you'll get a field house an' gym thrown in with the park? Elliott, I've just been thinkin'. I never did get a good look at the mural. I bust out laughin' so on my first view, I had to leave before I got to the parts with the local boys in 'em. You got pull enough to get me into the post office on Sunday?"

Elliott smiled, and brushed imaginary dust from the lapels of his coat.

"Have I got pull? Asey, I have a gold plated key, all my

own. On a chain, with a tag that's very tastefully inscribed, calling me all sorts of endearing names. I'm positive they had that inscription marked before I cast that vote. If you want to get into the post office, we'll go to my house and get the key, and have a private view of Quanomet's Public Eyesore Number One."

"I'll trail you over," Asey said.

Elliott's house was a long rambling place with so many ells and additions that even an architect would have had trouble picking out the original Cape Cod half house that had been the basis of it all.

"My daughter's around somewhere," Elliott said. "I think she knows where the key is—Jean! Hey, Jean—where are you? Jeanie, you know Asey Mayo, don't you? My daughter, Mrs. Dunn. Jean, where's that gold post office key, d'you know?"

"That thing?" Jean wrinkled up her forehead. "Teddy had it last. He was playing St. Peter and the Gates of Heaven with it—didn't you give it to him?"

"Well, yes, I guess I did," Elliott said. "But I need it now. Find it for me, will you?"

"Father darling, when Ted plays with things, it's not the easiest thing in the world to find them on two seconds' notice. You shouldn't have given him the key, if you really wanted it intact. But I'll see what I can do. Maybe Della'll know where it is—"

Della, a slightly distraught looking nursemaid, admitted that she hadn't seen the key since the baby played with it Saturday morning.

"Maybe he swallowed it," Jean said, as though that were the simplest solution.

"Oh, no!" Della protested. "I'm sure he didn't. He hasn't swallowed anything for a week. Perhaps the little Westover girl would know. She was playing with Teddy—"

"Come, come," Elliott said, "come, come! We've got to find that key! Really, Jean, I know I let Ted play with it, but I see no reason why the whole damn countryside has to use it as a plaything!"

"Darling, climb down," Jean said. "Remember what you did with that gold trowel you laid the library cornerstone with! If I hadn't just happened to find it out in the iris bed, the day before the delegation came for the lawn party—"

"Don't beat about the bush!" Elliott grinned in spite of himself. "Don't get off the subject—I want that key! You go find it. Go shake the children by their heels. Stand 'em on their heads. Peer into their tonsils, if you want. But go find that key!"

"Sometimes," Jean said, "I wish you were a simple tax-payer. Della, come on. We'll see if the Westover infant has any thoughts on the matter. What did they put in that mole hole, d'you know—"

"No respect, that's what," Elliott said. "They treat me like an elderly neighbor, the whole lot of 'em, and—"

"An' you love it," Asey said.

"Well, yes, I suppose I do. Come on in, and we'll wait for 'em to find the key. It'll turn up. You can't lose things like that. I've got a collection of teeth I've been trying to mislay for years. I've often wondered, why do people think that Congressmen want teeth? I've got whale teeth and dog teeth and Indian teeth. All kinds. But would they stand me a new upper set? Not on your tintype."

At the end of an hour, Jean wandered out to the barn game room.

"Oh, here you are," she said. "Look, it's awfully funny. The Westover child let the little Lake boy have the key, and he says with bland finality that someone took it away from him."

"Come now, Jean!"

"That's true, Father. I won't go into the details of the game they were playing—"

"Who? The Lake boy or the someone, or what?"

"Don't be so impatient, dear. They were playing jail delivery, and the Westover child was the gangster in prison, and the little Lake boy was the mob that was going to get him out—"

"The youth of this country," Elliott began.

"Ssh, dear. It took hours to make sense out of things, and I want to tell you while I still have things straight. The Lake boy went off to consult with Ted—Ted was the G-man who was foiling things, if that makes you any happier—and he left the key with his gun, over by the lilac hedge. And someone took it. The Lake boy saw him running off, and yelled, but the person beat it, and the Lake boy thinks he went off in a car. Lake didn't dare tell anyone at the time. He just said he'd mislaid it, and Ted was so busy with his new croquet set that Ray brought him yesterday afternoon that he forgot all about the key. So there you are."

"It's a mad house, Asey," Elliott said sadly. "Other people's houses run all right. Why can't mine? Here's a simple little key. Can it be found? No. It's St. Peter's key to heaven, it's the prime factor in a jail delivery. Babies teethe on it. And finally, strangers swoop out of my lilac hedge and snatch it from the mouths of babes and sucklings, or words to that effect. I ask you! What's the matter, Asey? What did you say?"

"I said," Asey told him, "that I wish you'd call up the post master, an' tell him to meet us over in Quanomet as soon as he can make it."

"What—oh, Jonah, you mean? All right, I'll call him. But you don't really think anyone took the key, do you? What ever for? Who'd have known what key it was?"

Elliott sounded a little anxious.

"Wasn't there a public presentation of keys, on the day the office opened?" Asey asked. "Seems to me Jennie murmured somethin' about it."

"Well, yes. It was a sort of incident in the opening. You know, sandwiched in after the soprano sang, and before the band had its fling. They gave out half a dozen keys, to the Governor and a Senator or two, and me—"

"An' plenty of people," Asey said, "saw you bein' presented with it."

"Yes, yes, I suppose they did. But how would anyone know that the little Lake child was going to play jail delivery with it over by the lilac hedge the next afternoon?" Elliott demanded.

"They wouldn't," Asey said. "But if someone was waitin'

around, waitin' for the chance to swipe your key, I don't see but what they could swipe it from the Lake child with the greatest of ease. An' after all, it'd be easier to swipe from you than from the Gov'nor or the rest—when did they take the key, in the aft'noon?"

"The early afternoon some time," Jean said. "Of course the children don't know the exact time. It's rather a wonder they remember the day. Look, I've been thinking—is it right to go strewing post office keys around in any such loose fashion? I thought the interior of post offices were like altars, sort of sacred and all."

"They're just keys to the front part," Elliott said. "They don't let you in to anything but the front part where the mural is. But look here, why wouldn't someone steal the keys from Jonah? From the post master? Why should they pick on me?"

"I wouldn't know," Asey said tactfully. But it occurred to him that it would be far simpler to swipe a key from this easy going household than from the Quanomet post master, who took himself and his job with great seriousness. "I wouldn't know, unless it'd be that Jonah'd miss the keys sooner than you would, on account of usin' 'em more."

"Oh, this is all a lot of nonsense!" Elliott said. "We're making mountains out of mole hills. I don't believe anyone took the key. Probably we can find it if we get out rakes and scrape around. I don't think anyone wanted to steal the key. I don't believe that they did steal it. It's just a child's story. I—what are you waiting for, Asey?"

He continued before Asey had a chance to protest that he was not delaying the expedition.

"What *are* you waiting for? Let's get over and get into the place and see if anything has happened. But of course it hasn't," he added, as though he wanted to convince himself on the point. "Of course not. The child made up that story. No one took the key—my God, *my* key! *My* key! If someone has got into that place with my key—hurry up, Asey! But it's nonsense. They wouldn't dare break into the post office—"

"They wouldn't be breakin' in," Asey pointed out, with a grin. "They've got a key."

"Well," Elliott said, "I'm sure there's some law that covers it. Defacing government property—oh, my God! This means still more headlines for Quanomet! Asey, can't we keep it out of the papers, don't you think?"

Half an hour later, in the front part of the Quanomet post office, Asey answered Elliott's anxious question.

"Nope," he said, "I don't think you *can* keep this out of the headlines. This is too complete."

17.

"THE miscreants!" Elliott said. "The miscreants! This is an outrage. This is—why, there's not a single inch of that mural or of the side panels left! Not an inch that isn't covered by that red paint! It's— Jonah, don't you think that this is an outrage?"

Jonah, the dour post master, looked carefully at Elliott and then at the red smeared walls before replying.

"Well," he said cautiously, "yes, an' no. Yes, an' no, if you ask me. It's a crime to hurt gov'ment prop'ty. They hadn't ought to of touched gov'ment prop'ty. But I tell you, it seems awful good to be able to look around the inside of this place without blinkin' an' wincin'. Red lead, ain't it, Asey?"

Asey nodded. Red lead seemed to be playing quite a part in this case.

"Put on," Jonah continued, thrusting out an exploratory forefinger, "put on around the middle of last night, I'd say. Kind of a neat job. They didn't spill much paint, an' they didn't do any tramplin' around in what they did spill, either. No, sir, this wasn't no mad job. This was delib'rate."

"I am profoundly shocked," Elliott said. "Profoundly. I'm at a loss."

His voice was entirely serious, and so was his face, and both were impressing Jonah enormously. But it seemed to Asey that underneath his seriousness, Elliott was considerably pleased, and considerably relieved. It had solved his problems, anyway.

"I s'pose the picture's ruined?" Jonah asked hopefully. "Seems so."

Elliott looked inquiringly at Asey.

"I guess so," Asey said. "I don't think you'll be able to do much reclaimin', an' it'll cost a pretty penny—"

"Asey," Elliott said, "you have hit the nail squarely on the head. Any sort of reclamation would necessarily be a most expensive job, a burden on the taxpayers, already burdened— and so on. And after all, you can't expect the government to pour more money down the sewer—I mean, down the pipe."

"You don't figger there's any chance that they might, do you?" Jonah asked.

"I would not like to go on record," Elliott cleared his throat, "but I think I may safely say that—I'm speaking for myself, you understand. This is not an official statement. It should not be construed as such."

Jonah nodded. "I see."

"But I think I may safely say," Elliott went on, "that the chances of this work of—er—art, this work of art being reclaimed or renovated are—well, they're remote, Jonah. They're remote."

He spoke with such relish that for a moment Asey wondered if Elliott might possibly have lost his key on purpose.

"That's fine," Jonah said. "I don't mind tellin' you, I sort of wanted to paint the thing out, myself."

"Off record," Elliott said heartily, "me too, Jonah. Well, well, what's to be done? Do we call in the police, or notify

Washington, or what? The post office is out of my line entirely—"

"Say!" Jonah, who had walked over to the front door, beckoned to them. "Say, looky here, in the inside of the lock here. Looky! This gold key. This—"

"In the door?" Elliott asked unhappily.

"Right smack in the front door—it's unlocked, an' this key's sittin' here on the inside. Say—well, what do you know about that, this's your key, Elliott!"

"Impossible," Elliott said with prompt firmness. "Absolutely impossible. I don't believe it!"

"Well, it's got your name on the tag," Jonah said, "L. P. Elliott. That's you, ain't it? Say," his dour face lighted up. "Say, you oughtn't of forgotten this, El. You'd ought to of been more careful—"

"Jonah, you don't think that I—"

Jonah winked elaborately.

"But, man alive, I had nothing to do with this! If that is my key, it was stolen. As a matter of fact, I knew it had been stolen. A man came out of my hedge—" Elliott stopped in confusion.

"It is," Asey said sympathetically, "kind of a silly story, ain't it?"

"But it's true! Jonah, you've got to believe me—"

"I won't say a word," Jonah said. "Not a word. Here, take it. Now, you know what I think? We came in the back way, an' no one seen us. But if they did, we can fix that up. I think we better get along—"

"What?" Elliott said. "Justice—"

"I know," Jonah returned. "But there still might be time for someone to salvage that damn painting, for all we know, but if we wait till tomorrow—when it's good an' dry—"

"We can't do any such thing!"

"Come on, El," Jonah said. "Let's let it get found tomorrow, just to be on the safe side. I'll find it myself, when I come over early tomorrow for the up mail. If anything's said about your bein' here this evenin', why, you just come out back with me to get a valuable doc'ment that got mailed by mistake. We didn't even come in this part of the buildin' at all. Come on, now. We don't want to be in here too long— hurry!"

He shepherded them out, despite Elliott's voluble protests.

"Now see here," Elliott said as they paused on the rear steps, "see here, Jonah, I did *not* have a thing to do with this! I give you my word of honor that I did not—"

"Go long," Jonah said. "I was your sergeant in France, remember. I know how straight a face you can lie with!"

"But I didn't!"

"Listen," Jonah inserted a finger in Elliott's vest buttonhole. "Listen, this'll get Quanomet and the towns around all so roused up in your favor—why, a hundred per cent! Just you consider the next election all over an' done with, El. We thought you was shilly-shallyin', not wantin' to get involved with Strutt's uncle in Washington that chose Lorne's picture. They been callin' you a fake, an' a straddler. But this'll save you, this will. An' don't think anyone'll ever let on, or give you away. You won't get involved a mite. I'll see to that, if Asey don't. We'll—what's the word, Asey?"

"Alibi, I think," Asey said in a strained voice.

"That's it! If it should happen that you get mixed up, why, we'll alibi you. We'll lay it all to the tourists in that mess last night," Jonah patted Elliott on the shoulder. "Now, you get along, El. I'm goin' to be late for evenin' services, as 'tis. An' don't you give this a thought—we all wanted to do it ourselves, an' we'll show you how we appreciate your doin' it for us. We know now that you got our wishes right to heart!"

Elliott gazed blankly after Jonah as he got into his car and went off.

"My God!" he said weakly. "My God!"

Asey, having restrained himself as long as any human being could, laughed until the tears streamed down his cheeks in rivulets.

After a moment, Elliott joined him.

"Whee," Asey said at last, "I'm exhausted. I'm all wore out. Oh, golly, I think this is the funniest thing that's happened to you yet about this edifice, Elliott. I think—say, you didn't do it, did you?"

"What?" Elliott yelled at the top of his voice. "What? Listen to me!"

After ten minutes, Asey stopped him.

"I didn't really think so," he said. "Honest, I didn't. Look, I got to get over to see Roddy Strutt. I'm ashamed of myself for not havin' been there hours ago. Are you comin' with me?"

"Well," Elliott said with resignation, "I've apparently got the native vote, solid. Maybe I don't need the Strutts. Who

knows? Sure, I'll come along, but if you find me being po-
litical, please don't take it seriously. If Roddy Strutt actually is involved in this, I'll do everything in my power to
help you get the worm. Only, it's just possible that I may
have to pretend otherwise."

"I understand," Asey said. "Let's get on."

He stopped by the telephone exchange to talk with Hanson, who hailed him wildly from the sidewalk.

"Just a sec," Asey called to Elliott in the car, "there's
things that got to be done here."

"Asey," Hanson said, "why can't you stay in one place
so—"

"I ain't got time," Asey said, drawing Hanson aside, "to
go into a lot of details, but this's what I want you to do. I
want you to check up on Elliott—"

"Him? The Congressman?"

"Lower your voice, an' don't point," Asey said. "I mean
him, the Congressman. Check up on him from when the
post office closed last night till this afternoon. Got that? And
for the love of heaven, don't let him or anyone else suspect
that you're doin' any checkin', either. Then you phone your
boss in Boston, an' tell him that I want him to get from the
newspapers the best pictures he can find of the mural. The
best pictures, of all of it, and I want 'em enlarged so's I can
see all the details. Got that?"

"But you can go over to the post office, an' see it for yourself," Hanson said.

Asey drew a long breath. "Will you do what I tell you,
or—listen, do I usually ask you to chase wild geese? Well,

then! You get after them two items, pronto, an' I'll see you later. Keep someone over at Octagon House—"

"I have," Hanson said. "And Jack Lorne's all worked up, because his drawings—"

"Were burned up," Asey said. "I know. Now, I'm goin' over to chat with Roddy Strutt. I—that car that's comin' has a press card on the windshield—so long!"

On the way to the Strutt house, Elliott asked for the inside story of the murder, and Asey briefly summed it up for him.

"And you think Marina saw the ambergris first?" Elliott said, "from the plane— Asey, have you thought that if she saw it, any number of others, whoever they were, might have seen it from the plane, too?"

Asey admitted that he had given that angle a considerable amount of attention.

"As for Roddy himself," Elliott said, "I personally can't say a kind word for him. I don't think he's got the brains of an ox. I don't think it's ever been my misfortune to meet a weaker and stupider young man. But somehow I feel that if Roddy had killed that woman, you'd have been extremely positive about him by now. Roddy wouldn't have had the wit to use Pam Frye's knife, for example. If Roddy ever got up courage enough to kill anyone, he'd lay such a stupidly elaborate plan that you've have seen through it in a second. Like this business of crashing the plane for an alibi. It was expensive, and it was spectacular, and it was elaborate, but it wasn't very bright. He might have killed himself. And he doesn't seem to have taken Brigham into consideration at all."

"That's true," Asey said. "He wasn't even bright enough to be solicitous about Brigham an' his hurts. If he'd had an ounce of sense, Roddy'd have taken him to the hospital himself, an' called in every specialist within a hundred miles. Then he'd have had Brigham on his side, instead of havin' Brigham hatin' him, an' wonderin' what the whole business meant anyway. Well, we'll soon be seein' things."

The Filipino with the cauliflower ears was guarding the closed entrance to the driveway. If he recognized Asey as the man who had tried to come in the day before, he gave no sign of it, but he refused to let them through until he had called the house.

"Mr. Strutt," he said at last, "he come."

Carveth Strutt tripped down the driveway with the odd springy walk that Asey noticed so often in short, fat men.

"Mayo!" he said. "And—why, it's Elliott! Larry, old man, I'm so glad you've come! This is very decent of you, very. I assure you that we won't forget this!"

Elliott cleared his throat. "It's all," he said cautiously, "all most unfortunate. Can we—er—drive through?"

"Of course, of course! Let the bar down, Manuel," Carveth said. "And perhaps you'll let me ride back with you. Ah, thank you."

Up in the house, Carveth set in motion half a dozen servants.

When things quieted down, Asey and Elliott found themselves sitting out on the terrace that faced the ocean. They were almost entirely surrounded by a series of large silver trays.

"Cigars," Elliott sniffed, and helped himself to a handful. "Cigarettes—all very monogrammed and crested and—phew! Turkish. Three kinds of whiskey. Soda, ginger ales, white rock. My, my—" he stood off and eyed the plates of hors d'oeuvres, "just look at those things!"

Asey laughed. "I never see 'em," he said, "that I don't think of the time that I took Jennie an' Syl to a birthday party of Bill Porter's. Jennie, she had a fine time, but I knew there was somethin' worryin' her, an' when we got home, I asked her what it was. 'Twas about the hors d'oeuvres. She kept worryin' if the hired help had to make up those things every day, just on the chance of comp'ny droppin' in, or if they was somethin' special. She knocked the Ladies' Aid cold, at the next meetin', with her versions. Look, now the smoke of battle's cleared away, whatever became of Carveth?"

Elliott shrugged.

"He said he was going out to fetch Roddy."

"I wish," Asey said, "he'd be quick about it."

"Relax," Elliott advised. "Have a drink and eat up some of these things. There's one kind I want to tackle, but I want you to tackle 'em first. If it's fish, I want to be warned. Jean has some kind of fish paste that makes my stomach writhe just to look at it."

Asey picked up a plate of sandwiches, and methodically ate his way, layer by layer, to the bottom.

"I didn't," he explained, "have any dinner today. D'you suppose the coffee's any good here?"

"There's something you pull or push—here. I'll order

some," Elliott said. "After all, he told us to make ourselves at home."

He asked the boy who brought the coffee where Mr. Strutt had gone, but the boy didn't know.

"You go find Carveth," Asey said, "an' tell him to bring Roddy here—oho, you speak Spanish, don't you? Well," he repeated his order, to Elliott's delight.

"I don't see why you get so s'prised," Asey said. "I was one of them as helped annex our little brown brothers."

"And you did things in China during the Boxer business, too, didn't you?" Elliott asked.

"I know a few words of Chinese, if that's what you mean," Asey returned.

"Don't you ever reminisce?" Elliott wanted to know.

Asey smiled. "I'm tryin' to stave off the age of reminiscence," he said, "as long as I can. When I begin to rem'nisce, then I'll know I'm gettin' old. Let's see—you was to Château Thierry, wasn't you?"

With the aid of cigarettes, matches, hors d'oeuvres and a trayful of glasses, Elliott fought the battle of Château Thierry for him on the floor.

"And then the French," he said, "they—say, where the hell *is* Carveth anyway?"

"I'm beginnin' to have a horrid feelin'," Asey said, "that we been foxed. Come on. Let's leave the World War for one of the brown brothers to clean up, an' find out just what'n time is goin' on here."

Elliott pulled the bell cords, but no one answered the summons.

"Why," Asey inquired as they went into the house, "why does all this put me in mind of your daughter's fish paste? Answer, the odor. Let's try yellin'. There was people enough flittin' around when we come!"

They yelled.

No one came.

"Well, we'll pull every damn bell cord in sight, simultaneously," Elliott said, "and see what happens then!"

But nothing happened.

"I'm damned!" Elliott said angrily. "I'm everlastingly damned! What do these birds think they're trying to pull, I'd like to know!"

"Let's hunt," Asey said.

They hunted through the house, and around the house.

Finally, Asey drew out his old Colt, and fired it into the air.

"That," he said, "ought to do something!"

In a minute, a house boy appeared. He was followed by more servants.

At last Carveth wearily walked up to where Asey and Elliott stood.

"Have you found him?"

"Have we," Asey asked, "found who?"

"Roddy!"

"Listen," Asey said. "This is not funny. This is not smart. This is—"

"It's a damned outrage!" Elliott was thoroughly aroused. "We come here to help you, and to help your precious nephew—and what happens? You stick us—you maroon us!

You maroon us on a piazza and go away, leaving us to cool our heels while you flit around—damn it, man! I'd not used to being kept waiting! I'm not used to such treatment! What's the meaning of all this? Where is Roddy?"

"He's disappeared," Carveth was so excited that he squeaked. "He's disappeared! He's gone!"

"Yeah," Asey said.

"But he has! Manuel—Pedro—hasn't he disappeared? You tell them!"

"Oh, sure," Asey said. "They'll tell us, all right. I don't doubt that a bit."

"But Roddy is gone!"

"All I got to say," Asey twirled the Colt, "is that you better find him an' bring him back in just fifteen minutes, Brother Strutt, or you'll be struttin' into a jail. Do I make myself clear?"

Carveth was almost in tears. "But I tell you—"

"Neither Elliott nor me," Asey said, "was born yesterday. You find Roddy, an' find him quick, or the house of Strutt'll be cold turkey—"

"He's gone," Carveth sobbed. "He was here before you came, an' now he's gone. That man's got him!"

"If this is an act," Asey said, "it's one of the best I ever seen outside a theater. Elliott, will you explain to him that I want Roddy, without any more tears or squeaks?"

"But it's that man Jennings!" Carveth said. "It's that man Jennings!"

"Oho, it is? You mean Earl Jennings, the plumber?"

"Yes," Carveth said. "Yes. It—it was a most unfortunate incident, all around, but boys will be boys—" his voice was practically inaudible, "natural exuberance of youth, as I told him, and I'm sure we did everything in our power to make things right, and then this mural—"

"What's the unfortunate incident?" Asey asked.

"Jennings' daughter," Elliott explained while Carveth blew his nose.

"And now," Carveth said, "he's done what he threatened— he's kidnaped Roddy—and why don't you two do something about it?"

"Earl Jennings," Asey said "is over in the Pochet hospital. I seen him there myself—"

"Most unfortunate his being hurt in that plane crash," Carveth said. "Most unfortunate, as I told Roddy, why couldn't he have picked someone else. But of course that would have been satisfactorily adjusted by the family, just as the other unfortunate incident was adjusted. I told Jennings that myself, last night."

"He was in the hospital last night," Asey said.

"Oh, no, he was not!" Carveth retorted with a show of spirit. "He was there, here, threatening us! After I saw you at Octagon House. And threatening Roddy, too. He seemed to think that he had been put into that mural because Roddy told Ma— I mean, told Lorne to put him in. And that accident—"

"You mean to say that Jennings, Earl Jennings the plumber—he was here last night?" Asey's eyes lighted up.

"He was," Carveth said.

Asey smiled, and remembered the conversation he had had with the nurse about Jennings. If he had had the slightest bit of intelligence, he should have guessed. What was it she'd said? Something about "So Asey had heard what went on about Jennings—"

"It seems to me," Elliott said, "that I did hear something about Jennings on the loose last night. He goes off on busts, you know. They're the talk of Quanomet. They used to be the talk even of Company B, in the old days."

"Listen to me," Asey said to Carveth. "I'm comin' back here in an hour, an' you produce Roddy for me. Elliott's go-in' to stay here with you an' see that you do, ain't you, Elliott? Right. You see he finds Roddy, if you have to fight another Château Thierry. Here," he handed over the forty-five. "You take this, an' find Roddy. I'm goin' over to the Pochet hospital an' see Jennings. I happen to know that he'll be there."

The nurses crowded around him by the desk.

"Asey," Susan said, "you certainly did the trick! We haven't had a peek out of Jennings since you were here. He went to sleep like a little lamb—"

"I want to see him," Asey said. "Quick—tell me if he got out last night."

"Yesterday afternoon, shortly after you were here. They say he was on a tear, but he really hadn't had much to drink. His wife and the doctor made him come back this morning —they simply couldn't quiet him down. It's that mural and the pipes that have got on his nerves—" she opened the door carefully. "I think he's asleep—" she flicked on the light. "Oh, Mr. Jennings— Mis—"

She and Asey stared at the empty room.

18. ASEY brushed past Susan into the hall, and raced back to the desk.

" 'Scuse me," he said, and grabbed the telephone. "Hello, this is Asey Mayo. I want to talk with Hanson of the state police—that's right. Ask the Quanomet exchange where he is—right."

Susan whispered breathlessly to the other nurse.

"Hello, Hanson? Oh, Lane. Listen. Take some men, go over to the Strutt place by the beach. Hunt for a fellow named Earl Jennings, and for the young Strutt boy. There's a Congressman there named Elliott. He'll explain everything to you. You want Earl Jennings, an' Roddy Strutt. Got that?"

He listened for a moment.

"That's it, Lane. What do you do when you get them? You sit on them both. Oh, an' phone to the barracks—get Jennings' car plate numbers from someone. Have the roads watched, for fun. That's right. I'll be over."

He put the phone down, stared reflectively at a chart on the desk, and then picked up the receiver again.

"I want Octagon House, over in Quanomet," he said.

He whistled under his breath as he waited.

"Octagon House—that you, Tim? Tim, have you got

troopers there? Well, leave one at the house, take the other an' go over to Lorne's—he's still there? Okay. Take a trooper an' go over an' stay. The biffer's loose again, an' he might come for Lorne. That's right. No chases, this time, Tim. Tell those fellers to get him."

"What—" Susan began.

"I ain't got time to tell you," Asey said. "Oh, why didn't we tie that fellow up!"

He hurried out to Tim's car and swung it back toward Quanomet.

At the cross roads he hesitated the fraction of a second. It would be a little longer to go past the Octagon House but, on the other hand, it might be wise to drop in there on his way back to the Strutt's.

Tim howled at him as he turned up the Lornes' drive.

"Asey! Come here—my God, come here—"

"What's happened?" Asey didn't even bother to turn off the engine.

"Lorne—"

"Lorne, what? What?"

"Come and see," Tim held open the door. "In the studio."

Lorne lay face down on the couch, his shoulders shaking convulsively.

"What's the matter?" Asey demanded.

Lorne lifted up a tear stained face, looked at Asey, and then dove back into a pillow.

"He's been spanked," Tim explained cheerfully.

"What?"

"Believe it or not, he's been spanked. It took me ten minutes to get the information out of him. I thought he was having convulsions when we first came in."

"Who spanked him?"

"That," Tim said, "is something I don't know. I haven't got that far yet. He's terribly reticent. You'd think he'd had his tongue spanked."

Asey walked over and shook Lorne by the shoulder.

"Come to! What happened, an' who done it?"

Lorne sobbed bitterly.

"See here," Asey said, "you told me that artists had to suffer. This ain't no way to take a spankin'. You'd ought to consider it a thrillin' experience that'll prob'ly make you another Mike Angelo."

"He—he sus-spup-panked me!"

"Sooner or later," Tim said, "spankings come to all men. Brace up. We want to know who the hero was."

"Earl Jennings!"

Asey sat down. "How long ago," he asked, "did this happen? Come on, come to, Lorne! When did he do it?"

"I don't know. A long time. Two hours. Maybe less. I don't know. But," Lorne sat up, "I know one thing, if I ever see the man again, I'll kill him, d'you hear me? I'll kill him! I'll tear him apart with my bare hands!"

The idea of the slender Jack Lorne tearing Jennings apart was somehow irresistibly funny to Asey. It appealed also to Timothy.

"Does he mean he'll do that to the biffer?" the latter wanted to know. "He does? Oh, no, Jack! No. I've had some brief experience with your spanker, and I'll tell you for your own good, just you let him have his way, and forgive him freely."

"I'll murder him, I'll—"

"If you insist," Tim said, "let me give you the address of this lad I know. He's a professional builder-upper. Maybe inside of two or three years, you might take a whack at Jennings, but I'd just give the whole idea up."

"No one can do that," Lorne said dramatically, "to me! And live!"

He got up from the couch and strode around the studio.

"No one!" he yelled, and hurled a glass vase at the fireplace. "No one—"

"Not that," Tim said. "Don't throw that, Jack. That's a nice Toby, far too good for you to smash for demonstration purposes. Take this highball glass, if you have to express yourself in crockery."

Asey waited for Lorne to calm down. "Now," he said, "how long ago was Jennings here? Figger it out, because it makes a lot of dif'rence."

"Oh, about a quarter to eight—between seven-thirty and eight or so," Lorne said. "No earlier than seven-thirty. He came in, and picked me up, and—and spanked me!"

"Then what did he do? Where did he go?"

"I don't know, but when I see him again—oh, you can laugh, but the next time I see him, I'll break every bone—"

Asey looked toward the doorway and began to chuckle.

"And if you don't stop insulting me," Lorne said, "I'll begin on you. I mean what I say about Jennings—"

Tim smiled. "Well, begin," he said. "Aren't you," he inquired politely of the man standing in the doorway, "aren't you Mr. Jennings, of the tall, dark and mad Jenningses?"

Lorne wheeled around.

"You—you—"

"Wait," Jennings said. "Don't start anything you might regret. I told you that once I had my innings with you, I lost all my hard feelin's. All of 'em. But," he added simply, "if I hadn't had my innings, I'd have gone plumb off my head. Asey, I just had to sneak out of that hospital. I *had* to."

"Where've you been since you spanked our friend Lorne?" Asey asked him.

"Down fixing up the tank and the drain," Jennings said. "That's what I came in for. I got to get into the garage and it's locked. Got the keys, Lorne? Honest, I know it was a dirty trick to stop your plumbing up, but I said to myself, I said, I'll show the little cuss how pipes can leak!"

Asey pointed to a chair. "Sit down, an' let's weed. You beat it from the hospital soon after I seen you yesterday. Why?"

With utter honesty, Jennings explained.

"The money there was being made," he said. "I just couldn't bear lying there and thinking of that money, and me getting none of it. And then up town, a reporter spotted me and asked if I was the man with the leaking pipes— lots of people who'd seen the mural, they all recognized me and they kept kidding me, and I got sore. And by the time I got all set to cash in on the tourist money, why the outsiders had come with their midways, and there wasn't any money for me to make. And then I had a couple of drinks, and then more people recognized me, and I kept getting sorer."

"And started off after Lorne."

"Yes. Honest," Jennings said, "I'm sorry I whacked you. I was so mad, I didn't know what I was doing. And I thought you was Jerry Chase. And those troopers, they got in my way. And then I sneaked in this house, and I thought it was Lorne coming, but it was Aaron—I'm *awful* sorry about that. I'll pay all his bills and damages and all. You know, I did think he was Lorne. And then when I seen what I done, I beat it. And then I said to myself, Earl, I said, you go back and see how much damage you done, and be a man about it. But when I come back, the troopers was out, and they chased me—"

"To the river, an' you foxed 'em at the pond," Asey finished up. "If it'll make you feel any worse, neither one of 'em can swim worth a cent, and it was the will of God that they somehow managed to land on Dune Island and not in Davy Jones's locker."

Jennings shook his head sorrowfully. "Well," he said, "I guess I got a lot to be ashamed of. Anyway, I went back to town and had a few more drinks, and then I went to Strutts'. I was sore at Roddy by then. Honest, I don't why it is, but the minute I get a few drinks in me, I seem to get mad."

"You do," Tim said.

"And then," Jennings went on, "my wife made me come home, and this morning she got the doctor, and they made me go back to the hospital. Then I met Jerry Chase, and he got me mad again, kidding about those pipes, and then this afternoon—well, I had to leave, Asey. I'd have burst if I hadn't come over here and given Lorne what was coming to him. Of course, if I'd got hold of him last night, I might have hurt him bad. But just spanking him, it eased my feelings right away. Like magic. Ain't that strange?"

"Strange," Asey said, "an' beautiful. Beautiful to think you're back to normal again. Now, when you came back here last night an' biffed Aaron—"

"That's something I want to talk to you about," Jennings said. "I thought of this plan last night before I come back, and the troopers chased me. Pam's been wanting water laid on, and a bathroom, over to Octagon House. Do you suppose, if I fixed 'em up free, they'd forgive me? I like Aaron, and I'm awful sorry this happened. I didn't know he was hurt so bad till I heard them talking in the hospital. I didn't throw him down the stairs, either. He must just have lost his balance. Do you suppose I could fix things up?"

"You could try," Asey said. "What do Tim an' I get? An' the troopers?"

Jennings sighed. "Can I take it out in plumbing?"

"What about my drawings," Jack Lorne demanded, "that you stole? Oh, don't stare and pretend you don't know! You can pull the wool over Mayo's eyes, but you can't fool me. What about my drawings?"

"I don't know anything about your drawings," Jennings protested. "Except that thing in the post office—now, why do you have to keep reminding me of that, just as soon as I get my mind off of it? Serves you right, if someone stole your drawings. They ought to be burned—say," he added regretfully, "Whyn't *I* think to! Why—"

"Then who stole them if you didn't?" Jack asked. "There isn't anyone else who could have!"

Jennings looked pityingly at him, and then turned to Asey.

"I'm sorry," he said. "That's about all I can say, I guess. I'm sorry I banged you up, and the rest. But mostly Aaron. He's a good man. I'll try to make things up, somehow."

"Been to Roddy's this evenin'?" Asey asked.

"No. I had to thumb a ride to get here," Jennings said. "I found this pair of overalls and this sweater out in the hospital shed. I didn't have my clothes, or the car. I just came over here and tended to Lorne, and then I went to work on the pipes, just to show *I* hadn't any hard feelings at all."

Timothy was grinning broadly, and Asey couldn't hold back a chuckle. There was something rather amazing about this big husk of a man, and the simple directness with which he went to his point.

"What about Roddy an' your daughter?" Asey asked. "An' Roddy an' the plane crashin' into you, an' his uncle in Washington that got the contract for Lorne, an' that got your face in the mural—"

"He did not get that contract for me!" Lorne said.

"Ssh! What about all of them, Jennings? Ain't you still mad about them?"

"To tell you the candid truth, Asey," Jennings said, "Edith wasn't much better than she should of been. Her mother and

I always had a time with her. I just give her Roddy's money and told her to take it and go. She wasn't," he added meaningly, "much different from Marina, except she didn't have as many brains, and she wasn't so nice looking. And as for the plane—well, Strutt'll pay for that. And the mural—well," he waved his hand, "I got that all out of my system on Lorne, here."

"Come over here," Asey said, "an' let me see your hands."

"Sure, look away. There's some poison ivy on this one, I got it last night in the woods."

"Done any painting with red lead, lately?"

"Not since I was here the other day—see, here's some under my thumb nail. It's hell to get off, that stuff is. My wife's got some soap she makes me use, but what's the use? That takes off the skin, too."

Asey looked at him. "Can you prove what time you got over here, or when you left the hospital?" he said.

"Why, I don't know as I could tell you exactly. They got my watch at the hospital, you know. But it was the minister that give me the lift. I guess he could tell you, all right. Look, can I get into the garage?"

Asey shook his head. "The cops got the key."

"Well, then," Jennings turned to Lorne, "I can't do any more till that's open. Say, Asey, can I see Aaron? I'd like to get it over as soon as I can. If I could just make Pam and Aaron understand that I really didn't mean a thing—"

"Just playful, that's all." Timothy rubbed his chin reflectively. "Emma Goldman, as a kitten, used to lay open my arm from wrist to elbow with that same disarming and engaging candor. But the barn burning, Jennings. And the contents of the barn. You'll have quite a time before the Fryes forgive you that—"

"How'd you know about the contents of the barn?" Asey asked sharply.

"Pam told me. She—"

"She did?" Asey sighed. "Has she told everyone? An' I give her credit for so much sense!"

"I think she was sensible," Tim said. "And anyway, the stuff's gone. But it'll take more than pipes and a tiled bath to make Aaron and Pam forget. Why *did* you burn the barn, Jennings? Why didn't you burn two other barns?"

"But I didn't burn any!" Jennings said.

Tim looked at Asey.

"Jennings hit you," Asey said, "an' then started for Lorne's. On the way he laid out the troopers—what'd you use, your bare fist?"

"I did on you. I used my billy on the others. My old M.P. billy."

"I see. Well, after the troopers, he came here an' smacked Aaron, thinkin' it was Jack. N'en he beat it. He wasn't around while the barn was burned, though he may have been while the fire was bein' set, earlier."

Tim raised his eyebrows.

"Then he came back again," Asey said, "and O'Malley and Shorty chased him, an' some time durin' the interval, him an' me had our set-to. If you really want to go into it, we can take a pad an' time it out. But that's the way it all happened, an' it all fits."

"I must have been out a long time," Tim said.

"Nope, when you consider what you got hit with, an' the stump you landed on. You got to remember you was copin' with the pride of Comp'ny B."

"I see," Tim sounded dubious. "But are you quite sure, Jennings, that you didn't fire the barn?"

"Honest, I didn't. I smelled smoke later, but I thought it come from town. They'd been starting fires there. Asey, you believe me, don't you?"

"I'm inclined to," Asey said, "but I honestly don't know why. Just your winnin' personality, I guess. Now, I got to get along. I'll see Pam before I—"

"What about me?" Lorne asked. "Me, and my drawings, and my—my sufferings? And—"

"Just you consider them," Asey said, "the sufferin's of a true artist, an' thank God Jennings didn't do more than spank you."

"You defend the man!"

"I don't, but I know the part he played in this—"

"You defend him, you excuse him, you believe every word he says! You don't seem to think it matters, what he did to me, and my drawings, and all! You're in league with him—"

"Would you," Asey asked with a purr in his voice, "like another spankin'? Would you?"

"Well," Lorne said, "well, why do you uphold him?"

"I don't! I'd figgered what part the biffer played, an' I was right. I worried for fear he might really be after Roddy, but he's proved that's all Roddy an' Carveth, puttin' on an act. Now, Lorne, take the advice of the old Philistine, an' pipe down. Tim, what become of the trooper you brought over?"

"He's outside. I didn't know until he popped in," Timothy said, "that Jennings was here. I told the trooper to go outside and keep watch. He's there now, I suppose—"

"Who is he?"

"No one I ever saw before."

"That's a relief," Asey said. "If it was Shorty or O'Malley, Jennings might have his hands full. Coming over to see Pam an' Aaron?"

Jennings squared his shoulders. "Uh-huh."

Over at Octagon House, Pam greeted them wearily.

"Don't speak above a whisper," she said. "We've just got Aaron asleep—I don't know if Cummings gave him too many pills, or not enough, but he's been fretful and nervous —he's even been fussing about the clocks. I've called Dr. Cummings and told him to drop over before he finishes for the night. I'm worried—"

"Pam," Jennings said, "I did it."

"What?"

"I hit him, but I didn't mean to, I thought it was Lorne. I didn't throw him down the stairs, he fell. And I'm awful sorry—can I fix you up with water and a bathroom, free— and the doctor's bills, and honest, I'm awful sorry," Jennings paused for breath. "Honest, I am."

Asey didn't know whether Pam was going to laugh or cry, or just whack Jennings in the nose.

"Did you burn the barn?" she said at last.

"No, I didn't."

"Well—oh, damn, there's that phone, and it'll wake Father—damn you, stop ringing!"

"Think she's mad?" Jennings whispered as Pam raced off to the phone.

"I think you're lucky," Asey said, "in havin' a reasonable woman to deal with—"

"It was for you, Asey," Pam said, coming back. "It was Elliott, and he wants you over at Roddy's. He didn't say— Peg, grab Emma, that wretch is reducing the rubber plant to elastic bands again! He didn't say what he wanted you for, but he said to hurry, and I said you would."

"Okay," Asey said. "You an' Jennings solve your problems. I'll be back here for the night—oh, have someone get me some clean clothes from home, will you? Phone Jennie or Syl."

Elliott was waiting for him at the driveway to the Strutt estate.

"They weren't lying," he said. "They weren't putting on an act, Asey."

"You mean, Roddy *has* disappeared?" Asey said. "Well, maybe. But I've solved Jennings, and I know no menacer got hold of Roddy. He may have gone elsewhere, but he went of his own accord. You don't really think that Roddy is seriously missin', do you?"

"Well," Elliott said briefly, "he's dead, anyway."

19.

TWO hours later, in the enormous living room at the Strutt house, Asey puffed on his pipe and listened wearily to the argument going on between Dr. Cummings and Carveth on the subject of Roddy's death.

They had probably been arguing less than ten minutes, but it seemed to Asey that they had been yelling and spitting at each other for weeks and weeks. Ordinarily he would have stopped their wrangling, but he had too many problems staring him in the face to make any efforts as an arbitrator.

"Mr. Strutt," Cummings dropped his angry bellow and spoke in a voice so tautly controlled that it startled even Asey, "I know that Roddy was your favorite nephew, and I know you've been upset during the last day or so, and I know you've suffered a tremendous blow tonight. But Roddy didn't kill himself. He was murdered."

"Roddy was driven to suicide!" Carveth said.

"Look," Cummings' voice soared again, "I've tried to explain that I know how you feel, but I know the facts in the case. That's my job. I've spent the last couple of hours just finding out facts. Roddy was murdered."

"The boy was driven to suicide," Carveth said with stubborn persistence. "Everyone knows that suicides always go into a garage, shut the door and start a car—"

"But they don't lock the garage doors on the outside!" Cummings said. "With a padlock!"

"Everyone knows it," Strutt went on, "and that's just what happened here. Roddy was so intimidated and so over-wrought by these threats—why, he went out of his mind! He wasn't responsible for what he did. And it's all the fault of that Jennings—"

"Carbon monoxide," Cummings said, "is a favorite with suicides. But Roddy was killed. He went into the garage, and someone—either someone with him or someone waiting for him—hit him on the base of the skull, hard enough to stun him. Then they moved him so that his head rested under the exhaust of his Porter roadster, and they started the roadster, and then they went out, snapping the padlock after them. Certainly you don't think that Roddy locked that padlock, and then crawled back through a crack!"

"What do *you* think?" Carveth appealed to Asey.

"I don't think," Asey said, "that I could ever prove it was suicide."

"Oh, I don't know what to do!" Carveth seemed to crumple back into his chair. "I don't know what to do, or what to think!"

Dr. Cummings, too thoroughly annoyed with Strutt to stop and be sympathetic, hammered away at his point.

"Sheer reason," he said, "should convince you—"

Asey motioned for him to be silent. This was no time to attempt to reach any possible better judgment Carveth might possess.

"I wonder, Mr. Strutt," he said, embarking on his tentative

plan, "about the newspaper angle. We kept this quiet up to now, but before long the reporters'll come. There's a lot in town, an' you'll have to see 'em, an' talk with 'em—"

"I couldn't face the press," Carveth said brokenly. "I simply couldn't!"

"Well," Asey said, "I don't blame you. But they'll insist —say, how about lettin' Elliott an' me write some sort of statement for you?"

"Oh, would you?" Carveth asked eagerly.

The doctor raised his eyebrows and looked at Asey. That man could get more places with a little honey and molasses!

"But you got to consider," Asey went on, "the papers' angle, an' the position you an' your family hold. I wonder if, on the whole, it mightn't be wise to call it murder?"

"Why?"

"Of course," Asey was very diffident, "I don't want to go against your wishes, but if we admit this is suicide, wouldn't it sort of be a—a—"

"Blemish," the doctor suggested. "Blemish. A stain on the family escutcheon."

"Just so. Now, you knew that your nephew was involved in the Marina Lorne business, didn't you, Mr. Strutt?"

Carveth grudgingly admitted that he had guessed it.

"An' if we say that he committed suicide, then—well, folks'll start talkin' an' sayin' that Roddy probably had reason to kill himself. People are always awful willin' to believe the unpleasantest things they can about anyone who kills himself. They want a reason, an' I'm afraid that

Marina's murder might turn out to be it. But if we say Roddy was murdered, people will be sorry. P'raps sorry enough to forget some of the—uh—unpleasant incidents, an' all."

Carveth thought for a moment.

"By George," he said. "I never thought of that! I think you're right. You and Elliott fix up something—perhaps this will be the way to get Jennings. Yes. Yes, indeed."

"Now why," Cummings asked as he and Asey walked down the hall together a few minutes later, "why did you twist him over to our way of thinking, just to let him go off on a tangent about Jennings? He'll talk with Hanson, and you can't tell what will happen. You're sure Jennings didn't kill him, aren't you?"

Asey nodded. "But I don't want two conflictin' stories on this," he said, "and I do want Hanson an' Carveth to provide a distractin' element. Anyone would do, but Jennings is handiest."

"In other words, you want the right hand in action, while the left brings forth rabbits. I see. Asey, are you so sure about Jennings? He certainly menaced magnificently last night, if you can believe Carveth. And biffing Roddy over the head has a touch of Jennings about it."

"It's neat," Asey said. "The whole thing is neat, so much neater than I'd imagined at first that it makes my spine curl."

"Can you alibi Jennings?" the doctor asked, as he paused to pick up his black bag from the hall table.

"I can," Asey said. "I done some phonin' an' checkin'

while you was busy out in the garage. Jennings is alibied by time, an' the Methodist minister. You see, Roddy'd disappeared just a little while before Elliott an' I come here, that was around seven-thirty this evenin', or maybe a bit after. At just about that same time, the minister was pickin' up Jennings, about a hundred yards from the Pochet hospital. At a quarter to eight, Lorne claims that Jennings was spankin' him. So you see, Jennings didn't have time to come here. The nurses can prove he was in his room at the hospital about fifteen minutes before the minister picked him up. They got him on a chart. There you are."

"But where will Jennings be, when Carveth and Hanson get going?"

"He's safe. I'll get him out, if they get him in too deep. I want a red herrin' here, an' it won't harm him to be it. He can take it. An' I hope he'll keep everyone busy—"

"While you sneak off and ferret out the murderers?" Cummings asked.

"The murderer," Asey corrected. "Just one."

"Forgotten Marina?"

"Nope," Asey said. "Oh, I know what you're goin' to say, Doc. The first murder was a stabbin' an' this is a carbon monoxide by force, an' they don't seem alike. But they're alike in one thing. The knife they used was Pam's, an' the idea here, I think, is for us to land on Jennings."

Cummings set his bag down.

"Then you think that Roddy was being menaced, but not by Jennings?" he asked.

"I thought," Asey admitted, "all this menacin' was a yarn,

at first. Now I wonder if perhaps Roddy wasn't bein' threatened all right. An' of course when Jennings turned up last night, naturally the Strutts thought that he was the menacer. Only he wasn't."

The doctor sighed. "It gives you an unknown menacer to start with, I suppose, but I don't feel that's much of a foundation. How would anyone *know* that Jennings was the basher who went after you and the rest?"

"They wouldn't have to know," Asey said, "about that business in the woods, or any specific bashin'. Jennings has a reputation for violence. Everyone knows what he thinks an' how he feels about Roddy. An' they know he's mad at the mural. He's a nice, likely person to pick out, just as Pam was. Are you ready? Then let's get goin' before the reporters swarm."

Elliott met them as they walked down to the garage where the doctor's car was parked.

"Hanson's come and gone," he said, "and he left two messages for Asey. That he'd done all the checking, and it was okay. And what you wanted is on its way to you from Boston. Look, why did you check on me? Don't look so guileless, Hanson made a break!"

"The nicest people," Asey said, "do the strangest things. Elliott, you got to compose a statement for the press—an' then will you hang around here? Carveth's in a state, an' if you're helpful enough, you might get a new school. Besides, someone ought to be here who can make decisions."

Elliott took copious notes on the backs of envelopes.

"There," he said. "Where'll you be?"

"Octagon House," Asey said. "Got anything, Lane?" he asked the officer who came over to them.

"No prints on the padlock, the car keys, the wheel, door, or anything. Everything's clean. Wiped off. He got hit with that piece of wood you thought, but that's clean, too. And the padlock was not forced. Asey, I don't get this at all!"

"You think we do?" Cummings asked.

"Strutt said they expected trouble," Lane said. "They don't seem to know just what kind, but they expected it. They had the place all armed and fortified. Under those circumstances, how did anyone get here without being seen? And why did Strutt unlock the garage and go in? He must have, too. The garage key is on the same ring with the car keys that were in the roadster, and they tell me that no one else had a key to this garage. Seems there'd been a bit of trouble with the servants swiping the roadster for their joy rides, and that's why it was here all by itself. What was the idea, Asey?"

"No one knows any ideas," Asey said wearily. "It's my opinion that the servants was fed up with this armin' an' fortifyin', and that except for the two at the driveway gates, no one was doin' any guardin' at all. I've got some pretty good evidence that the rest was mostly occupied with a crap game an' field day, in the basement. It was gettin' dark when Roddy disappeared. Someone could have sneaked along the shore all right, without bein' seen. I can't find out why Roddy come here."

"Date, maybe?" Lane suggested. "I hear he was a lad with the ladies."

"He had every opportunity to make dates," Asey said. "He's been phonin' people right an' left all day, an' they been phonin' him. Carveth put his foot down on a couple of parties Roddy'd planned here for today, but you can't tell how many other dates he might have made."

"But if they were afraid of trouble," Lane said, "would Roddy have made dates, or come down here without telling anyone? And if he'd seen a prowler, whyn't he yell?"

Asey shrugged. "I think, myself, that he must of had a date with someone that he wanted to keep quiet about, or one with someone he never thought of as bein' a menace. He came here, met 'em, went into the garage for a chat—this is a secluded sort of place, here. An' durin' the chat, he got his. Did you find anythin' in the garage, by the way?"

"Clews? No. It's a clean garage. There were things in the car, but just the sort of things you'd expect to find in a car of his. Hairpins and a lipstick or two, and a glass bead, and compacts, and a powder puff—all shades lead me to feel that he preferred blondes. Come on and look."

Asey went into the garage.

"You know," Lane said, displaying the articles, "you don't get clews in a thing of this sort, unless—"

" 'Less," Asey said, "you have someone step into some fresh cement, or write names an' addresses an' phone numbers on the corpse's shirt front. Doc, I'm drivin' back in Tim's car. You're comin' to see Aaron, ain't you? Well, I'll meet you at the Octagon House. Thanks, Lane. Happy huntin'."

Offhand, he thought as he drove along home, offhand he couldn't remember when he had ever felt more bitterly ashamed of himself. If only he had gone to the Strutt home the night before! If only he had gone to see Roddy, and ironed out the situation. If only he had shown some trace of common sense! If only he had, Roddy might still be alive.

He reproached himself steadily and forcefully all the way along the beach road.

Of course, even if he had gone, he'd only have learned about the Jennings episode, and considered Jennings the menace. That wouldn't have helped matters much. He might have talked with Roddy, but he wouldn't have gone far without Brigham's side of the story to use as a crowbar in prying out the truth.

The chances were that whoever set out to kill Roddy would have killed him in any case. Everyone in the town knew of the guarding and the fortifications of the Strutt house, but the preparations had not deterred the murderer in the least. He had made up his mind to kill Roddy, and he did just that.

And Marina had been killed in that same grimly determined way. The barn had been burned by someone with the same determination and disregard for consequences. The mural had been obliterated with finality and deliberation. The key stealing was neat and deliberate. Everything, in fact, that seemed to matter was characterized by the same quiet and efficient force. By neat timing, and firm thinking. The fellow thought things out, and things went with a fine smoothness for him.

He turned into the driveway of the Octagon House.

Mrs. Carr, followed by Emma on her leash, walked down from the porch to meet him.

They were the only ones up, she informed him, except for a lone, wandering trooper.

"Pam and Peg were tired to death, and so was Tim. I packed them to bed. Aaron's asleep, mercifully, but he— Asey, what's happened now, you seem so dejected—I know. You need food!"

"I always wondered," Asey said as they went indoors, "why a woman always thinks that all anyone needs to make 'em feel better is just a little food. I *do*," he added hurriedly, before Mrs. Carr could retort, "need food. An' if you can find me some super-spinach that'll give me the brains to settle this—don't yell at the news—this murder of Roddy Strutt, I'll be willin' to trail you around on Emma's leash."

"So he's been killed, has he?" She didn't seem perturbed by the information. "It doesn't surprise me—oh, here's the chicken Pam was saving—no, not a bit. Nothing would surprise me at this point. Why was he killed?"

"I ain't at the who or why stage yet," Asey said, attacking the chicken.

"Is it the same one who killed Marina that did this? Really? Why?"

"I can't give you facts," Asey said. "Only a sort of gentle philosophizin' about the simple murder. I don't think I ever seen anythin' more simple than these two murders. Girl stabbed with someone else's knife. No clews. Man stunned an' stuck under exhaust pipe. No clews. There you are. Smart. Smooth. Unobtrusive, like. Use guns, an' ballistics'll get you. Use poison, an' toxicol'gists'll get you. But use a stolen knife an' carbon monoxide, an' combine 'em with a passion for removin' finger prints, an' a lack of collar buttons an' false teeth left behind—oh, you got somethin' here, you have! We got to prove you took the knife. We got to prove you started the car, so to speak. An' very few murderers invite audiences."

"What were the motives?" Mrs. Carr asked.

"Roddy an' Marina," Asey said, "sort of inspired motives. The place is littered with reasons for people to kill 'em."

"Why," Mrs. Carr asked, "do people kill people, anyway? I was trying to think, today, just why I wanted to kill Marina, and all I could think of was, she'd hurt Tim. That seems so vague!"

"Usually it's love or money," Asey said, "or variations on 'em. There are others, of course. I once knew a man who killed another man on account of bein' unduly sensitive about his toupé, but that ain't a normal one."

"Well, murderers aren't normal, anyway," Mrs. Carr said, replenishing his plate.

"Emma," Asey said, "is a normal cat. She eats, an' she sleeps, an' she's bright enough to be trained to a leash. How normal would Emma be, if she got a real chance at that parrot?"

"I almost wish," Mrs. Carr said sincerely, "that she would. Toots is the most inhuman bird—just sits and stares and stares, and never a word! I suppose that Toots and Emma, between them, know the whole story. They pretend to, anyway. But Asey, murderers aren't normal. They can't be."

"I don't see why there's this far-reachin' theory," Asey said, "that murderers have to be either eccentric people with too many brains, or dumb clods without any. More often than not, it's a nice person who turns out to be a murderer. 'Course, by the time the papers get through, they've got all the symptoms listed in the doc's book, an' you wonder why they wasn't put away behind bars at the age of three an' a half."

"You think it was some nice person who killed Marina and Roddy?" Mrs. Carr asked anxiously. "Oh, dear, I thought it would be someone—well, not with a beard, and teeth missing, but someone—"

"With a leer and no socks," Asey said. "I know. P'raps it is. But they got a nice way of thinkin'. I give 'em credit."

"How'll you find him?"

"By time," Asey said. "Time, an' some other odds an' ends, like who ruined the mural—"

"Oh, has that been ruined? How perfectly splendid! How perfectly wonderful! Look, don't you want what's left of this odd Spanish cream? It looks peculiar, but it tastes very good. Oh, I'm delighted about that mural. I'm sure that everyone in Quanomet will be so much happier to have that horrid thing out of the way!"

Asey chuckled. "An' I got to find out who burned the barn," he said, "an' who saw Roddy Strutt on Friday night—"

"That sounds *ter*ribly difficult!"

"It is," Asey said. "An' I got to find out if Lorne's drawings was burned for spite, or a purpose. An' just the time

element alone is enough to keep one man busy for the end
of his days. I s'pose you could find someone willin' to sit,
an' go through the entire population of this town an' the
surroundin' countryside, an' find out where every man, chick
an' child was from around seven-fifteen—that's about when
Carveth first lost track of Roddy. Thought he'd just gone
out on the terrace. Anyway, from seven-fifteen, on for the
next half or three-quarters of an hour. An' even if you narrowed it down to seven-thirty to eight, you'd still have a lot
of ground to cover."

"But someone at the Strutt house must have seen something! They must know something!"

"They ought to, but they don't. An' there you are."

"Seven-thirty to eight," Mrs. Carr said reflectively. "Dear
me, how hard it is to remember things, even six hours later.
Let's see—I was up trying to amuse Aaron, and getting radio
programs for him on that strange battery set. Tim went to
the village for cigarettes—we were running short. Peg went
with him to get her car—she left it up town last night, you
know, and they did all sorts of things to it, in that riot.
Poured beer into the crank case, or the gas tank, or something. Pam was making jelly—"

"What?"

"Yes, I thought it was a little too much, myself. But she
said the currants wouldn't be any good tomorrow, and after
all the work she went to in getting them, she wasn't going
to have them go to waste—isn't New England amazing,
Asey? It makes me feel I'm so plastic, and useless, and fu-
tile, and ineffective. I probably am. Anyway, Pam made

jelly. I suppose it at least had the virtue of taking her mind off things—and particularly the ambergris. I do feel so badly about that!"

"So," Asey said, "do I. That's another item on my list. I got to find that."

"Find it? But my dear man, it was burned up—Pam said it was! I—"

"Wait," Asey said. "I think I hear the doc—it should be him. He was comin' right over from Roddy's."

Mrs. Carr looked out of the window. "It's lots of cars at Jack Lorne's," she said. "But—yes, here's the doctor—"

Cummings came into the kitchen.

"They didn't even think of Jennings, Asey," he said. "They pulled a fast one. And the hell of it is, they've got him cold. On ice."

20.

DR. CUMMINGS was bitterly disappointed with Asey's reactions to his bombshell of news.

The man didn't seem at all disconcerted. He didn't ask who, or how. He just nodded interestedly and pulled out that damned pipe. That—Cummings searched for a word —that damned ubiquitous pipe!

"Well," the doctor said finally, *"say* something!"

"I'm thinkin'," Asey returned, "Lorne must of got back from Roddy's about seven-thirty-five, or seven-forty. Just in time for Jennings to spank him. Who saw him?"

"The Hepplewhites," Cummings sounded very annoyed. "They have the place next to Roddy's—you know? Yes, yes, probably you *do* know, probably you have dinner with them on alternate Tuesdays. Asey, how do you get to know things, anyway?"

"An' the Hepplewhites seen Lorne?"

"They did, and so did their aged grandmother—she's one of those women who see everything. She watched him edge through the woods—"

"Didn't she," Asey interrupted, "say, 'slink'?"

Cummings drew a long breath. "Sometimes, Asey, you infuriate me to the point of utter speechlessness. Anyway, the Hepplewhites reported when they heard about Roddy. Someone else saw his car parked by the lane."

"Lorne has an alibi for Marina's death," Asey said.

"Yes, but Hanson's figured it all out. Roddy killed Marina. Hanson's been working on that angle all along, it seems. After the news of Roddy leaked out, Nettie Hobbs crashed through and filled in the blank spaces."

Asey grinned.

"After," he said, "the gold mine give out. Uh-huh. Wonder how she'll explain her speed in cashin' that check, an' the delay in tellin' about it. Prob'ly she'll bring in her pasture, an' how it dawned on her that Roddy didn't want to buy it, he was just payin' hush money. I see. So Roddy killed Marina, an' Lorne's the outraged husband. Think of the headlines, doc! 'Outraged Husband Kills Lover-Murderer. Artist Slays Playboy on Quaint Cape Cod, as Thousands Stare at Mural. Inset—Mural.' Yup, this'll be more of a blemish than suicide, I guess!"

"You haven't heard it all," Cummings said. "On Friday night, Marina went to a party. It began before that artist left, the one she was going to pose for when he came back. I forget who gave the binge, but it was one of that bunch up at the shore. Anyway, Marina'd got this posing job, and she was tickled to death, and did more than her share of drinking—I said she'd been drinking a lot, after I looked at her later that night. And Roddy breezed into this party a little after eight. Didn't stay more than half an hour, but while he was there, he and Marina had a fight. She wanted him to do something for her, and he said he wouldn't, and she said he would, and that he'd better, or words to that effect— I'm just giving you the barest outline."

Asey nodded. Translated, it meant that Marina had something on Roddy that would force him into staging the ambergris holdup on herself and Pam, whether he wanted to or not. He was convinced that a holdup had been Marina's plan.

"Marina left around nine-thirty," the doctor said, "and Hanson figures that Roddy came back over here to the garage, waited till she came, and got her. There you are. They say that Roddy was sore at her taking that posing job, and that he'd found out she was playing around with someone else—Hanson has it all worked out. Plenty of motive, plenty of opportunity—Roddy didn't like Pam, so he used her knife. It all figures out very nicely."

"What's Hanson's notion of the plane crash?"

"Just like yours. He's been over and talked with that pilot, too. Now, I'll see to Aaron—"

"He's asleep," Pam said as she came into the kitchen. "And you'll wake him over my dead body—have you got that medicine?"

Cummings passed her two small bottles.

"Directions are on 'em," he said. "Well, if he's asleep, I'll be over the first thing in the morning."

"And what," Pam said, "has gone and happened now? Something has. I can tell by your faces."

She blinked when Mrs. Carr told her.

"Oh!" she said. "I—I can't believe it! Roddy—and Jack? Asey, is that so? Does—oh, of course! It means there's no hope left at all for the ambergris to turn up, now! Doesn't it?"

"It's a damned shame about that, Pam," Cummings said. "I'm awfully sorry about it. I'd sort of hoped that with the mural, and this place—what do the papers call it? The Incredible Background to these Startling Events—well, I'd hoped that Asey would delve into the incredible background, and pick up one clew from the mural, say, and one from this place—"

"You been readin' books," Asey said gloomily. "That's your trouble—"

"And then I thought," Cummings continued, "that he'd twitch the ambergris out of thin air for you. But—well, it can't be helped, I suppose. Coming home, Asey? I'll drive you over."

"Yup," Asey said. "I guess so."

Over in his own home, he sat down in the kitchen rocker and lighted his pipe.

Ordinarily that rocker was a restful chair, and he liked it. But now it squeaked reproachfully at him. No reason, he thought, why it shouldn't. All this ripping and tearing around he'd done since Friday, and where was he? The whole business had been just as headlong and breathless as a ride on a roller coaster—and where was he now? He was right smack back at the entrance again.

There were just two things of which he was certain: that Roddy had not killed Marina, and that Jack had not killed Roddy.

Roddy, he felt sure, had come to the garage after the murder, and his plane wrecking and all the rest had been inspired by his more or less justifiable fear that he would be arrested for the killing. He paid his hush money to Nettie because he was scared stiff.

Jack Lorne might have gone to Roddy's, he might have slunk through the woods near the Hepplewhites'. But it was Asey's guess that Lorne had been summoned on the phone by Roddy, and that he had immediately returned home when Roddy—probably already dead in the garage, or at least already there with someone else—failed to show up.

Asey rocked back and forth.

While he and the rest raced their heads off, chasing Jennings, rescuing troopers, pulling Aaron out of cellars, hunting gold keys—during all that, the murderer was laughing up his sleeve. Why shouldn't he? He'd covered his tracks as nicely as anyone could. He hadn't thrust any obstacles around that would trip him up later. He hadn't tried to thwart anyone. He hadn't left any clews.

But he must have left clews. You couldn't kill two people, ruin a mural, burn a barn, steal a gold key from a Congressman, drawings from an artist, a knife from a back door—you couldn't begin to do all those things without slipping up somewhere. There was a clew. There were clews. There must be. Probably there were clews all over the place —if only he and the rest had wit enough to recognize 'em.

Wearily, Asey forced his mind back to Friday night and the beginning of everything.

He had worked his way up to the barn burning when he heard two cars pull up in his drive.

"Hanson," Asey murmured grimly to himself as he went to answer the knocker. "Hanson, jubilant an' crowin'—"

Far from being pleased with himself and his solution, Hanson was worried and despondent-looking.

"Asey," he said, "I'm stuck. Did Cummings tell you about Lorne? Well, it won't work. It ought to, but—my God, you've got to believe him! Lorne claims that Roddy called him up and urged him to come over on a matter of great importance. Lorne didn't want to, he said, because he was busy working on a picture for someone's dining room—now, isn't that crazy!"

"Not," Asey returned, "if you've had many dealin's with Lorne, it ain't. But he went, just the same?"

"Roddy kept calling and calling. So Lorne went, at last. When Roddy didn't show up by the boathouse, where he said he'd be, why Lorne turned around and came home, and went back to work on his picture. That's his story, and he's sticking to it. And I can't break it. We can't. None of us. I can't get him to change a thing, and honestly, Asey, I'm beginning to think that he's telling the truth! What do you think?"

"There's the matter of his drawin's," Asey said. "Someone burned 'em, an' it wasn't Jennings. An' the mural. It's been painted out, you know. I think both of 'em have got something to do with this affair, an' I think Lorne's the last person on earth to harm his own work."

"I guessed something happened to the mural," Hanson said. "Look, can I come in and talk things over with you? I've got pictures of the mural, they just came from Boston. For the love of God, Asey, if you think there's any clew in this thing, will you look?"

Asey spread the photographs out on the kitchen table.

In many ways, he thought, the reproductions were better than the original. They lacked Lorne's violent coloring, but without that to distract you, you could really see a lot more.

He spent little time on the main panel, other than to chuckle at the resemblance of ailing Capital to Carveth Strutt.

"These side panels," he said to Hanson, "are the things, I think. Now, let's see. This one here's all Pilgrims an' Indians an' history. Local faces. That's past history, I guess, an' this one's the future, with more local faces. Yup, here's Jennings as Industry Mending the Leaking Pipes of Civilization—"

"What industry?" Hanson looked puzzled.

"Dunno," Asey said. "It ain't a bit clear in my mind as to what industry'd have pipes that size in Quanomet. That's the picture that got Jennings so mad. Reflected on his business, he thought. There's the minister with the wart, an' here's Jerry Chase. Oh, boy, here's Nettie bein' the fish wife, an' Roddy bein'—lust, I guess."

"Where's Pam Frye and her father?"

"They're in the main one," Asey said. "She's one of them tired-lookin' women that's stirrin' things in the kettle, an' he's either Time or the tax collector, floatin' on top. Oh, here's Peg Boone, on the history side. She's the Indian girl skinnin'—Hanson, what'n time is that critter she's skinnin'?"

"It might be almost anything," Hanson said. "It's got four front legs. She looks pretty good, compared to some.

He did her a lot better than Pam. Asey, there's the milkman, and here's the Portygee we ran in so many times for bootlegging, the one that had the uncle that was a judge—"

At the end of an hour, Hanson sighed.

"I can't make anything out of this," he said. "Not a thing. Can you? Oh, don't tell me you're going to go through it all over again! Don't! Tell me more about the ambergris part of things. That ambergris gets me—"

"It gets me, too," Asey said. "Hanson, I wish we had Lorne here. I'd like to know for sure what was what and who was who. If I was this feller lyin' on the dung heap in the corner, I don't know as I wouldn't get sore enough to kill someone, myself. Yes, I'm thinkin' about that ambergris, but I'm goin' over this picture till I get somewhere—"

"Lorne's out in the car with my fellows," Hanson said. "I'll bring him in."

Lorne's general annoyance, anger and irritation all characteristically gave way to pleasure at the excellence of the mural photographs.

"Those are good!" he said. "Those are the finest pictures —why, they're damned near as good as my—"

"Get goin'," Asey said, "an' name people! Hustle!"

"Why should I—"

"Name people," Asey said, "or I go cut a paddle—"

With very bad grace, Lorne went through the series of pictures.

"Now," Hanson said when he got through, "what good did all that do? We're back just where we started, Asey. We are right back—"

"No, we ain't!" Asey said suddenly. "No sireebob! Hanson, we been goin' at this from the wrong angle! It wasn't the way the person was pictured as a person, but the way they was pictured, an' what it told—"

"What! What? You—"

Before Asey could explain, the door knocker sounded again.

"See," Asey pointed gleefully. "Look!"

Hanson looked, and his mouth opened.

"My God—but how can you prove—oh, damn that person, he'll have that door down!"

"I'll go," Asey said.

Jennie Mayo and her pint-sized husband, Syl, stood on the doorstep.

"So it's you, is it, an' not burglars?" Jennie said. "I seen the lights when I got up, an' I made Syl come over. I thought it might be burglars—"

"It's just me," Asey said, tactfully not adding that if he was a burglar, she had hardly picked the most sensible way to catch him.

"Look at you!" Jennie said. "Still in them paint duds! An' you ain't been to bed tonight, have you? Oh, it's the police you got in there, is it? Asey, are you most done with this case? Because if you are, I want you to make me a promise!"

"What?"

"I want you to promise me," Jennie said seriously, "that you'll change your clothes before you let the reporters take your pictures for the papers. You can look *so* nice when you've a mind to! Will you change into some of your nice clothes, please?"

"Jennie," Asey said, "sometimes I wonder how Syl's stood—"

"An' it's six o'clock," Jennie said—"look, Syl's not goin' out till the tide shifts—s'pose you let me get breakfast for the lot, huh? All of you look tired to death, and a nice hot breakfast'll do you good—what're you laughin' about? You know it will! Syl, run get cream from home, while I set to work." She bustled past Asey into the hall. "Hullo, Mr. Hanson, is it true that Roddy's murdered an' you've taken Jack —oh. Oh, I didn't see you, Mr. Lorne!"

Hanson grinned. "How do you know so much about things?" he demanded.

"It's the twenty-one party line," Asey said. "She's on it, an' nothin' escapes her—"

"He's just laughin' at me," Jennie said amiably. "He used to have a phone on that line himself, Mr. Hanson, an' he listened just as much as anyone—say, it's kind of too bad about Roddy, ain't it?"

"Too bad what?" Asey asked, surprised at the sympathetic concern in her voice.

"Why, I don't know exactly how to say it," Jennie said, "but the first call I heard this mornin', it sort of seemed there might of been somethin' good to Roddy, after all. Seems like he'd been tryin' to—well, not exactly to reform, but kind of make an effort—"

"What kind of an effort?" Asey ignored Hanson's signal to ease Jennie into the kitchen.

"Well, it seems that Saturday mornin', he went into the library—you know, the one that his father give the town? He'd never set foot in it before, an' Miss Perkins—she's the head one there—she was talkin' to her aunt, Liza Perkins, over the Neck way. She said that Roddy was sort of embarrassed, like. He come in the library an' wanted a book."

"So he could read, could he?" Asey said.

"I think you're horrid, talkin' that way about the dead! Anyway, he asked for that book that his grandfather wrote, and was just as nice as he could be. Left some money for a new encyclopaedia, too. He said the one they had wasn't no good. An' he said he'd have the whalin' book rebound in leather with nice gold trimmings before he returned it— wasn't that nice of him? At least, it's nicer than he ever bothered to be about things like that, before."

"Jennie Mayo," Asey said, "are you sure about this book business?"

"Sure? Why, I heard that Miss Perkins tell all about it, with my own ears!"

"Jennie," Asey said, "who built Octagon House?"

"Who? I don't know!"

Asey took her by the shoulders and propelled her to the phone.

"See that?" he said. "Well, you go ring the twenty-one line, man by man. You find out, Jennie, who built the Octagon House! Hurry—"

"But—"

"If you find out," Asey said, "I'll do anythin' you want! I'll buy you a new dress— I'll buy you a new car— I'll give you a Porter, all for yourself! I'll—"

"Will you," Jennie asked, "put on some decent clothes before the reporters take pictures of you?"

"White flannels, an' a blue coat," Asey promised, "an' my best yachtin' cap. Now, get goin'. Don't ask questions now, Hanson. Wait'll we see if this turns out—you see, he didn't know about the ambergris, at first. That is, he didn't know the value—"

"Who didn't?"

"Roddy," Asey said. "Then, after his plane crash, an' before he begun flingin' money to Nettie, an' offerin' rewards, an' bein' so lavish—sure, he'd bind it in gold! Why not? He remembered his grandfather's book, see? About whalin', an' ambergris. Looked up ambergris in encyclopaedias, too— man, don't you see? It was Roddy who moved that ambergris out of the barn, Roddy Strutt! Roddy found out by then how much the ambergris was worth! An' Roddy has his savin' streak, an' the fam'ly yen to get money—Roddy moved it! I knew there had to be another person, an' some reason for him bein' killed! Got someone, Jennie?"

"Well, if it don't beat all," Jennie said. "The line was busy—I thought it would be, it most always is. But Emmaline, up to the office—she hadn't gone home yet, she phoned her great-aunt for me. Old Mrs. Foss. She just knows everything that happened in days gone by, an' Mrs. Foss knew about the Octagon House. Just got up, she had, to start her stove. Awful brisk for an old lady, up every mornin' at six—"

"Who built Octagon House?"

"Earl Jennings' father, he built it. But I'm sure I don't know what—"

"Hanson," Asey said happily, "here's where we start in our provin'!"

21. A FEW minutes before nine that same morning, Asey slid his long Porter roadster up the Octagon House drive—so quietly that the woman standing by the back door didn't even turn her head.

With a grin, Asey recognized Nettie Hobbs in the trailing black dress she reserved for funerals, and doing good.

"I tell you," Nettie said shrilly, "it's some calves' foot jelly for poor dear Aaron—"

Pam's laugh rippled out.

"Nettie," she said, "I'm sure you mean well, but the last thing father wants to put into his mouth at this point is a calf's foot. He can just manage a thin straw."

"I must say," Nettie observed acidly, "I guess I know when I'm not wanted!"

"As a matter of fact," Pam returned, "you don't. If you did, you'd have gone straight home Friday night, and all this wouldn't have happened. It's a painful point, but very true."

"You're mad," Nettie said, "because I thought you killed your sister. And if you want to know, I'm not at all sure that you didn't, so there!"

"Oh, come," Pam said. "Would you want to be even the step-mother of a murderer?"

Nettie switched around so quickly that she nearly tripped. Her eyes lighted on the roadster, and she stopped her flouncing-off-in-indignation act.

"Oh, it's Mis-ter Mayo!" she said, walking over. "Mis-ter—Mister—oh." An odd expression came over her face. "Oh."

"Yup," Asey said, fishing in his pocket. "Mister Mayo. You can tell him by his car. When he has the car with him. Nettie, here's a nice shiny fifty-cent piece, an' a nice shiny dime. Ord'narily I don't make no refunds, but this sixty cents has been burnin' holes in my pockets—"

He held out the money, but Nettie fled. Pam strolled out of the house.

"Asey, what *did* you do to her? She's simply deflated! She scuttled!"

"If ever you have any trouble with her," Asey said, "just ask if she needs a good paint job done. Where's everyone, an' how's Aaron?"

"Peg's up with him now," Pam said. "He's loads better, even managed to eat a soft-boiled egg for breakfast. Tim and Gran went tearing off—a telegram came. Some friends of theirs landed in Provincetown, or something. Good Lord, Asey," she added as he got out of the roadster, "what sartorial splendor! What—what elegance! I hadn't got the full force of you, in the car. Ain't you somethin'?"

"Uh-huh," Asey said. He saw no need of telling her that Jennie Mayo had stood over him and almost forcibly removed his paint clothes, and thrust him into the white flannels, the while keeping up a steady conversation about his promise to dress up. "So Aaron's really better?"

"He seems almost himself. But I thought," Pam said, "that I'd better nip the calves' foot jelly in the bud. I mean, on the hoof—where are you going?" she asked Peg Boone, as they met her at the door.

Peg smiled.

"Whenever possible," she said, "I avoid the hour. Nine o'clock is going to strike, very shortly. I do wish I hadn't this complex about clocks! What about Jack, Asey? Does Hanson still have him?"

"Oh, Hanson's wanderin' around with him. I guess he's got his case, all right."

The clocks began to strike as he and Pam went into the circular hall.

Asey listened appreciatively, and stared intently at the smallest clock, in the shape of a cat.

"Seems to of lost an eye," he said, knowing full well that the eye was lost, and where it had been found.

"That little one? He drips eyes," Pam said. "I've got an old evening bag, an old yellow beaded thing, that I just use to replace that cat's eyes."

"Yellow evenin' bag, huh?" Asey said. "I hadn't got that far."

"Cats," Pam chatted on gaily, "are a sore subject here this morning. Emma Goldman went for Toots at last, and we rescued Toots just as her tail feathers were going down Emma's throat. Toots was very ruffled. I thought for a moment she was going to talk—she never has, you know, since I salvaged her from Marina. Some Argentine gave her to her, or it to her—or for all I know, him to her. Look, Asey, if it's my hands you're staring at, don't stare any longer. I can explain what seems to be gore. It's red lead. You see, Tim and Peg and I had one last grand final hunt for the ambergris in the cellar this morning, and I tipped over the red lead—"

"That your father got from Sears'," Asey said. "He ordered twenty gallons of yellow to paint the house with, but it turned out to be ten gallons of yellow an' ten of red lead, when it come, an' bein' Aaron, he just took it philosophical like an' never done nothin' about returnin' it. Yup. I know. He just supplied the neighborhood an' everyone else with red lead. Don't I hear someone at the door?"

There should be someone there, he knew, if Aaron's clocks were right.

"Just Peg—oh, who is it, Peg?"

"Your plumber friend, Jennings," she said. "He wants to come in. I think you're about to have water laid on, from the looks of his truck."

Pam sighed, and went back to the door. Asey strolled after her.

"Earl," Pam said, "I told you—"

"Mornin'," Jennings said blithely. "I'm a mite late, but somethin' come up that required me as a selectman. Somehow my two jobs always seem to be gettin' in each other's way. If I got a pipe to fix, then I got papers to sign, and if—"

"Earl," Pam said, "I told you yesterday that Aaron and I will forgive your bashing around. You were drunk, and you weren't responsible, and if you pay the doctor's bills, that's all right. But don't try me, Earl! Please don't rouse me! Because if I should begin to think of what you did in burning that barn—"

"I didn't, I keep telling you—"

"Then," Pam went on, "I might lose my temper, and it's a fiendish thing."

"Pam," Jennings said, "when you get to be able to r'lax in your new tiled tub, when you can loll around in the porcelain luxury—"

Asey bit his lip to keep the corners of his mouth from turning up into a broad grin. Jennings was doing well. He was almost doing too well. That lolling in the tub business was an obvious crib from his own conversation.

"You know perfectly well that it's silly to talk about tiled baths," Pam said. "We haven't water, and we can't afford electricity—"

"Pam," Jennings said, "I got that all thought out. You know, it was my grandfather that built this place, and I found the original plans to home. We'll just fill in that well you got now, and the cistern, too, and then we'll go back to the original well. It's a spring, really—"

"The old well, out by the barn?" Pam said.

Jennings nodded. "Used to be a windmill on the top of it," he said. "The old octagonal well. I forgot you had one till I looked it up on them old plans. It's about a hundred feet west of the barn, and we can build your—look, let me see Aaron, will you, an' talk with him?"

"What octagonal well?" Peggy Boone demanded.

"It used to be Marina's favorite thing about the place,"

Pam explained. "She loved it. She fell into it so often that Aaron had the top boarded up, years ago, when we were children. Marina used to brag that she lived in an eight-sided house, with an eight-sided barn, and an eight-sided well. It never mattered then if some other child said that her father made more money than our father. Marina would just curl her lip and say that *they* didn't live in an eight-sided house with eight-sided barns and wells. There was something final about that. Well, come on up, Earl, and talk to Father. Maybe something can be done, if you think so. But we simply haven't got a cent to put into anything. Come on and advise us, Asey. Come on, Peg."

"Wait'll I get some cigarettes—did that Timothy take all his with him?"

"I hope so," Pam said. "It's disgraceful, the way you've been bumming them and making them run out of their own fancy kind. Come on, and let's get this settled."

Jennings looked at Asey, as they followed Pam up to Aaron's room.

"Talk!" Asey barely moved his lips. "Talk!"

Jennings embarked on a discussion of electricity, its cost and upkeep, and the advantages of a modern water system.

"If you think," Pam said rather crossly, "that we keep a hand pump because we don't hold with these modern innovations, or we're scared of a faucet—you're crazy! No one would be more modern than I, if I were given half a chance. I personally want a house that looks like a tin biscuit box, with inserts of glass and colored bricks, and a top that tilts —Aaron, here's Earl Jennings again. Can you trust yourself to listen to his newest ideas? He seems to mean what he said about laying on water."

"What a Biblical sound that has!" Aaron said. "Come in—"

They had got to the stage of figuring things interminably on the block used by Aaron for his conversations the day before, when Asey heard a car in the drive.

He got up casually and looked out of the window.

Pam and Aaron were too engrossed in the figures to hear his snort of annoyance.

"Be right back," Asey said, and rushed for the stairs.

Those Carrs! That Carr family! He had told them to go away and stay away, and here they were, blundering back at this time, of all times!

Before he reached the bottom of the stairs, a flock of shots rang out.

Hanson bumped into him at the doorway.

"We had to shoot, Asey!" he said breathlessly. "We had to! She went for the Carrs—she'd got it out of the well, and into the barrow, and she was just making for your roadster when the Carrs came back. And without a second's warning, she pulled that gun and shot at Tim—we had to shoot her!"

"How's Tim?"

"She just winged him, but—well, we got her," Hanson said. "Tim didn't mean to do anything but help her with the barrow, I guess, but she thought—"

Asey pushed past Hanson out doors.

Timothy, gripping his shoulder, was sitting on the running board of the little coupé. Beyond, in the grass, lay Peg Boone.

"Is it all real?" Tim asked blankly, "is all this real? Is it —was it Peg?"

Asey nodded. "We had to let her know where it was to get her. We just meant for her to—to hang herself, as you might say. We—"

"Well, you certainly did," Mrs. Carr, hugging Emma to her bosom, peered out of the coupé. "You certainly did. Asey, what's in that barrow, that she was wheeling? Whatever made her go for Tim like that? Why, she—she went for him! Like—like Emma went for the bird! Whatever did she have in that barrow?"

"You can come out now, Gran," Tim said. "I wish you would, my arm needs fixing—what is that stuff, Asey?"

"That stuff in the barrow," Asey said, "that is ambergris."

Half an hour later, Cummings spread a final piece of adhesive on Timothy's arm, and leaned down to put the roll back in his bag.

"That," he said, "that'll hold you, I guess. Now just you keep quiet, and—"

"Keep quiet nothing," Tim said. "Asey, explanations are tedious, but you'd best begin. How did you know it was her? How did you know it was a woman?"

"I went back to the beginnin'," Asey said, "an' it come over me that first off, it was sort of a fem'nine touch to pin that note back on the door for Pam, after takin' the knife. An' it was a fem'nine temper. An' she had one. She told Nettie so, an' Jack said so. An' she smoked cig'rettes—an' she liked your Turkish best. An' she's an athletic sort. I thought so when she vaulted the barbed wire barricade the other day."

"How?" Mrs. Carr said. "Why? I don't—somehow, I can't get this through my head."

"She was up in Roddy's plane," Asey said. "She seen that lump after Marina did. Brigham remembered her. She was over there that day—only no one remembered till we started askin'. She was—"

"Unobtrusive," Tim said, "but there. Everywhere. Well, I got that much, didn't I, Pam? I said she was all over the place. So she saw the ambergris from the plane—"

"But Marina had taken the beach wagon, when she got to land," Asey said. "Peg didn't have any way of gettin' out there. From what we been able to discover, she took her car out around the other side of the point, as far as she could, and then walked. But the stuff was gone. I s'pose she seen the tire tracks, an' done her own figurin' as to what Marina wanted Roddy's beach wagon for. She got her car an' come back here, an' took Pam's knife—"

"Why didn't she take the ambergris right away, after Sister and I came back?" Pam demanded.

"You was here, Nettie was here—she begun to do some figurin'. We know she was at that party where Roddy and Marina were, an' she left before Marina did. And—"

"What part did Roddy play, exactly?" Tim asked.

"First off, Marina got him to say he'd play holdup, and take the ambergris from her and Pam. He came over here to do that. An' he found Marina dead, an' beat it—"

"Why didn't *he* take the ambergris?" Mrs. Carr demanded.

"He didn't, because he didn't know how valuable it was," Asey said. "Not till later, when he looked into the matter through encyclopaedias an' his grandfather's book on whal-in'. That had a nice lot about ambergris. So Roddy come over, ingratiatin' himself by offerin' rewards, an' he must of seen Aaron take it to the barn. Later, he took it out an' dumped it in the well. One of the troopers remembers Roddy helped."

"Well," Tim said. "Stop at the well—I never heard of an octagonal well! How would Roddy know?"

"It was one of Marina's pet spots," Asey said. "Pam says she often showed it to people. That's how he knew about it. He dumped it in before the barn burned. That same night, Peg went for Jack's drawin's while we was all huntin' the troopers. The mural was done from her drawin's, you know. Marina swiped 'em—"

"What?" Tim said. "You mean, like she swiped my old drawings—didn't Lorne know? He really didn't?"

"He really didn't," Asey said. "Peggy Boone didn't know, either, not until she seen the whole mural when the post office was opened. The—what d'you call it? The design of it was hers. An' add that to the ambergris—"

"And Marina's taking Jack away from her in the first place," Pam said. "I think I see—"

"Nettie brought that point up," Asey said. "About Jack an' Peg. Well, she got out some time after three, Peg did, Saturday night, an' painted out the mural with red lead. From Aaron's stock. Got out the tree, same as you did, Pam, that same night. That afternoon, she'd snatched Elliott's gold key to the post office from the kid playin' with it. We got him out of bed, an' he said it might of been a woman in pants. She wears dungarees all the time."

"But why didn't she take the ambergris at once?" Pam said. "Why not?"

"Gimme time," Asey said. "She had the same trouble you did—transportation. You'd fixed the garage doors, an' Marina had the car key. That meant she had to take the ambergris out, through the side door. We'll have to guess at a lot. Like maybe she went to that party where Marina was, to try to get the car key. That'd of been the simplest way. Her car ain't much more'n a wreck. An' she knew if she started with the ambergris, she had to keep on goin'. Anyway, when she come here, she had to kill Marina to get the stuff. An' Roddy was around. You see, he thought that Nettie seen him, that's why he paid her hush money. Actually, Peg seen him, but she wasn't sure who it was. That's why she went to Nettie that day I overheard 'em, to find out if Nettie seen her. Then she realized later, it must of been Roddy. That's why he got menaced. She begun to dope out his part in the ambergris. That's why finally she killed him."

"But how did you know? How can you prove—"

"There's always clews," Asey said, "if you can find 'em to fit. In Roddy's car was a glass bead, a yellow glass bead. Didn't mean anythin' to me till I got to thinkin' about the clocks here, an' that littlest cat, with the little beady eyes. You see, Peggy Boone didn't like clocks—she's the first woman I've seen for a long while that ain't got a white strip around her wrist, from wearin' a watch. She didn't like the ticking of clocks and watches. She didn't have one. But when she set out to kill Roddy, she knew she needed a time check. So she took that smallest cat along—that was durin' the time that she was presumably gettin' her car from the garage. She got it. She timed it beautifully. Took Hanson some time to follow her moves, this mornin'. But she left the little glass bead from the clock in the roadster, when she started it. It's the only thing she left behind, too."

"But the mural—why was that ruined?"

Asey smiled. "Everyone was sore," he said, "at the way they was pictured in that thing. What they was made to look like. When I looked at the pictures of it a while ago, I thought I'd been barkin' up the wrong tree. Peg Boone was an Indian girl. Lorne hadn't distorted her any. She was nice lookin', an' he hadn't made her do anythin' disgraceful—"

"She was skinning some sort of animal," Pam said.

"Yup. An' she was skinnin' it with a knife," Asey said, "held in her left hand. See what I mean? There you are, anyway. That's how things happened. Marina took Jack from her, Marina swiped her drawings, Marina got the ambergris first. An' Peg Boone was vindictive, just as she told Nettie."

"Her left hand!" Pam said. "Why, I never thought of that —but why didn't we think of her?"

"Why should we of, at first?" Asey said. "She was so solicitous about you—why not? You pointed to the ambergris! When she come back to get that, after killin' Marina an' all, you'd taken it, you see. But the minute she found you didn't know, she stopped bein' solicitous. Hanson, I see O'Malley an' Shorty gettin' out of that car, an' Jennings is here—I'm goin' down to avert some wholesale murders!"

The two troopers and Jennings were carrying on what seemed to be a first-class rough and tumble when he got out on the lawn.

"Come on!" Asey said. "Snap out of it—"

"Okay," Shorty said. "I suppose it ain't dignified—say, it's the first time we seen him since Company B disbanded—"

"What?"

"Yes, sir," Jennings said, playfully giving O'Malley a dig in the ribs that sent him sprawling. "First time—what did you say, Asey? And look, didn't I do a good job for you?"

"You did," Asey told him. "And all I said was, let sleepin' dogs lie. P'raps it's better you don't know, 'less the subject crops up of its own accord. Okay, have your reunion—"

He went back to the house and started up the stairs just as the clocks struck eleven.

The noise died away, and he heard voices drifting down from Aaron's room.

"Asey," Pam said, "is marvelous—"

"All his work," Hanson said. "All of it!"

"Naturally," Cummings told them. "Naturally, Asey is a—"

Asey hesitated at the foot of the stairs.

Perhaps it would be just as well if he left the reporters and the rest of it all to Hanson and Cummings. There was the *Mary B* waiting for him, and his clothes hadn't been unpacked. He would, he guessed, run along home.

A noise made him turn as he started out of the hall.

Toots, the parrot, was staring at him from his cage.

"Ah," Toots said, speaking for the first and only time in his life, "ah, brains! Brains, brains, brains, brains, brains!"

"Ain't it," Asey said, "the truth?"

Tipping his yachting cap to a rakish angle, he strode out to the Porter.

Available from Foul Play Press

The perennially popular Phoebe Atwood Taylor whose droll "Codfish Sherlock," Asey Mayo, and "Shakespeare lookalike," Leonidas Witherall, have been eliciting guffaws from proper Bostonian Brahmins for over half a century.

Asey Mayo Cape Cod Mysteries

The Annulet of Gilt	288 pages	$5.95
The Asey Mayo Trio	256 pages	$5.95
Banbury Bog	176 pages	$4.95
The Cape Cod Mystery	192 pages	$5.95
The Criminal C.O.D.	288 pages	$5.95
The Crimson Patch	240 pages	$5.95
The Deadly Sunshade	297 pages	$5.95
Death Lights a Candle	304 pages	$5.95
Diplomatic Corpse	256 pages	$5.95
Figure Away	288 pages	$5.95
Going, Going, Gone	218 pages	$5.95
The Mystery of the Cape Cod Players	272 pages	$5.95
The Mystery of the Cape Cod Tavern	283 pages	$5.95
Octagon House	304 pages	$5.95
Out of Order	280 pages	$5.95
The Perennial Boarder	288 pages	$5.95
Proof of the Pudding	192 pages	$5.95
Sandbar Sinister	296 pages	$5.95
Spring Harrowing	288 pages	$5.95
Three Plots for Asey Mayo	320 pages	$6.95

"Surely, under whichever pseudonym, Mrs. Taylor is the mystery equivalent of Buster Keaton."   —Dilys Winn

Leonidas Witherall Mysteries (by "Alice Tilton")

Beginning with a Bash	284 pages	$5.95
File for Record	287 pages	$5.95
Hollow Chest	284 pages	$5.95
The Left Leg	275 pages	$5.95

Available from bookshops, or by mail from the publisher: The Countryman Press, Box 175, Woodstock, Vermont 05091-0175. Please include $2.50 for shipping your order. Visa or Mastercard orders ($20.00 minimum), call 802-457-1049, 9-5 EST, Monday–Friday.

Now Back in Print

Margot Arnold

The complete adventures of Margot Arnold's beloved pair of peripatetic sleuths, Penny Spring and Sir Toby Glendower:

The Cape Cod Caper	*192 pages*	*$ 4.95*
The Catacomb Conspiracy	*260 pages*	*$18.95*
Death of a Voodoo Doll	*220 pages*	*$ 4.95*
Death on the Dragon's Tongue	*224 pages*	*$ 4.95*
Exit Actors, Dying	*176 pages*	*$ 4.95*
Lament for a Lady Laird	*221 pages*	*$ 5.95*
The Menehune Murders	*272 pages*	*$ 5.95*
Toby's Folly (hardcover)	*256 pages*	*$18.95*
Zadock's Treasure	*192 pages*	*$ 4.95*

Joyce Porter

American readers, having faced several lean years deprived of the company of Chief Inspector Wilfred Dover, will rejoice (so to speak) in the reappearance of "the most idle and avaricious policeman in the United Kingdom (and, possibly, the world)." Here is the series that introduced the bane of Scotland Yard and his hapless assistant, Sgt. MacGregor, to international acclaim.

Dover One	*192 pages*	*$ 5.95*
Dover Two	*222 pages*	*$ 4.95*
Dover Three	*192 pages*	*$ 4.95*
Dead Easy for Dover	*176 pages*	*$ 5.95*
Dover and the Unkindest Cut of All	*188 pages*	*$ 5.95*
Dover Beats the Band (hardcover)	*176 pages*	*$ 17.95*
Dover Goes to Pott	*192 pages*	*$ 5.95*
Dover Strikes Again	*202 pages*	*$ 5.95*

"Meet Detective Chief Inspector Wilfred Dover. He's fat, lazy, a scrounger and the worst detective at Scotland Yard. But you will love him."
—*Manchester Evening News*

Available from bookshops, or by mail from the publisher: The Countryman Press, Box 175, Woodstock, Vermont 05091-0175. Please include $2.50 for shipping your order. Visa or Mastercard orders ($20.00 minimum), call 802-457-1049, 9-5 EST, Monday–Friday.

Prices and availability subject to change.